# SINLESS

---

## DEADLY OMEN BOOK ONE

### JENICA SAREN

Sloth Gluttony

Lust Envy Greed

Pride and Wrath

All start as a seed


Sins begin small

Seductive and sweet

Alluring tempting

Naughty petite


Then oh so slow

They slither they grow

They entice they please

They strip they tease


Off with the gloves

The shoulder strap slips

The gown falls down

To the breast, to the hips


Wants become needs

Needs become habits

They feed the breed

Like cancer like rabbits


Habits to addictions

Addiction to obsession

Obsession to abuse

Abuse to aggression


Who to hurt

Besides me myself and I

Who to damage

Who shall I make cry


My elevation to evil

My soul I do sell

When I lure you

Into my little hell -Keith Smith

*To my favourite authors, for instilling in me a passion for words that can't be tamed or satisfied, regardless of the hours spent creating or exploring. Thank you.*

my mother stealing the father-daughter dance because she was possessive that way.

But that would never happen, not in my lifetime. My father was a reverend at a tiny church out in my equally tiny hometown near Cottage Grove. My mother was just his little groupie and had been for as long as I'd been alive. I had once found some old photos of her out clubbing, with big hair and bold makeup, a cigarette in one hand and a drink in the other, but as soon as my dad found out about my little discovery, he took them all out back and burned them to ash. My mother stood by, staring wistfully, but nodding her approval anyway.

Once I decided that on the stage, dancing, was where I was meant to be, I thought my parents would be proud, but I was instead castigated for choosing to "show off" my body. I figured that if they thought so little of me and that I was showing off my body, I would do just that, then they would see that a pair of tights wasn't so bad by comparison.

Boy, did that backfire. I found myself loving every single moment that my feet were on that stage, the pole in my hands, the burn in my muscles as I folded myself into various shapes in the air. Better yet, the praise, the adoration, the *freedom*. It was like it was something I was born to do. Which, when I think about it, sounds really... Odd. *Oh hey, how's it going? Yeah, I was born to be a stripper.*

Oh well. Nobody else had to like it.

I took a deep breath, reapplied my lip gloss, and headed toward the door.

My fans were waiting.

◆ ◆ ◆

MY BREATH LEFT me in little puffs of white condensation as I hurried back toward my car. Downside to being paid in cash: always needing to get your change after paying for gas, even when it's fucking cold as tits outside.

As I slid behind the wheel and started the car, I crossed my arms and waited for the heat to get to work. Perks of being paid in cash: heated seats. When you can buy a car in straight cash, no one questions your apparent need for heated seats, they just make it happen. But heated seats don't follow me into the gas station, so there's that. Someone should probably invent those. It might save a life or something. Granted, carrying your seat with you would be a pain in the ass, but I'd still like to have the option.

After I was satisfied that my heaters weren't seconds away from being fired for slacking, I threw the car into drive and made my way down the dark, winding road toward my house. I used to be totally freaked by the idea of driving down such a twisty, unlit, creepy road in the middle of the night – I mean, what if I was so damn tired that I fell asleep at the wheel and ended up headfirst in one of those massive pine trees? – but after I saw the house, I couldn't pass it up. It was isolated, but not rural, surrounded by all the comforts of nature's beauty, and the house itself was *uh-mazing*; two stories, old Victorian mixed with just enough contemporary and modern to not feel haunted, and the couple that was renting out to me had furnished the whole thing, sans mattress. A used mattress would have freaked me out, anyway.

It was so weird to think about how far I had come in such a short few years. My own place, brand new car, a job I loved, and a boyfriend – sorry, *fiancé* that I was completely enamoured with. It might have had something to do with the lack of finger-pinching. My friend and co-worker, Mercedes, had helped me pick out the perfect ensemble for our honeymoon, and I was as stoked as stoked could be. He adored me just as much as I adored him. So much so that he would probably faint where he stood if he saw me before the honeymoon in my new getup, but I had already warned him that this was a very real possibility. You know, to give him time to prepare himself.

I giggled to myself as I pulled into the freshly re-paved driveway, courtesy of the hardworking Lex. He really did so much. No, not just menial labour, but also in our relationship. Nearly every night that I came home from the club, he had a surprise waiting for me. It wasn't unusual for him to already be asleep by the time that I dragged my ass inside, but he knew that I was prone to feeling a lack of affection when I came home to a quiet house. There's just something so lonely about having such a big house and feeling all alone in it. *Anyway*, he knew how lonely I felt, so before he moved in with me, he had taken to dropping by my house in the evenings and leaving a small gift on the doorstep for me; it could have been a slice of cheesecake from the Italian restaurant where he proposed, or just a little note. It was all so perfect. Since he moved in, he still did it, but the gifts started feeling more comforting and homey. It never failed to amaze me how thoughtful he could be.

As I shut off the car absently, I found myself looking toward my bedroom window which seemed to be dimly lit. A huge, shit-eating grin stole over my face, and I concocted a quick plan. If he was awake, and the lights were dim, then he obviously had a present for me. And by present, I mean sex. Best. Present. Ever.

I was home a little earlier than normal since it was my last night, so I didn't want to open the garage door and have him hear me coming.

*He. Hehe. Hehehehe.*

I fell into a fit of snickers and giggles at my dirty little pun and had to cover my mouth and mentally kick my own shin to get the laughter to begin subsiding. *Coming.* I bit the inside of my check a little harder than necessary to quell my juvenile cackling.

After I was convinced that my inner teenager had finally taken a chill pill, I got out of my car, slowly and quietly bumping the door with my hip while I juggled my purse, makeup case, and little cake from the club that said, *"Bye, Ria! See you next week!"* in bright crimson icing. *Thanks for that, Rory.* Joke's on him, I wouldn't be back. At least he remembered my favourite colour.

I sidled up to the front door and quickly punched in the code to unlock it before easing it open and reminding myself to give Lex an extra big... Thank you. For oiling the hinges. Just the hinges. Just a thank you. Maybe a kiss... and...

*Focus!* I reprimanded myself while gently closing the door. *Penis later, mission impenisable now.* I mentally smacked myself. Impossible. I really did mean impossible. God, myself was such a dirty-minded weirdo.

As I tiptoed toward my bedroom door, I could smell my favourite lavender and vanilla oils, and the seductive sound of Enya echoed around the first floor, just loud enough to mask my footsteps.

Halfway past the dining table, I saw something that made me nearly drop all of my things in a heap. I put them down gently (and intentionally) as I examined the glittery, white, faux fur scarf that hung leisurely over the back of the chair nearest me.

I stroked it once, delicately, eyes glued to it like it might fly away.

Most of Lex's gifts he had given me had been relatively inexpensive, but meaningful. This, though. I knew exactly how much this gem cost, and I also know he knew how much I wanted it.

He must be going all out since we would be married in two days. I had never met a more perfect man before I met Lex; he was thoughtful, he was kind, he was loving, he was hot as hell, and he was faithful. He basically ticked every little relationship checkbox that I had, and that was certainly a first.

A tremor of excitement skittered down my spine, and I couldn't contain myself for a minute more. I rushed to the bedroom door, flung it wide, and promptly froze in my tracks, all feelings of joy fleeing me as the image before me started to sink in. I felt cold, then hot, then cold again. I was having trouble processing the horrifying, obvious scene before me, it was like it was just refusing to sink in. I couldn't think. I couldn't breathe. I couldn't figure out how I was still standing when the whole world just seemed to tilt on its axis before my very reliable eyes. Then I did what any rational young woman would do.

I screamed like a banshee.

My voice sounded shrill and psychotic, even to my own ears, as my screaming subsided. I couldn't believe my eyes. Everything I loved, everything about my new life, up in smoke. And the man I loved, the man that I gave myself to completely... he... he...

He was a filthy, disgusting, rotten cheater.

"Get out." My words were almost a whisper, like the rage inside me had swallowed them whole, wrapping them in its fiery inferno.

Lex was sitting in the bed, his eyes wide and hands in front of him as though he was warding off an attack. If I wanted to attack him, these stilettos would make some excellent holes in his excellent target of a face, and his hands wouldn't stop them. "Babe, listen," he started, his voice shaking. "It's not- "

"It's not what it looks like?" I snarled, my voice finally returning to me. "Because it looks like you're laying naked in *my* bed, with *my* best friend." I had been trying so hard to ignore the soft, angelic face that was peeking up from beneath the covers, but the words were out, and I couldn't ignore it now. It wasn't even a pretty face. It was a horrible face. She had a horrible, homewrecking face that I would love to punch, and I loved acting on instinct.

So that's what I did.

I leapt across the bed with all my might and slammed my fist into her not-pretty face. Before I could land another solid blow, strong arms wrapped around me and I was suddenly flying backward against a somewhat squishy wall of flesh. He wasn't even that hot. He had flab. I was better than flab. Flab didn't have any room to go cheating on their sexy fiancées.

I kicked back as hard as I could, but I couldn't seem to find a good vantage point from my current position. "Let me go!" I screamed, hitting octaves that I'm sure would have landed me an award or five. I threw my head backwards into his and felt a satisfying crunch behind the throbbing in my skull. Lex wailed and released me as I spun on my heel to see his bleeding face. Looked like I got the nose. It was a shitty nose, anyway. "*Get out!*" I repeated, more forcefully, before turning on Mercedes and her rapidly swelling eye. "And you..." I started, lowering my voice as I stalked toward her.

She let out a frightened squeal as she jumped up from the bed, black hair flying and grabbing pieces of clothing as she went. She made it look like she was a pro at picking up clothes in a hurry, and considering the circumstances, I'd guess she was. She seemed to have a lot of experience in this particular field. I watched her grab the scarf on her way out and I had to fight down the despair and heartbreak that was threatening to overtake me.

After taking a few calming breaths, I turned back toward Lex and fixed him with the glare that my mom used to give me when she caught me sneaking food into my room. It was a scary look, I swear it. And I was apparently doing it well, because the cheating scum before me dropped to his knees and started wringing his hands.

"Babe, I'm sorry, j-just hear me out!" He stammered. He looked so sad and pitiful, that I almost dropped to my knees beside him, but his words started to hit home and I regained my center. I was strong, beautiful, successful, and I sure as hell didn't need to depend on this sorry excuse of a man to make me happy. Myself made me happy. My outer self and... place internal exasperated sigh here... and my bitch of an inner self.

After my little internal pep talk monolog, I squared my shoulders and pulled myself up to my full height of five feet and two inches. Plus six inches, because stilettos. "I don't want to hear one more fucking word from your sorry ass. I just want you gone." I told him, locking my eyes with his.

All of a sudden, he seemed to have decided that the sad and pathetic act wasn't working, so he stood up to his full height as well, which wasn't much taller than me when I was in my heels. His bland, brown eyes stared straight back at me. How had I never noticed how bland they were? They were like wet cardboard, and no one liked that colour. "I'm not going anywhere. We'll work this out, I promise, and I'm not leaving you until we do." The seemingly heartfelt sentiment sounded like it had an underlying threat, because I'm paranoid that way and I'm a woman, so when he reached out as if to cup my chin, all I could do was swing my leg up as hard and fast as it would go.

*Ding, ding, ding! We have a winner, folks!*

I watched him crumple to the floor like the toys from *Toy Story* when Andy showed up. On that note, I was done. I whirled around and made a mad dash for my closet where I started throwing essentials into my big red suitcase. He wanted to play hard ball? Fine. He didn't want to leave? Fine. He didn't want me? Not fine, but whatever. I was a big girl. After I finished throwing half the contents of my closet into the unreasonably large suitcase, I moved for my shoes and underwear. I didn't even bother with toiletries; I could grab more later.

Suitcase in tow, I marched toward the door, not daring to even sneak a peek back at the man who had not only ripped my heart out, but stomped it into the ground like a cigarette butt. My chest definitely hurt, but it didn't hurt nearly as bad as the sudden grip on my wrist. I hissed at the nails digging into the sensitive flesh and dropped my suitcase to turn and drag my nails across Lex's face. Why couldn't he take a hint? His grip budged slightly, and I yanked my arm free, feeling the pins and needles of blood rushing back into the limb. I yanked up my suitcase once more and looked my former love dead in the eye. "You can stay here, I don't care, but I don't want you anywhere near me." I said flatly. I couldn't even muster the energy to glare anymore. "And if you touch me again, it will be the last thing you ever do." With that, I spun on my heel and stalked toward the kitchen sink, where I ripped off my previously beloved engagement ring and tossed it down the drain. I heard Lex's yelp behind me, which only made me more sadistic. So, of course, I turned on the garbage disposal.

*Have fun with that, dickhead.*

I didn't look back again as I closed the front door behind me with a slam.

THE SUN WAS STARTING to come up by the time my eyes finally felt too heavy for me to keep going much longer. I kept telling myself just to find a hotel, and that would be okay. I could sleep on the... Nope. I shuddered at the idea of sleeping on a mattress that had been used and abused too many times to count. Not happening. I wasn't a clean freak or anything, the idea of sleeping on a used mattress just majorly freaked me the fuck out. I couldn't do it. No, I could just sleep in my car once I found a comfortably populated area.

Not a moment after the thought had crossed my mind, I approached a sign saying that I was entering a town called Willow Tree, the sign boasting a hearty population of 1, 777. Large enough to get lost in, and small enough to not feel crowded. It seemed perfect.

I kept driving, perked up by the sudden possibility of a new town. Just when I thought that the sign was placed as a joke, I started seeing little signs of civilization; a quaint-looking farmhouse that I'd never be caught dead in, a little gas station that wasn't even open yet. As I continued a little farther, I passed a tiny little church that was set into the trees like it was trying to be forgotten, but the sprawling cemetery attached made it a little difficult to miss. A chill ran up my spine and I turned back to focus on the road again. I avoided churches like the plague since rebelling against my parents nearly four years ago; they just made me wholly uncomfortable for some reason. I actually knew the reason, but I was stubborn.

*It's because they try to strip away everything you are.* My inner self chimed in, uninvited but welcome. I was wondering where she had been this entire trip. But, she was right. I mean, I was right. Myself was right? Ugh, whatever.

As I mentally opened my mouth to start bickering with myself, I saw the town itself begin to come into view.

I breathed out a little gasp. "It's perfect." I whispered to myself. And perfect it was. It was like one of those small towns from Hallmark movies, the ones that are called small towns, but they're actually really sizeable and stylish.

I drove around the roundabout that circled a statue of a man I didn't recognize and spotted my first target: a little coffee shop, aptly named "Little Coffee Shop". Sounded like my kind of place. I drove around the back of the cute little building, where a hand-painted sign for parking directed me toward an adorable alcove with ivy covered walls and multihued leaves littering the ground.

I grabbed my purse, checked my reflection in the rearview mirror, and brushed my hair out with the little compact brush that I never left home without. I started to walk inside when I wobbled a bit and realized I was still in my heels. Oops. I quickly exchanged my intimidating stilettos for a pair of heels that looked like Air Jordans - what can I say? I love heels. After the quick change, I finally deemed myself worthy of being seen by the public eye.

The second I opened the door, I was greeted by a delightful jingling bell and the aroma of my drug of choice.

*Mmmm...coffee...* I could see my inner self practically drooling over the idea of caffeine. I was right there with her.

I walked up to the counter where a friendly-looking girl stood, patiently waiting for me to peruse the menu or whatever. It made me a little uncomfortable to just stand there, so I walked up to the counter and leaned my hip against it casually.

"Hi!" The girl behind the counter said cheerfully. "What can I get you today?" She was seriously adorable, with long, curly brown hair, big hazel eyes, and those cute lips that always look curved up at the edges, like a cat. And oh god, she was so short.

I decided to forego my initial urge to ask for her number.

"I'd love your name." I told her with a warm smile. Or at least, I hoped it was warm, since I was practically dying of caffeine withdrawals.

The girl blinked once, slowly, before a giant grin took over her elfish features. "I'm Andrea! But everyone just calls me Drea." She said while extending her hand over the counter. I took it and shook it gently.

"I'm Ria, and no it's not short for anything." I told her, grinning back. I liked Drea. She seemed really cool, and I definitely could have chosen a worse person to make my first impression on.

"Ooooh! That's so exotic-sounding! I'm so jealous!" She seemed like the chatty type, and right now that was fine by me. "How about I get you something while we chat? The shop is always dead this early, but we always get the odd straggler that really needs their fix before they can face the day." She giggled behind her hand like a little girl, and the tiny she-devil inside me was salivating at the chance to corrupt.

*Down, girl. First the coffee, then the sexploits.*

She seemed content with my argument. Not that there was any real argument since I was basically just talking to myself and answering myself like a complete and total nutjob. "I'll take a venti vanilla frap with extra whip and caramel drizzle, please." I said as not-crazily as possible. Which, in all honesty, probably made me look crazy as hell. But if it did, Drea wasn't going to make a big deal out of it, which I seriously appreciated.

She nodded her approval and got to work on my coffee, and didn't even flinch when I interrupted her to add two extra espresso shots, she just nodded again and carried on her chatting. By the tome my coffee was placed in front of me with a flourish that I was pretty sure I could come to expect from Drea, I realized how eerily quiet the little shop was.

"Hey," I began, taking a sip from my Frappuccino. "Why is it so quiet in here?"

Drea hopped up to sit on the counter, swinging her legs. "Sorry. I open the place most days, and it just feels so weird to have music going in here when I'm all by myself." Her cheeks turned a sweet, pale pink as she said this. "But I'll throw some on real quick. After all, the customer is always right." She hopped off the counter with a wink and turned on the soundbar above the counter.

The erotic, tantalizing sound of *Florence + The Machine* filled the space around us and I couldn't help closing my eyes and swaying to the hypnotic sound. I always thought that music had some kind of power of premonition to it, like the music could sometimes tell us our future without us even being aware of it. Of course, sometimes it couldn't be anything more than a really good song, but it was fun to imagine.

I felt a little tap on my shoulder and opened my eyes to see Drea standing there with a meek smile, gesturing toward the tiny dancefloor with colourful lights shining down on it where I guessed they usually did things like karaoke night. "Wanna go?" She asked.

I grinned and grabbed her hand. "Uh, duh." I said as I dragged her along behind me. Seriously, like I would ever give up a chance to dance, regardless of my currently fragile emotional and mental state. We started swaying to the music, each of us finding our own little way to move just a couple of feet from each other. It wasn't intimate like slow dancing, but it was nice to have someone let loose with you a little sometimes, to connect with on a deeper level than conversation ever could. Even if dancing with a stranger in an empty coffee shop was pretty damn weird.

*"Seven devils all around you...seven devils in my house..."*

It was so easy for me to just fall into the music, and I could tell that Drea was the same, despite her earlier statement about music in the empty space. Just as the song started coming to a close, I heard a familiar jingling sound.

"Andrea, dear!" I turned to the source of the voice and found an old woman standing by the counter. She had long wispy, delicate white hair that made her appear almost mystical, bright blue eyes that could be defined clear across the shop, and a strong, angular face that was anything but hard or rough looking. She looked like she had worked hard her whole life, but wouldn't dare touch a tool with her delicate, perfectly manicured hands. I don't even know how I could call this woman "old". She may have been up there in years, but she was spritely, standing tall, and dressed in a kaleidoscope of colours and long flowy skirts. I instantly loved her. "How about you get me a hot cup of tea? I feel like today is going to be a good one!" She stated with a beaming smile in my direction.

Drea skipped to the counter and got to work. "Sure thing, Miss Clove!" She chirped.

Miss Clove moved to the table nearest me and patted the chair beside her. I noticed that she was decorated on every visible part of her body with various, mismatched jewelry. I didn't feel alarmed or nervous, so I decided to comply, despite that fact that I maybe should have been reciting my mother's lessons regarding "stranger danger". I moved to sit in the chair next to her and stumbled over one of the mismatched rugs that were scattered around the shop. She caught my arm in a surprisingly firm grasp and helped me into the chair.

"Tsk, tsk, tsk. You're going to snap your ankle in those, my dear." She said with mock sternness. Then she leaned in and whispered conspiratorially, "it's alright though, we can hold each other up." She winked as she lifted the bottom of her skirts to reveal some of the most adorable wedges I had ever seen. We sat there and giggled together for a moment, and then Drea was there with Miss Clove's tea.

"Piping hot, two sugars!" She said, placing it on the table with the same flourish that I had noted earlier. She sat down opposite us and leaned her forearms on the table. "So, what are you two old hens gossiping about?"

Miss Clove and I looked at each other and then back at Drea. "Shoes!" We said unanimously, falling into another fit of giggles. Miss Clove sounded so young when she laughed, that I wouldn't have guessed she was any older than I was if I had heard her voice through a curtain, or any other device preventing face-to-face interaction.

I wiped little tears from my eyes. "Miss Clove saved my life while you were off slacking."

Miss Clove gasped and placed a heavily decorated hand over her heart. "Darling, Andrea here calls me 'Miss Clove' because her parents are apparently set in their ways, but you may call me Clove. I'm not nearly as old as I look, so there's no need for formalities." She put her hand over mine on the table and gave me a small smile while Drea rolled her eyes and propped her chin on her hand, feigning boredom.

I took a moment to wonder if this was normal for little towns, or if I just happened to be that approachable. I met Drea maybe twenty minutes ago and Clove probably five minutes ago, but they were both acting as though it was perfectly normal to dance around, sit, and talk with a complete stranger. I mean, I did it for a living, but that was different... Wasn't it?

The sound of Clove clearing her throat brought me back to the present. "So..."

"Oh, Ria." I supplied.

Clove beamed, her luminous blue eyes twinkling. "So, Ria, what brings you to our little township?" She asked, pulling a stray lock of ashen hair behind her ear.

I looked down at my hands twined together on the table and contemplated how to phrase my situation without giving these, although kind, strangers a complete run down of my life. "I'm... Between places right now. I just needed a change of scenery, and I just found this place by accident and decided to stop to rest." I said it all slowly, chewing over my words.

Drea practically started bouncing in her seat, abandoning her disinterested ruse. "Oh! My mom works at the inn up the road, and I can totally get you a discount on a room."

She looked so excited that I was having trouble thinking of a polite way to refuse, when Clove jumped to my rescue.

"Nonsense! I still have space in that old house, and dear Ria here is more than welcome to stay." She gave me a knowing look that gave me chills, but not the creepy kind.

I started fumbling with my words in the face of this woman's generosity. "I-I have a fear of used beds." I finally blurted, my brain failing me for the umpteenth time in my life.

Clove nodded her head in understanding while Drea gave me a kind of funny look. Not mean funny, just weird funny. "Totally understandable." Clove agreed. "You don't know what's been done to it – or in it. So, you will be glad to know that there is a brand-new mattress in one of the rooms, complete with plastic wrapping." She grabbed my hand and looked at me earnestly. "I would be more than happy to help, and I live in the cottage next door, so I'm there when things get too stressful." Her words were comforting, and despite hardly knowing her, I found her offer lifting a weight off my shoulders and settling my mind into a state of easy peace. Just one thing bothered me...

Why would things get stressful?

## 3 RIA

I stepped outside under the pretense of needing something from my car, but I was honestly just torn between getting the fuck out of this town filled with too-friendly people and taking Clove up on her offer. I mean, where else would I go? I texted Marie, my current landlady, on the way out of town. I explained the whole situation and she was extremely understanding. She may have possibly, maybe, kinda mentioned that Norman, her husband, was very fond of his medieval torture collection. They were a really fucking weird couple, but they were old, sweet, and very generous, so I obviously liked them anyway.

But... My home. I had just left, and there was no way I could go back to that place after the things I saw. I was scarred for life. So, could I just move to a place where no one knows me? Where I don't have a job or friends? What about the club? There's no way I could just give up the club that I called my home away from house.

*You already called it quits, dumbass.* My inner self reminded me, folding her arms across her chest while rolling her eyes at my insolence. *You said you wouldn't be back, and now you can stick to it.*

I knew she was right, and that sucked big ones. I couldn't argue, so I settled for glaring inwardly, as I often found myself doing.

I paced around my car, trying to clear my head with a little bit of menial movement. I couldn't think sitting still. On the one hand, I didn't have anything waiting for me back home. I had a hog-faced ex-best friend, a hopefully sexually crippled ex-fiancé, and an ex-job that would mock me until the day I died if I returned. I was a bit of a masochist sometimes, but I sure as hell wasn't an idiot. This town was nice, with its historic structure, quietness, and friendly citizens, but it really wasn't the place for a stripper. It's all I had to my name, and I wasn't so sure I was willing to give it up so easily.

But... Would starting over really be so bad?

The question caught me by surprise and my steady cadence

faltered. Would it? I could reinvent myself. Small town girl, Ria. I had plenty of cash stashed away for now in my giant popcorn tin, so I could get by for a few months if I was careless, or a year if I was frugal. That would buy me time to figure out what it was that the new Ria wanted to do. My inner self was doing a jig, and by jig, I mean that she was doing some pretty risqué moves that my outer self wouldn't have been caught dead doing, which says a lot because, you know, the whole stripper thing. At least someone was happy. I mean, I was happy, but *I* wasn't happy. The I inside I was happy. That was kinda the same I, right? My outer I was making my inner brain hurt. Not that I had an outer brain. Son of a-

Spurred on by my internal ramblings, I stood up straighter, took a deep breath and plowed inside before my brain could regain cognitive function over my mouth. I stepped back through the front door and found Drea and Clove standing by the counter, having what seemed to be a hilarious conversation, if their snickering was anything to judge by.

I cleared my throat quietly as I approached Clove. "Clove, I'm so grateful for your offer, I really and truly am," I started, holding her well-groomed hands in my own. Before I could finish my sentence, Drea was up, up, and away.

"Ria, you can't turn her down! She was just saying she wasn't even going to charge you rent! It's really no trouble, and you wouldn't wanna stay at the inn anyway, it's old and musty, and some of the rooms have roaches, so it's really best if-"

Clove extracted one of her hands from mine and gently clamped it over the outraged girl's mouth. She let out an exasperated sigh and focused her startling eyes on me once more. "What were you saying, dear girl?"

I shot a halfhearted glare at my little curly-haired friend and continued. "I'd be really honoured if you'd let me rent out that room. I think I need a bigger change than what I was looking for, and I hope I can find it here, if even for just a little while." I let out a long breath while I stared at her, waiting for her thoughtful expression to reveal her thoughts.

"Dear girl, you little star, I'm absolutely positive that you'll find the change you need here, even if it's not quite what you might expect it to be." Her eyes were both earnest and sad, so I braced myself for her next words. "But I can't let you rent out that room." I opened my mouth to object, apologize, or beg, I'm not really sure which, but she quickly held up the hand that was previously blockading the onslaught of words that were pouring from Drea's mouth.

"What our little chatterbox here was saying before I so rudely interrupted is true; I would like to help a wandering soul and give you the room for free as long as you're staying. And since you've already accepted the room, I would take it as a great personal offensive if you tried to persuade me to accept money from you." This gentle woman seemed to stand a little taller as she said all of this, and I was nearly standing there with my mouth agape and jaw unhinged. "Of course, fruit baskets are always welcome. Yes, a monthly fruit basket sounds lovely. I will accept one fruit basket per month as your rent."

This time, I'm pretty sure my jowls hit the floor with an audible *thunk*. I swiveled my eyes to Drea, the question of Clove's sanity being forced at her through all of the telepathy abilities that I possessed. I talked to myself in my mind all the time, how hard could it be? But the evil little barista just focused intently on her task of removing an invisible spot from the counter, looking like she was channeling all of her energy into not laughing.

*Thanks a lot, you traitor.* I thought loudly at her. Of course, she didn't respond, but it was worth a shot.

I directed my attention to Clove once again and nodded, smiling as meekly as I could possibly meek.

Clove clapped her hands together once and grinned a grin that belonged on a billboard. "Wonderful!" She exclaimed. "I will happily show you to the house, as I'm sure you could really use the rest. Get yourself a nice cup of tea on our dearest Andrea. I need to run to Hall's and I will be right back to lead the way." She gathered up the small clutch that was lying on the counter beside her, and strode through the door with a gentle jingle.

I turned on Drea, my eyes intending to pierce her flesh with lasers or something equally as impressive and painful. "No, she's not crazy," she said, finally facing me, smiling kindly, but not without humour. "She's a little out there, but she's harmless and we all love it." She hopped clumsily over the counter and started heating up various machines. "So what'll it be, newcomer?"

I smiled almost unwillingly and pulled myself onto the countertop. "Same as before. I can barely function right now. Shouldn't it be illegal to coerce someone into a deal when they're under the influence?" I rambled a little, shamelessly, until Drea turned a wary eye on me. I rolled mine in response. "Under the influence of sleep deprivation. Fuck. I need to rethink the number of shots I need. Espresso, not alcohol, though I could totally go for some tonight. Oh, do you have a liquor store? Better stock up for a room warming party." Okay, I rambled more than a little. I was halfway off the mental diving board to asking if there were any hot guys to invite when my chest received a painful stab. Oh yeah. Hot guys suck. Not that Lex was hot. He was ugly. Not so ugly that he'd lower my standards, but I mean, he was ugly to me now. Cheaters were ugly.

Drea plopped my coffee beside me on the counter with what I'm going to guess is a natural flourish and not just a work thing like I had first been thinking, and leaned her hip against the counter. "So you're really doing it, huh?" She asked. "We haven't had anyone new in town for a few years now. It's like no one even knows the town exists half the time." She swiped a bagel from the display case and took a nibble.

"Yeah," I said, mildly distracted. I pinched off a piece of her bagel and chewed while I thought. "I need a change, and I think this could be a good one. Besides, the whole town is kinda cute." My inner self nodded her agreement, appearing serene and pleased with herself. I started sipping at my coffee and gazed out the storefront windows. I really did like the place, despite it seeming so small. It seemed like a great place to meet decent people and build a little life for myself. And best yet, if it was really as forgotten as Drea said, then my parents would remain a distant, painful memory and stay the hell away from me.

I hopped off the counter and stretched, feeling the caffeine wake me up a bit more. I needed sleep soon, otherwise I was going to have permanent bags under my eyes. "I'm gonna head out to my car and wait for Clove. I'll see you later, okay?" I glanced at Drea and she nodded, picking up a damp cloth and wiping the space where crumbs had fallen on the counter.

"We'll be open until midnight tonight for karaoke. You should swing by. I won't be behind the counter, but I'll be at the bar, enjoying the perks of being twenty-one." The way she grinned and worded the sentence made me curious.

I narrowed my eyes at her for a brief moment. "Is today your birthday, Drea?" I asked slowly, trying to seem disinterested but curious.

She nodded rapidly, her curls flying around her like a possessed squid or something. "Yes ma'am! So you'll be there?" She asked earnestly, her eyes sparkling.

I grinned back, infected by her enthusiasm. "Yeah, I'll be there. Promise." I told her, crossing my heart like I was twelve. "I'll see you tonight." I made a little heart with my hands as I backed out the door with a jingle.

I made my way back to my car and unlocked it before practically falling into my seat. I figured I'd just sit there and play some games on my phone while I waited for Clove. As I was about to press the little *Candy Crush* icon on my home screen, I noticed my message icon said that I had forty-four new text messages. I opened the app and found the first one, from my landlady.

*He'll be out by tomorrow. If you want to come back let us know, otherwise we'll move your belongings to the storage container on the property. Be safe.*

Aww, that was sweet. I shot her a quick message back

explaining that I wasn't sure of my return at the moment and thanking her for her help.

Next, I tapped on the tab labeled "Merc" and found a dozen or so photos of me dancing, along with a message that she probably expected to scare me. *Tell anyone what happened and I'll send these to your parents!*

I actually laughed out loud and considered telling her to go ahead and do it, but I figured that would be a waste of my very valuable energy. I had a camera in my kitchen from the time I hired a plumber to install my new garbage disposal, and the reviews said he was kinda shady. Better safe than sorry, right? I'd log on later and see if I could find any good shots of her running naked through my house.

Then came the one I was dreading. The tab labeled "Baby Love" had twenty-seven messages in it. Trying to stall, I opened his contact and changed his name before going back to the tab that was now labeled "Cardboard". Seemed fitting. I took a deep breath and tried to prepare myself, then I tapped the tab.

Half of the messages were begging me to come back and work things out, another good few were trying to demean me by attacking my job, and the last of the others were threats of calling the police over my assault on him. Ha! That's cute. Trying to scare me back into a relationship wasn't exactly the best tactic, and if he had paid me any real attention while we were together, he would know that threats were not something that I responded to. It started to dawn on me that all of his thoughtfulness was just common sense. I had been infatuated and willing to accept any token of his affection that I hadn't even realized he wasn't really paying attention.

The pang in my heart was so painful that my vision went blurry with tears for a brief moment. I had given so much of myself to someone who only seemed to care about my status as a stripper, probably hoping to make me a trophy wife.

*I thought strippers were supposed to be hot and fun, but you're actually just a whore. Have fun fucking all your "clients".* He wrote in one of the last messages.

I threw my phone into the passenger seat and leaned my head against the steering wheel. Fuck him. Guys who said shit just to hurt their exes after a breakup were the absolute shittiest. I deserved better. Way better. I'm pretty sure a one night stand in this town would be more rewarding than all the time Cardboard and I had been together. I refused to even say his name. I was going to treat him like Voldemort, because I was certain that saying his name would bring death and destruction to my already fragile world.

I closed my eyes for a second, just to get my bearings, when I heard I car honk behind me. I looked up to find Clove behind the wheel of a little blue Honda, obviously older but well cared for. She made a motion with her hand for me to follow her, and she pulled out of the lot. I started my car with the press of a button and started down the winding streets behind my new landlady.

I SLOWLY PULLED down a twisted gravel driveway and my jaw all but dropped through my floorboard as the house came into sight. If I thought my last home was big, boy was I in for a shocker today.

It was a glorified dollhouse, with two stories and immaculate Victorian spires reaching up into the trees that canopied the whole house. It was painted white, with a large wrap-around porch in a muted gray that somehow didn't make the place look dull or desolate. Rose bushes adorned the spaces nearest the porch, with a large flowerbed of flourishing and colourful flowers that I didn't have names for stretching out into a small courtyard. Fruit trees decorated the drive way, all sporting a different variety and also appearing to be flourishing. I questioned how these plants all seemed to be doing so well, seeing as it was autumn, but I didn't think too hard on the subject. The windows that I could see from the front were tall and embellished, with a stained glass pain in what appeared to be an attic window. I made a mental note to go see it up close.

The two cars came to a halt and I stepped out of my car, walking to meet Clove.

"It's lovely, isn't it?" She asked, almost distractedly, as she fumbled in the backseat for a couple of tote bags. I extended an arm to help her and she shot me a look that was similar to a toddler who wanted to slide by himself.

I followed her up the front steps and to the door, where she just walked right in, no lock or anything. She led me first to the living room which seemed almost more like a small ballroom with its high ceiling and crystal chandelier. "Here is the main living space, with all the creature comforts." She introduced, gesturing around her in an exaggerated circle. She proceeded with the tour to the conjoined kitchen and dining room, separated only by a breakfast bar. "This is the kitchen area, with the newest appliances and updated plumbing and electric." She went to each appliance and gestured, as though I had difficulty seeing them, then she took off for the stairs, surprisingly nimble for such an older lady.

The stairs spiraled upward, like the stairs from every girl's dream fairytale, and they seemed really sturdy. Clove was talking again, but I was way too busy looking at the marvelous space laid out before me. When we finally reached a hall atop the stairs, she led us to the right. "And this, little star, is your room." She opened the door slowly, and we stepped inside. I nearly fell to my knees at the gorgeous sight before me and had to hang on to the doorframe to keep myself upright. The space was light an airy, with an antique fourposter canopy bed, dark toned wood furniture, and a huge set of windows set into one of the false spires. A little bench seat had been set in front of the window, and I felt like I'd be spending many of my evenings right there, just enjoying the serenity of the landscapes around me.

And, as promised, there was a brand new mattress, still covered in its shipping plastic and sitting on the bed in anticipation of a new owner.

Clove set down her totes and started pulling things out and handing them to me. The first was a set of new sheets in a crisp white, with matching pillow cases. The next was a cell phone charger, and then a notebook. I was about to hug her and give my thanks when she pulled out a bright crimson, silken comforter. My eyes must have been the size of dinner plates, because I was absolutely in love. It was not only my favourite colour, but it was lavish and exciting, and a huge contrast to the light and sweet energy the room had to it right now. This time, I actually did throw my arms around her.

"Thank you!" I squealed. "How did you know red was my favourite?" It was down to the shade, I mean *wow*!

Clove patted my back gently. "It just seemed like a good fit, dear. Now let's get this all on the bed, and I'll get out of your hair so you can sleep."

I nodded my agreement a little hastily and got to work immediately. "This house must have a dozen bedrooms. Why'd you give me this one?" I was actually thinking the question to myself, but it came out of my physical mouth instead of my mental one.

"It just seemed more your style, little star." She said sweetly. "Of course, you're more than welcome to explore the place, I'm just not claiming any responsibility for what you find." She started chuckling softly to herself.

My interest was certainly peaking as we folded the comforter over the top sheet. "What's in the other rooms?"

Clove started laughing quietly again and took a moment to answer. "Just furniture and nothing that pays rent." She said with a wink in my direction. I started giggling too, because I wasn't paying rent either.

We finished with the bed and Clove wrote her phone number in the notebook she gave me before taking off with strict instructions for me to sleep. Of course, I didn't waste a single second, and I curled up between the sheets and passed out.

## 4 RIA

WHEN I OPENED MY EYES, I BARELY EVEN REALIZED where I was, and it took a moment for my brain to catch up with my vision. I could see soft moonlight filtering through the leaves above, and it very delicately lit the rest of the bedroom. It almost looked like something out of a fairytale. I stretched beneath my covers and then slipped out of bed. I couldn't remember the last time I had slept so long or so late, but I felt renewed and refreshed.

My stomached decided then was the time to make its presence known, and I tried to think about any food places that I may have seen in town. I still had to get ready for Drea's birthday party, and I didn't particularly feel like going all the way back into town just to double back. Then I remembered that Clove had said something about food in the fridge before she left, and my stomach gurgled out a victory shout.

*Down girl, I have to actually get to the kitchen first.*

I opened my door and peeked down the hallway, getting an eerie feeling of not being alone. It was an old house, and the night probably just made it seem haunted. Besides, ghosts weren't a real thing. So, I pushed on, tiptoeing down the stairs carefully so I didn't trip and turn into a ghost myself. As I reached the ground floor, I heard a creak and jumped what felt like half a mile into the air.

*Calm your tits, dude! It's just the floor of an old house, now put your big girl thong on and get your ass in gear.* My inner self wasn't pleased with my scaredy cat shenanigans and took to chastising me in her silken pajamas; the look on her face said she wasn't in the mood to take any shit and going back to sleep was a perfectly feasible option. No way. Nuh-uh. This girl needed food before getting trashed at a karaoke birthday bash, and oversleeping did absolutely nothing for potential wrinkles.

I took a deep breath and pushed on, guided by the moonlight and warm glow coming from the kitchen. I stepped through the arched walkway and saw that the hood light was on over the stovetop. Had it been that way when I came through? I didn't think so, but Clove might've turned it on, anticipating my vampiric rise from the dead after dark.

Shrugging, I opened the left door on the huge fridge and perused the contents. Milk, eggs, biscuits, a random assortment of fruits and vegetables, some thawed steaks, and a few six packs. My sweet, possibly psychotic landlady didn't really seem the type to crack open a cold one, but she was a stranger after all. Who knew?

I grabbed the eggs and located a slab of bacon, deciding that you could never go wrong with breakfast food when you've just woken up. I heard another random creak and jumped again. I reopened the fridge and grabbed one of the beers, deciding that you can never go wrong with alcohol when you're acting like a dumbass in a haunted/non-haunted house. As I closed the fridge door, I could have swore I saw a man standing behind it. I closed my eyes and shook my head.

"What the actual fuck?" A rich, baritone voice said directly in front of me. I popped my eyes open and screamed like I've never screamed before, moving to turn and run for a drawer with knives, but I twisted too fast and found myself falling. Turning mid-fall to catch myself, I landed against something soft and warm, my cheek pressed against the object.

Bright lights flashed on overhead, and I heard scuffling and swearing from all directions. I moved to lift my head and felt my face turn from warm, to hot, to flaming, to a burning inferno with the intensity of a California forest fire.

A dick. I landed on a *dick*.

I squealed and was on my feet, scuttling backward before you could say "penis". I kept backing up, my eyes squeezed shut, until I backed against a body. Warm, large hands gripped my shoulders and spun me around, and when I opened my eyes, I was suddenly pretty sure that I had screamed myself straight to heaven when I found He-Who-Must-Not-Be-Named in bed with The Wicked Witch of the West Coast. You must be wondering why, so I'll go ahead and kill the suspense.

Suddenly, I was staring into the face of an actual, living and breathing angel. He had hair that was a seamless meld from bronze to gold, tousled as though he had just rolled out of bed, his eyes a fierce and intense silver that appeared to shine like headlights in the dark, and a strong, squared off jaw that every *Superman* actor would die for. It had just enough stubble to look rough, yet well maintained.

I found myself going slack-jawed and wide eyed, and seriously considered saying a few Hail Marys.

"Who the fuck are you? What are you doing in our house?" The angel practically growled the questions and his voice sent some very non-angelic, but *very* heavenly tingles straight to some very exciting places. I still found myself unable to speak and he started glowering at me, seeming to analyze me, but in a way that seemed to ask if I was mentally slow.

"Can she even speak?" A very melodic, quiet voice asked to my right.

"She can certainly scream." Another voice replied lazily behind me. I recognized it as the voice that started this whole mess. The penis.

Something seemed to click inside my very flustered, confused brain. Unfortunately, my rational inner self appeared to be momentarily absent, so the next word out of my mouth was probably something that would haunt me to my grave.

"A-angel!" I blurted, my mouth suddenly deciding that consent to speak no longer applied.

I heard a snort to my right. "Oh, it does speak." The voice was clipped with a light accent, like someone born in England, but raised around Americans.

The specimen before me looked like he'd been splashed with cold water, looking surprised and disturbed. He blinked slowly, never taking his shining eyes off me. "Angel?" He repeated, slowly, as if not to frighten me. I nodded once, deciding to roll with whatever madness my mouth was spewing without my consent, and his lips turned up at the corners. "Listen sweetheart," he said, lowering his voice and leaning toward me. We were nearly nose to nose, and I could smell something like burnt sugar and bourbon. It was intoxicating. "I'm no angel."

He suddenly released my shoulders and simultaneously shoved me – not too hard – sending me stumbling backward. Luckily, the only thing I backed into this time was the breakfast bar. Which furnished a very sturdy, heavy looking wooden vase thing. I grabbed it quickly and spun to meet the strangers that had turned my night on its head, brandishing it like a powerful weapon.

"Okay," I said, probably a little too shrilly. "Here's what's going to happen: one of you, and I don't care who, is going to tell me who the fuck you are and what in god's good name is going on here." I felt strong and sure, despite being basically stuck in front of... One... Two... Three... Four... Five. Five very large, very muscled, very... Manly men.

*Sexy. The word you're looking for is sexy.* And my inner self was back. Bring some testosterone into the room, and *BAM!* There she was, bright eyed and her bushy trimmed.

"Hey, it's okay." Said a voice I had heard earlier. I sought out his face and found a very handsome man looking back at me. He appeared refined, yet edgy with his mane of chestnut hair pulled back, a few strands hanging around his face. He looked Russian, with his angular face structure, five o'clock shadow, deep amber coloured eyes, and built but slim physique. "We're just as confused as you are." He continued on with a small, friendly smile, his soft, melodic voice lulling me into a surely false sense of security.

"And pissed." The British guy interjected. I glanced from guy to guy before finding him standing behind the rest of the group. I couldn't clearly make out his face from where he was standing, but the splash of dirty blonde hair would have to serve as a temporary reminder.

The man in front of him spoke next. "It's not every day you find a chick in your kitchen, in nothing but a t-shirt." His voice was like honey, and I was the ant. I certainly felt like an ant; the guy was massive. He was built like a bear, and thanks to his lack of a shirt, I could see every single one of his defined muscles. He had short, wavy, hair in a brown so dark that reminded me of pure, unsweetened cocoa, and his eyes were a perfect ocean blue. He looked like he ate people for fun. More specifically, he looked like he wanted to eat *me*, and only halfway for fun.

I attempted to take a cautious step back, suddenly realizing the terrifying predicament I was in, only to be reminded that I was pressed tightly against the granite countertop. I brandished my wooden vase dangerously, as though it would fend off five men. My head whipped from side to side, trying to figure out how the hell I was going to get out of this literal hot mess, when my weapon was suddenly plucked from my hand. I jolted and spun around, facing the other side of the breakfast bar to find the weapon thief.

Attached to the wooden vase was an arm littered with tattoos. "That's *mine.*" The face attached to the arm growled. His dark hair was combed back in a sort of retro wave style, and his brown eyes couldn't have been glaring at me harder if they tried. He reminded me of the main character of a steamy Spanish soap opera I watched one time, just with way more ink.

And of course, my brain finally registered that six men was just way too much for my five-foot-two frame to handle, so I attempted a mad dash for the doorway–

And fell flat on my face.

I heard a collective groan sound around the room as I lay on the floor, trying to either gather the courage to get up, or the patience to feign death.

"Okay, I'm out." Said the British voice.

There was a shuffling of multiple sets of feet and the room felt lighter. Actually, *I* felt lighter. Like, really light. Because I was being lifted off the floor.

I squealed loudly and very girlishly, struggling to get free. When my basic struggling proved to be generally useless, I started slamming my fists against the torso of whichever giant was hauling me around.

"Would you just stop?" The giant asked. "You're not exactly causing damage, but I'd really hate to fall down the stairs with you." The dick. No really, it was the guy whose penis I landed on. He turned me so that I was actually facing a direction in which I could see, and I only halfway regretted it.

He was seriously gorgeous and looked kinda like one of those punk kids that used to hang out at the skatepark in my old town. His hair was cropped short on the sides and long up top, with the rich blue-black marred by a vibrant purple that covered the long part. He had a spiked stud in the middle of his lower lip, and a bar through his eyebrow. His eyes were probably the most heart-meltingly beautiful hazel I had ever seen in my entire life, with greens, browns, and golds that seemed to be both warring with each other and peacefully coexisting.

I realized that I must have been staring at him for entirely too long to be considered socially acceptable, because he looked down at me with one studded eyebrow raised.

I also know that I must have turned my favourite colour, because my cheeks were on fire and my inner self was giving me a cheeky grin. "Um," I began eloquently. "Hi?"

The giant shot me a lopsided grin as he pushed through my bedroom door and set me down on my feet, where I wobbled for a brief second before finding my balance again. "Hi." He replied, still looking at me with his goofy grin. He extended a hand out to me. "I'm Beck."

I cautiously gripped his hand in return. "I'm Ria." I replied, trying to sound a lot less confused and afraid for my life than I actually was. I mean, his hand was huge. What were they putting in the water out here?

Beck nudged his way past me and sat down on the edge of my bed. "So, from the top." He demanded lightly. I must have looked even more confused than I felt because he patted the bed next to him and explained, "who you are, why you're here, etcetera."

I meandered to the side of the bed where my head would rest and pulled my knees to my chest. Beck's gaze averted downward and I shifted my shirt to tuck under my toes. "Well, my name is Ria, I needed a change of scenery after a break up, and my apparently insane landlady offered me this place while also managing to *forget* to tell me I had roommates." I rambled everything off very shortly, trying to avoid telling the smoking hot guy at the foot of my bed my entire life story.

Beck looked thoughtful for a moment and then stood up. "Well, I'll leave you to it then, and I'll have one of the guys talk to Clove." He muttered something else under his breath and it took me a second to work it out.

*Crazy old bat.*

I chuckled quietly and immediately grew somber again. "So, uh," I started. "Sorry. About earlier, I mean." I gestured to his general personage.

He grinned again, almost wickedly this time. "I'll get even with you one day, *roomie.*" I could actually feel the lump in my throat I was trying to swallow. "But right now, I need that midnight snack that you so rudely interrupted." And then he was gone, door closed, nothing but the smell of peppermint remaining.

What.

The.

Fuck.

I looked at my phone for the time and saw that it was well past time to be ready and out the door. So, I had two options:

I could haul ass to the coffee shop and support my only real friend in town, or I could stick around here and try not to have waking nightmares of six guys roasting me on a spit. Well, five, because Beck actually seemed pretty nice. However, that mental image was enough to get my ass in gear, hunting through my bags and brushing my hair into something that resembled a fashionable style. I hunted around for my car keys and took off down the stairs, taking care not to stumble in my unreasonable choice of footwear.

Once I reached the bottom, I cautiously looked around for any immediate threats – mostly in the form of anything having a penis – and saw Beck at the breakfast bar with two bags of chips and several bowls of dip. Speaking of penises. He gave me a brief wave before I was out the door, out the driveway, and halfway out of my damn mind.

## 5 RIA

THE DRIVE FROM THE HOUSE AND BACK INTO TOWN WAS quick and uneventful. It was all kind of a blur though, because I'm pretty sure my brain hasn't entirely worked out the whole situation with my very unexpected roommates... Who, incidentally, were also not expecting me. Yay.

I circled around to the back of the coffee shop to find a

parking spot, but all of the spaces were filled. At least I knew where the popular hangout was. I was about two seconds away from deciding to park down the street when a flash of white caught my eye. I turned my attention to the distraction and couldn't help the brief laugh that escaped me; it was a handwritten sign in an empty parking space that read: *newbie parking.*

I could practically feel Drea's satisfaction as I pulled into the space. It was pretty obvious that I was the only newbie in town, and I found it a little endearing that she had reserved the spot for me without even knowing for sure that I would show up. But honestly, who was I to pass up a party?

I wrapped my little black bomber jacket around my shoulders as I stepped out of the cozy warmth of my car and into the cold night air, making a mad dash for the front door. Okay, this building was surprisingly big, and it was entirely too chilly. I rounded the corner and pushed through the cheerfully jingly door like a madwoman, trying not to stumble over the multiple rugs again. I had to stop for a second while my eyes adjusted to the scene before me.

As opposed to how the shop had been when I had arrived in the morning, the place was completely full to the brim and resembled an actual, low budget nightclub. The lights had been turned down low, and colourful spotlights and slow-moving lasers now filled the space. The music wasn't as loud as it was in the clubs I'd worked at, but it was certainly loud enough to enjoy while conversing. I scanned the scattered tables for my friend, but it was pretty hard to see with such low lighting.

"Ria!" I heard from my left. I turned toward the sound of

Drea's voice, trying to find her mane of curly hair in the crowd. Suddenly, I felt my wrist being ensnared, and I was being dragged through the mess of bodies and mismatched furniture. "We're sitting over here." Drea hollered unnecessarily. The music seriously wasn't that loud, otherwise I was going deaf prematurely. That thought had me getting a little paranoid, so I started trying to catch pieces of conversations as we passed different groups.

"If I go home and show them this grade, I'm deader than dead." One girl was complaining.

"She's still in an induced coma, so they're not sure..."

"Come on, baby, I'll make it special, I swear!" *Oh hell no.*

At the last one, I yanked my hand from Drea's surprisingly strong grip and feigned a drunk stumble into the guy's table, knocking his drink down his entire front.

He jumped up, locking his eyes to mine and failing pretty miserably at looking intimidating. "What the fuck, bitch?" He screamed at me, spittle flying. He was short and stocky, with ginger hair combed back and a large spattering of dark freckles all over his face. The worst part, though, is that his eyes were too small and too far apart. And they were the colour of wet cardboard.

My eyes shot to the small, blonde girl he was sitting with. She looked entirely uncomfortable and no older than maybe seventeen. It was like I temporarily had no control over my movements, like I was possessed, and before I could even register what was happening, my hand was cracking across his face. "How *dare* you try to sneak around behind my back?" I screeched, grabbing the girl's drink and throwing it in his face.

My inner self was doing a jig, obviously approving of my intervention.

The slimeball made a grab for me, his eyes filled with rage, but a larger hand wrapped around my waist at the last second.

"Finders keepers." Said a familiar voice attached to the hand. The beady-eyed guy started backing away with his hands slightly raised and completely red in the face, and with a last look of complete disgust in his direction, the girl was gone, fleeing into the crowd. *Thank god for that.*

Before I could open my mouth again, I was being steered in the opposite direction.

I turned and looked up at my saviour, who just happened to be built like a brick shithouse, and I very clearly recall him being shirtless the last time we saw each other, which was less than an hour ago.

"So, uh," I fumbled. "Hi?" Why did I keep saying that like a question? "Hi" wasn't a question, it was a greeting. As in, *Hi, my name is...*

*Get it together!* I scolded myself.

The guy just grunted in response and deposited me by a chair where Drea was sitting. And of course, just as I was about to thank him for taking me back to my friend, he sat down next to me. Just. My. Luck.

"Ria, what the hell?" Drea squealed. "You haven't even been here for twenty-four hours, and you're already hooking up with skeazey guys?" She looked absolutely appalled and started shaking her head like she was trying to get rid of a really bad mental image. I was seriously thinking about doing the same thing.

I did feel the need to defend myself, though. I wasn't *that* kind of ho. "No, I would never, ever, ever." I was shaking my head so hard that I could practically feel my brain rattling around. "He was trying to pressure some teenage girl into having sex with him." I explained, not even trying to mask my complete disgust.

Understanding dawned on Drea's face while confusion settled over Godzilla next to me.

"If Ria had tried to tell the girl not to feel pressured, she'd do it anyway and regret it later." She explained to our hulking companion.

The two of us watched the gears tuning and clicking into place. "So," he said slowly. "You needed her to see him as a lowlife, loser playboy so she'd choose to say no on her own?" He directed the question at me, settling his deep blue eyes on mine and making me squirm nervously.

"Bingo." I replied. "So, now that you've both seen my ass and saved it, care to introduce yourself?" I reached over and stole Drea's glass, taking a long swig without thinking it through, and nearly choked. It was disgustingly sweet. Gross.

Drea looked back and forth between the two of us. "I'm so confused. Didn't Miss Clove introduce you?"

I took another nauseatingly sweet sip. "Nope. She conveniently neglected to inform me –"

"Or any of us." The Big Friendly Giant interjected.

"That we were going to be roomies, or even that either party existed." I shrugged my shoulders and made to finish off Drea's drink before she yanked it out of my hands.

She shot me a glare and downed her drink. "Ria, Kellan, Kel, Ria. Now you've been introduced," she moved to get up from her seat and wobbled slightly. "And now I need another drink. It's my birthday." She added, glaring down the two of us. The two of us mumbled out our apologies as she took off for the bar, leaving the two of us in a very uncomfortable silence.

"So, Ria, how do you know Clove?" Kellan finally asked.

I gave a little shrug and stared intently at the wood grain on the table, the other partygoers, and even the lights – anything to avoid looking into those eyes. "I just met her here this morning, when I first got into town." I replied. I saw his eyebrow raise out of the corner of my eye and decided to put off his questioning until later. "So, how do you know Drea?" Divert, divert, divert. In the business I was in, conversation was never about me, and customers usually only asked about my personal life out of courtesy, and not really out of interest. Diverting the conversation back to them was always the best tactic.

Kellan looked out in the direction Drea went in and it was a few seconds before he spoke again. "You see all these people here tonight?" He asked, almost sadly. He turned back to look at me.

I took a quick look around before nodding.

He took a deep breath. "Out of all the people here, the only ones here to celebrate her birthday are you and I." He stared angrily down at the table, as if he was about to go Hulk on it. "Everyone else is here for the cheap booze and karaoke."

I had to take a second to mull that all over in my brain. It didn't make sense. "But she's so likeable, and she works one of the most sociable jobs ever." I was genuinely confused. I'd assume that she wasn't very good with people, or just didn't enjoy making friends, but my initial interaction with her said otherwise.

"This is an old town, and the people here are just as old fashioned, for the most part." His expression became solemn. I'm pretty sure that this was the closest this massive guy could ever come to tearing up. "Her sister is pretty popular around town, but Drea..." He looked like he was struggling to get the words out. "She plays for your team, if you know what I mean." He give me a sort of sad smile, which looked absolutely bizarre and out of place.

*Hold on two seconds.*

"The don't like her because she's *lesbian*?" I gasped. "What century are these people living in?" I was beyond appalled. I was completely aghast.

Kellan shook his head and looked out to the crowd again. "I know, it's fucked up, but it's their loss."

My heart swelled with admiration for both my beefy new roommate, and my sweet new friend. "I know, she's pretty damn awesome." I said, staring at the table again. My head whipped back up almost instantly. "Wait, how did you two become friends, then?" That was one thing that definitely baffled the ever loving fuck out of me.

He turned back to me and grinned a terrifying grin. It was

kinda hot. Uh, not that I noticed or anything. "She's something I can never have. I like that." Yep. Hot. Really, really, *really* hot.

*Totally noticing.* My inner self jeered.

I popped out of my seat before making a decision I'd seriously regret, which could have either been talking out loud to myself or jumping the missing Twin Tower before me. "I'm heading to the bar, want anything?" I asked.

Kellan slapped a twenty in my hand and said, "bourbon, two rocks."

I nodded and took off in the direction Drea had gone, suddenly realizing she'd been gone awhile. Once I reached the bar, I flagged down the bartender and ordered two bourbons, taking care to remember Kellan's two rocks, since he went to the trouble of requesting it in the first place. Once the drinks were ordered, I leaned back against the bar and surveyed the crowed.

*Where the actual fuck was she?*

No sooner had I thought the words, did my eyes land on the next karaoke contestant: my new friend. I had heard the girl hum earlier and it was not a sound I'd like to hear over a microphone, and considering how long she'd been gone and how drunk she already was, I wasn't about to let her embarrass herself.

I started pushing my way through the crush of bodies, calling her name. She didn't even bother to look up. Suddenly, the music started and it was too late. Drea opened her mouth, and mine gaped. That was one hundred percent *not* the voice I heard her humming with that morning, and I was at a total loss words. I listened to her belt out a couple of lines, stunned to bits, when I heard the bartender call out to me. I headed back to the bar and gathered the drinks, quickly moving to the table to drop Kellan's off with him so I could go back and support my friend.

"Here you go!" I said cheerily, plopping the glass on the table and turning to go back to the karaoke floor.

"Wait, Ria! Where are you going?"

I spun so fast that I gave myself a little bit of vertigo. "Drea?" I blinked rapidly a few times, staring at my friend who was sitting at the table, then turned to face the floor, where my friend was also standing and singing karaoke.

*Okay, so I entered the Matrix. Go me.* My inner self had propped herself up on a chaise lounge, a warm rag laid over her eyes in a show of dramatics.

"How...?" I trailed off, glancing between the two.

Drea rolled her eyes and gave Kellan a sidelong look, who took a sip of his drink and looked like he was thoroughly enjoying the show. "That would be my sister, Ana." She didn't say it with much distaste, more like halfhearted boredom, like it was a question that got asked way too frequently. Which, it probably did. "The whole twin thing throws people off, but I thought this jackass had already spilled the beans." She shoved Kellan playfully, and he grinned in return.

I watched the exchange with curiosity. "He told me you had a sister, but he seems to be channeling his inner Clove." I said as I rolled my eyes. Seriously, though. Ana? Drea? Andrea? Heh.

Kellan broke out in guffaws while Drea giggled.

They were actually a really cute pair, though I could definitely never see them as relationship material. They had this weird bond that was almost visible, like a cord stretching between them.

"So, uh, Kellan?" He continued laughing, likely not even hearing me. "Hey, Iron Giant!" I half-shouted.

He stopped laughing abruptly and raised an eyebrow at me, looking seconds away from breaking out in another round of uncontrollable laugher. "Iron Giant?" He repeated, deadpan.

"Good, I've got your attention." I was torn between being scared of his muscles crushing me and laughing my own ass off at the incredulous look on his face. Both would probably mean my own death. "I've got a question."

Kellan's face grew a little wary. "No personal questions, and you're good."

"Duly noted." I replied dryly. "I was actually wondering how everything at the house is going to work out. I'm pretty sure no one wants me there, and I wasn't exactly expecting roommates." He looked just the tiniest bit hurt before his face went carefully blank. "Not that I have a problem with you. Even Beck is kind of okay. I think." I amended.

He looked like he was thinking it all over for a second. "Well, whether or not the other guys want you around isn't really their choice to make. All votes have to be unanimous."

Drea chose that moment to jump back into the conversation. "Wait, your brothers don't want her around?" Drea looked so genuinely upset that I wanted to take back everything that had just came out of my stupid mouth.

Wait.

*Brothers?*

I tried so hard not to look shocked, I really did, but it was almost impossible with a news bomb like that dropped on my head. I forced myself to cool down for a second. Maybe not all of them were brothers. She didn't exactly say a number. It was entirely plausible that a couple of them were related.

Kellan rolled his eyes at Drea's dramatics. "No, I'm pretty sure Beck likes her fine. Besides, after the shock of her being there wears off, everything will be a-okay." He flashed her a completely heart-melting grin and she smiled timidly back.

She turned to look at me, then, fixing me with her innocent, earnest eyes. "If any one of those Severin boys gives you a hard time, just let me know and I'll sic Kel on them, 'kay?" She smiled at me and blew her a little kiss across the table.

"Thanks, boo." Severin? What a strange last name. Well, not that I had much room to talk.

"Don't mention it, cutie."

I stood up and stretched, looking at the rapidly thinning crowd around us. "I need to head out. I've still got to unpack." I told my two table companions. "Drea, do you need a ride home?" She'd had way too many drinks tonight for me to feel safe sending her home on her own.

She waved my worried expression away. "I'm fine, Ana's driving. She doesn't really drink." She told me, wrapping me in a big hug. "Thank you so much for coming! I know you don't really know me, but I really appreciate it."

I hugged her back hard before pulling back. "It was totally my pleasure. And happy birthday, girl." I zipped up the front of my jacket as I started out the door and turned to wave goodbye to the two of them before realizing that Kellan was following me. I almost freaked out before realizing he was probably heading the same way I was. You know, home.

Once outside the shop, the cold air biting at my nose and cheeks, I picked up the pace to my car.

"Where's the fire?" Kellan said from behind me.

I glanced back at him like he had grown an extra head. "It's cold as tits out here. I need heated seats." I told him, sounding a little prissy, but honestly not caring.

His eyebrows shot up into his hairline. "Heated seats?" He seemed like he was bouncing a little. "Can I ride with you?" Yep, definitely bouncing, and it was kind of adorable.

I laughed a little. "Calm down, Hulk, or you're gonna cause another west coast earthquake." He rolled his eyes at me but kept smiling his super sexy smile. "And didn't you bring your own ride?"

Kellan waved his hand like it might fend off the offending question. "I rode my bike here, and heated seats sound a hell of a lot better right now." The mental image of my giant, mouthwateringly sexy companion riding a bicycle almost made me crack up, but I knew he must have been talking about the gnarly Harley sitting down the parking lot from my own baby.

I couldn't bring myself to let him freeze, even if he did alternately scare the piss out of me and make me wanna jump his bones. "Oh, fine, come on." I told him, pressing the button to start the car. "Let's get home."

HEADING BACK DOWN THE DARK AND TWISTY ROAD TO the house, the silence in the car was borderline deafening. I kept flicking my eyes over to my enormous roommate, he was just staring out the window, completely silent and stoic. Every time I contemplated doing something to create a reprieve from the awkwardness, it would fall short in my mind. I had even considered turning on the radio, but I couldn't tell what kind of music he was into, and if he was into rap, I might have to throw one of us out of the car.

I kept staring at the dimly illuminated scenery around me, the waxing moon barely visible behind a spattering of clouds making the foliage appear almost menacing. I shook off one of those chills that people get when thinking about creepy stuff.

I tapped the steering wheel in frustration. Why was this drive taking so long?

Kellan cleared he throat beside me, startling me more than I would ever care to admit. "So, does the radio work?" He asked, his voice sounding a lot deeper and more tempting in the close quarters of my little car.

"Yeah, knock yourself out." I replied nonchalantly.

*Please don't be rap, please don't be rap.*

I kept the mantra going in my head while he fiddled with the stations, momentarily landing on a song that had a good rhythm before the rapper started doing his thing. Kellan made a sound like he was gagging, and I had to fight the hard fight to keep myself from doubling over. Finally, he found a station playing old rock and settled back into his seat, humming along with the song.

I nearly sighed out loud in relief and relaxed into the music.

"Where ya from?" Kellan asked, surprising the hell out of me.

*Someone's a chatterbox.*

I bit the inside of my cheek while I thought about how to answer. I didn't exactly want anyone following me back if I decided to head home, and while he had already seen me half-dressed, I wasn't about to share personal information with a strange, abnormally attractive, giant new roommate. "I grew up in Cottage Grove." I finally told him. At least if anyone went looking for me in my hometown, they'd be chased away with pitchforks and torches. They weren't actually that old fashioned, but they might as well have been – growing up, I never realized that pants were so comfortable and liberating. What a life.

Kellan eyed me suspiciously, obviously trying to chew over his next words. "You're a long way from home, then." He remarked.

I fought back an eyeroll. "That, I surely am." If I thought I'd be willing to jump from a moving vehicle before, that was nothing compared to how I was feeling right at that moment.

"What brought you all the way out here?" He persisted.

I bought myself a few seconds by turning onto the long driveway that led to the house. "Running. Life sucks sometimes, and it's easier to run than deal with the fallout, you know?"

He gave me a sad look. "I know."

I parked the car and got out, heading for the front door. I turned around and watched Kellan trying to get out of my little car and giggled a bit at his attempted maneuvering. "Need some help, Gigantor?" I called quietly, noting the lack of lights in the house.

Even in the dim lighting of the half-covered moon, I could see the scowl he shot at me as he squeezed himself out and I clutched my midsection while laughing. "Ha, ha." He mocked, coming up the steps.

Wiping a tear from my eye, I opened the front door and headed for the stairs. "'Night." I said to Kellan with a small smile. Back in the house, I was feeling a lot less bold and friendly.

He raised an eyebrow at me. "I'm gonna make some food, want any?" He offered.

I just shook my head. "No, that's fine. Thank you, though." I grinned and started back up the stairway, and I could have sworn I heard him say "goodnight", but when I looked back, he was nowhere in sight.

Back in my room, with the door firmly shut behind me, I turned on the lamp by my bed and started rifling through my bags for something with more sleep appeal and less cornered-by-six-guys-in-the-kitchen appeal. I quickly slipped into some capri yoga pants and a tank top, went to my adjoined bathroom and brushed my teeth, then curled up under the covers like a cat.

The idea of sleep was an attractive one, but the reality was evading me. My door didn't have a lock, so what if one of them decided to try something? My mind was at war with itself, the rational side fighting with my paranoia for dominance.

I decided to focus on counting the shadows of leaves on my floor, trying to make out the individual shapes and taking guesses at how many were in each indecipherable blob.

After who knows how long, I began drifting, dreaming of dark blue eyes and even darker hair.

I OPENED my eyes to bright morning sunlight and was half tempted to pull the covers over my eyes and go back to sleep. Mornings weren't my thing, I was a creature of the night. I rolled over to check the time on my phone and saw a glass of orange juice and two little white tablets, with a small folded paper sitting beside them.

I reached over and grabbed the note, propping myself up on my elbow.

*GOOD MORNING,*

*I DON'T KNOW how much you drank last night, but you didn't eat, so I assume you're hungover.*

*Thought this might help a little, and there's breakfast downstairs, if you can stomach it.*

*Oh, and the guys want to talk.*

*K*

OKAY, I'd have to be a complete moron not to think that was the absolute cutest thing ever. On one hand, the very thing I was afraid of happened and one of the guys came in while I was sleeping. On the other hand, that note was so sweet, and from someone who didn't even know my last name. It was like every girl's fantasy one-night stand with the perfect prince, sans sexy times.

Groaning, I rolled onto my back and threw my arm over my eyes. How I could have forgotten my roommate troubles so easily was beyond me. I hadn't even talked to clove, and believe me, I was definitely going to have a serious talk with her about necessary information and how to properly share it with the parties involved. But to do that I'd have to get out of bed and moving didn't exactly appeal to me at the moment. Even my little inner self was still snoring soundly. Not that I snored, because I didn't, but she definitely did.

Deciding that I was a one hundred percent capable and mature woman, I threw back my covers and walked to the bathroom. I got to washing my face, noting that my fair skin was slightly flushed, but since I didn't ever get acne, I knew it was just my nerves. I blotted my face with the hand towel on the side of the sink while I tried to collect my thoughts.

I knew who Beck and Kellan were, so that made things a little easier. However, I had no clue what the others were all about and that just didn't sit right with me. A house full of men that I knew absolutely nothing about was most certainly cause for nervousness, right?

I went back into my room and hunted for my hair brush. While pulling through the small tangles, I looked at the orange juice and aspirin again, feeling unreasonably guilty. I almost never had issues with hangovers so there was no need for the aspirin, and I really didn't like orange juice in the mornings because it made my mouth feel weird.

I decided that dumping the orange juice was the best course

of action, and quickly poured it down the bathroom sink before taking the glass with me down the stairs.

Once I rounded the corner into the kitchen, I prayed to anyone listening that my heart wasn't pounding loud enough for everyone to hear, because five pseudo-familiar sets of eyes landed on me all at once, locking me in place.

*Move. Just move. Fuck.*

I gave a little smile and waved. "Morning, boys." I greeted, as nonchalantly as I could manage. I focused very intently on walking to the sink to rinse my glass. "Is the dishwasher clean or dirty?" I was still avoiding eye contact, and I was doing a pretty great job of it, if I do say so myself.

"It's empty." I heard Kellan say, my knight in shining armour.

I simply nodded and opened the dishwasher, placing my glass up top and taking my time closing the door.

"Coffee?" I heard Beck ask.

Believe me when I say I turned around and nodded so fast that the world started going off kilter. "Please!" I replied excitedly. Coffee is love, coffee is life.

The purple-haired man got up from his seat and leaned across me to pull a mug from the cabinet. As he stretched, his loose black t-shirt rode up just enough for me to catch a mouthwatering glimpse of some seriously chiseled lower abs. *Yum.*

After getting the mug, he walked over to the Keurig in the corner and all but summoned a k-cup.

"Beck..." Another voice warned. I turned and found it was the soft-spoken guy with the long hair.

Beck continued making the coffee. "Gray..." He mocked back, never turning around.

The guy – Gray – narrowed his eyes at Beck's back, "E's going to be pissed if you use his coffee." He warned.

Beck made a talking motion with his hand and set the coffee to brew. "Well, then two things can happen." He held up one finger. "One, he can get the fuck over it and be a gentleman." He said. Then he held up the second finger while putting cream and sugar on the counter in front of me. "Or two, he can act like the brit he is and drink tea or some shit after I throw the whole lot into sea." He handed me the mug of steaming joe and retrieved a spoon from the drawer.

Kellan and the heavily tattooed guy snickered behind their mounds of pancakes, and I heard footsteps in the doorway.

"Well then," the brit in question began. "How's that for irony?" He yawned as he walked further into the kitchen making a beeline for me.

I nearly started flapping my mouth about, trying to figure out what to do or say. Maybe if I handed over the offending coffee, he'd leave it at that. Before I had time to formulate a rational thought, he was in front of me.

"Care to move, love? You're in my way." He said without a hint of the anger that I had been expecting I scooted to the side, dragging the creamer with me and reaching for the sugar when his hand caught mine. I gasped and froze, his fingers pulsing little bolts of lightning through my body in the strangest way. "Trust me, it's better without sugar." That's all he said before he released my hand and went back to making his own caffeinated beverage, taking his electric touch with him.

With slightly unsteady hands, I started pouring my cream and paused before grabbing the sugar, shooting a sideways glance at the British guy. Hot didn't even begin to cover it.

He had multihued dirty blonde hair that had a stylized messiness, as though he worked really hard to make it look that effortless. And his body was absolutely godly from what I could see, with wiry muscles banding around his arms and is sculpted collarbone. And, ugh, that jaw and five o'clock shadow; I was on the verge of swooning, while my inner self was already doing so, dramatic sigh and all.

I took a sip of the coffee sans sugar and my eyes widened. It had a smoky, chocolatey taste to it and I was completely hooked.

Kellan chuckled from his place at the table. "You've turned her over to the dark roast side, E." He teased.

The British guy turned to face me and I momentarily forgot how to draw breath. His eyes were the strangest, most exotic shade of violet that I had ever seen. I was pretty sure that if I stared too long, I'd be lost forever.

He smirked at me, showing off a cute little dimple that snapped me out of my brief daze. "I told you so, didn't I?"

I nodded and smiled a friendly smile. At least, I hoped it was friendly. "It's really good. What is it?" I asked, needing to stock up on a lifetime supply of the caffeinated goodness.

He raised an eyebrow at me. "I flavour it myself." He said

simply. "That's why I don't let that glutton over there touch the stuff. It's perfect, so enjoy."

Beck snorted. "I touched it." He chortled like he had gotten away with some big feat.

The guy rolled his eyes at Beck's childish behavior. "Come, we would like to speak with you." He gestured to the breakfast bar, where I obligingly took a seat on one of the barstools.

"*Chert, chuvak*," Gray groaned. "It's too early for this *der'mo*." He planted his face in his arms like he was about to fall asleep in class.

His use of foreign words had me curious. British accents were all over the place on the west coast, so that wasn't exactly surprising; I had even met a hot British guy at a marina in California once. Talk about a dream boat.

I leaned over and boldly poked the long-haired man's shoulder. He peeked up from his arm pillow with a question in his eyes. "I can't place your accent. Where are you from?" Okay, that was a safe question to ask, right? People got asked where they were from all the time.

He eyed me with both curiosity and wariness. "I spent my entire life all over, but my family was Russian." He explained quietly, as though we were in a fragile bubble. "Quiet, E's ready to get on with it and I need a nap."

Knowing damn well that it was only about eleven in the morning, I held back a snort. Boys.

E clapped his hands together once, getting the room's attention. "First thing's first: introductions." He said smoothly, sitting the opposite way on a dining chair. "I'm

Eliam." I was surprised by how much his name didn't surprise me. It just seemed to fit. "You've met Kellan and Beck." He nodded to each of them who nodded back.

"My name is Rafe." The heavily tattooed guy said. "Sorry about last night." He mumbled, rubbing the back of his neck. I smiled at him and nodded my head once.

"And this is Gatlin." Eliam gestured to the one I had called an angel, with his steely eyes and overall smouldering sexiness. He pinned Eliam with an angry glare, as though he was offended that he couldn't introduce himself.

There was silence in the kitchen as everyone looked at Gray's still form.

"And that sleeping heap of hair is Gray." Kellan finally supplied. Eliam shot him a glare that said he didn't appreciate his role as the introducer being usurped.

"I'm Ria." I said, looking to each set of eyes, except Gray's.

Eliam leaned forward on the back of his chair. "Good, now that all that is done, let's make one thing very clear: I don't dislike you, but I really don't want you here, or anywhere near my brothers." He said in a low voice. "All of our votes have to be unanimous, and the vote to remove you was not. So, here's the deal," he leaned closer toward me. "If there is any amount of money that will make you leave, name it and it shall be yours, so long as you just go and don't come back."

I jolted in my seat as though I'd been slapped. I'd been propositioned many times in my life for different activities and differing sums of money, but *never* had anyone attempted to chase me out of town with the promise of money for my cooperation. My face flushed with heat as I slowly stood from my seat, fixing Eliam with a glare that would make the devil sweat in hell.

And then there was the loud *snap* of my hand cracking across his face, my body shaking with rage and indignation.

"How *dare* you?" I hissed at him curling my fists. "I didn't choose to be here with you, but a stranger was kind enough to offer me a place to stay during a very difficult time in my life. I don't need your bullshit, you *pig!*."

I turned and stalked from the room, pushing past the men standing in the doorway, staring on in complete shock. My bare feet made a very unthreatening and undignified sound on the wooden stairs, but I couldn't bring myself to care very much.

Once in my room, I closed the door and went directly to the bathroom, which had a door with a lock and provided the moment of privacy that I needed so badly.

And then I cried and cried, loud enough that I could ignore the pounding on the door, the pain in my chest, and the worried male voices only a few feet away, separated from me only by a piece of wood.

I HADN'T BEEN ABLE TO GET HER OUT OF MY HEAD. THE beautiful girl with the reddish-blonde hair, blazing green eyes, and ethereal beauty.

From the moment I saw her, that I caught her backward retreat and turned her to face me, I was a goner. If I had ever needed redemption or forgiveness, it was for the dreams I had of her last night in my arms. Like the angel that she had called me, the dreams kept the line at snuggling... And stuff.

"Earth to Gat." Kellan called, waving his hand in front of my face.

I locked my gaze onto his, angry at him for disrupting my nefarious thoughts of the sleeping girl upstairs. "What?" I snapped.

Kellan notched his chin on his massive fist. "I want to be thinking whatever you're thinking because it's apparently very... *Entrancing.*" He drawled, wiggling his eyebrows suggestively at me.

Rolling my eyes, I stuffed another giant bite of pancakes in my mouth before I could say anything that might cause a fight. Strike three meant I had monitor duty for a month, and I was already on strike number two.

For a guy who compulsively ate every damn thing he could get his hands on, Beck was a damn good fucking cook, somehow managing to make enough to feed an entire army. So, basically, the six of us.

I had an entire mouth full of the fluffy, sweet creations when the object of my mental focus waltzed into the kitchen. I completely froze, as did my typically fearless brothers. She looked terrified, and I wanted so badly to erase that look from her face, to comfort her and tell her everything was okay. But I obviously couldn't, being a total stranger that she was so clearly afraid of. I had known the woman all of five seconds, and I'd already be willing to knock flat the sorry piece of shit that dared hurt or frighten her. Unfortunately for me, I was one of those pieces of shit and it was tearing me up inside.

She smiled meekly at the five of us in the kitchen, somehow looking sexy in her awkwardness. "Morning, boys." She greeted, her tone friendly, but her voice quiet, nervous.

She set about rinsing a glass, taking entirely too long to do so. She was stalling for time, but the reason escaped me. I knew I could be dense at times, but her skittishness still took me by surprise; I didn't get the sense that she was the timid type.

Eventually, she asked a question and Kellan answered, but I was tuning out. I couldn't stand to see her look at me that way, in fear and fascination. So, I took advantage of my own silence and used the time to appreciate the view.

She was dressed in tight capri yoga pants that shaped and clung to her ass like cling wrap. Her tank top was so form fitting that in the brief moments she turned in my direction, I could see her delicate buds straining through the thin fabric, drawing my attention to her perfect mounds and flat stomach. She was built like a gymnast, but with far more curves in all the right places. She was like a road map that I would kill to get the chance to explore.

Lost in my thoughts as I was, I didn't even see Eliam come into the room until he was giving a singular clap for attention.

We had spent the majority of the night holed up in E's room while we discussed the situation with our new houseguest. Obviously, E wanted her gone and we all understood his reasons, and we respected them. Rafe really didn't care so long as she didn't touch his things, big surprise there, and

Gray approved her staying, seeing he probably wouldn't see her much anyway. Beck was all for her being our new roommate, insisting that we needed a female presence around. No ulterior motives there. Kellan explained that, after spending a little time with her at the coffee shop, he thought she was a pretty decent person, and he wanted that kind of energy around. We all figured that his decision was more for Drea's benefit than his own, since they were pretty attached to one another.

However, I didn't say a word.

I wasn't against her staying, but the image of her in nothing but a white t-shirt and panties, sprawled on our kitchen floor, was forever burned into my mind and too great of a temptation.

Needless to say, there was no conclusive vote, seeing as all votes needed to be unanimous in nature. It was the way it had been ever since *her*.

I heard E speaking again and turned my focus to the present just in time to hear him introduce me, and I shot him a glare.

*I can speak for myself, dickhead.* I told him in my mind.

He shot me a look back that said, *yeah, sure you can.* He didn't even bother to use our connection to actually respond. Asshole.

Caught in a silent battle with Eliam – yeah, he was Eliam when I was mad at him – I missed the next part of the conversation.

"I'm Ria." She said kindly, gently. She looked both shy and

assertive, and I wasn't really sure how to approach her due to the conflicted energies I was getting from this end.

I watched as E's eyes hardened, though his face remained open and friendly as he leaned in closer to the confusing girl. I knew what was coming, and I had to clench my teeth hard enough to hear a crack to keep from lashing out at my brother. "Good, now that all that is done, let's make one thing very clear: I don't dislike you, but I really don't want you here, or anywhere near my brothers." *That fucking dickhead!* "All of our votes have to be unanimous, and the vote to remove you was not. So, here's the deal," E leaned in closer, and I clenched my fists under the table. "If there is any amount of money that will make you leave, name it and it shall be yours, so long as you just go and don't come back."

I was a split second from standing up and beating the shit out of my lousy brother for what he just said and the look he put on Ria's face, but she began rising to her feet, almost like she was simply floating there, looking every bit as sinfully gorgeous as she had in our kitchen the night before, but with an expression that made my palms sweat a little, no easy feat.

Then she slapped our oldest brother in the face.

Every single one of our jaws dropped to the floor, except Eliam. Even Gray had woken himself long enough to see it all go down.

"How *dare* you?" She hissed at him, her voice quiet and deadly, and admittedly sexy as hell. "I didn't choose to be here with you, but a stranger was kind enough to offer me a place to stay during a very difficult time in my life. I don't need your bullshit, you *pig!*"

She spat the last word in his face and fled the room, squeezing past Kel and Beck, and rushing up the stairs.

When I had first seen her the night before, I hadn't meant to be so scary. Her presence just caught me off guard, and I had no idea who she was or how she got there. I should have known it was the old crone playing her games, but I really didn't know, and I had never done well with the unknown. But what Eliam just said... He deserved more than a slap from a woman who's strength was nowhere near rivaling his own.

For a long moment, we all sat in silence, but then four of us were taking off up the stairs.

As started up the stairs, I could hear Gray's voice floating from the kitchen, full of distaste and pity, much more than our brother deserved.

"What the hell did you just do, man?"

And then I joined the rest of the guys at her bathroom door, pacing relentlessly, clenching and unclenching my fists as I struggled with what I should – or could – even do in a situation like this, one I had never been in before. All I could do was attempt to control the beast, the rage inside me, while hearing her tears and being helpless to stop them.

## 8 RIA

I DON'T LIKE CRYING. ASIDE FROM THE OBVIOUS RED nose, swollen eyes, and puffy cheeks, I had another big reason to not ever cry, no matter how bad things got.

I heaved heavily into the toilet beside me, by stomach contracting painfully as my delicious coffee was forced from my body by sadness.

Misery might love company, but sadness loved to be completely alone.

The banging and shouting outside the door had stopped, but the guys had started murmuring amongst themselves, and I could hear one of them pacing irritably in front of the door.

I didn't want to see anyone right now. I wasn't so much upset by Eliam's quick dismissal of me as I was that it had kind of struck me that I just wasn't the type of girl that guys wanted around for casual reasons. If I wasn't naked, drunk, or both no one gave a damn.

*"I don't dislike you, but I really don't want you here..."*

The words echoed around in my head for what felt like an eternity, fading away as I dry heaved over the toilet and returning just as I found the river of tears slowing, forcing me to repeat the vicious cycle. After the seventh or eighth time the tears came back my breath started becoming shallow and desperate, my heart racing as I struggled for air. The panic attack was grabbing at me, and no matter how many times my inner self tried to force it away, it just kept coming.

My vision was becoming hazy and black around the edges when I heard a metallic sound somewhere nearby, and I leaned my body up against the cabinets to keep from cracking my head open when I passed out. Darkness sounded nice right about now.

A figure crashed into the bathroom and fell in front of me, but I couldn't make out any features as my focus was solely on trying to steady my breathing.

"Ria." A calm, soft voice called out to me, laced with a strange accent that I was having issues identifying at the time. "Ria, are you okay?"

I couldn't bring myself to form words, so I simply shook my head limply, closing my eyes to avoid dizziness.

"Ria, just listen to my voice. You're going to be alright. Can you hear me?" The voice pressed on, calming my distressed nerves a little.

I nodded lightly, careful not to jostle my enraged stomach.

I felt a warm pressure on each of my hands in my lap, little soothing jolts of electricity weaving their way through my veins. I know I should have been alarmed, but having a panic attack makes just about anything seem normal.

"I'm going to count now, and I need you to start counting with me when you feel like you can, okay?" I nodded again and the voice started counting.

His voice was soothing in a strange sort of way, the words slow and emphasized in strange places. My muddled brain was trying to make sense of everything that was happening and who was sitting on the floor with me, but I was having a hard time forcing coherent thoughts to form.

*Eleven.*

*Twelve.*

*Thirteen.*

*Fourteen.*

I snapped my eyes open, my vision suddenly clear as I drew in a deep, steady breath. "Gray?" I asked in surprise.

"Just count with me." He instructed quietly, his hands warm and soft around my own. I took a moment to analyze him again, noting the raggedness about him and warm look in his amber eyes.

I shook my head. "I feel fine now." I told him gently, attempting to withdraw my hands.

He held on tighter and stared into my eyes like he could find the answer to life within them. "You had us scared, Ria. We heard you, and then you went quiet." He genuinely did look worried and it warmed my heart a little. Who cared what Eliam thought as long as I had those beautiful eyes to look at.

I gave him a small smile. "I could have been naked."

Gray gave me a cheeky grin. "But you weren't." He reminded me.

"But I could have been." I leveled a mock glare at him, still smiling to show I was absolutely not the least bit upset. I mean. I was kind of upset that he had picked the lock on my bathroom door, but thankful all the same.

A throat cleared from the doorway. "And then we would have had ourselves a party." Beck said as he grinned like a Cheshire cat.

I extracted one of my hands from Gray's grasp and pulled the hand towel from the counter. I raised an eyebrow at Beck, who raised one back as I threw the wadded up towel in his face. "Perv." I said with a roll of my eyes.

He chuckled. "I'll be back in the room with the guys." He told Gray before turning to me again. "Unless you want to take me up on that party?" He wiggled his brows and backed out of the doorway with his hands up as I searched for something heavier to throw.

Gray looked at me with a smile on his face and worry in his eyes. "Are you okay now?" He asked, squeezing the hand he still possessed.

I nodded my affirmation. "How did you do that?" I asked out of curiosity.

His smile turned sad for a moment. "I have a lot of experience with women and panic attacks." He got to his feet and hauled me up with him, holding onto my waist for a few seconds to make sure I had my balance. "Do you want me to get the guys out? They just want to make sure you're okay." He nodded to the open door, where I could see four frustrated-looking, giant, ripped, sexy as hell guys looking everywhere but in my direction.

I swallowed the lump in my throat and shook my head. I needed to let them know I was fine, and then I needed to figure out my next move. I wasn't about to stick around some place where even one dickhead didn't want me around. I was better than that.

My inner self and I squared our shoulders and took a deep breath as I forced my legs to move. I walked through the open doorway and flopped down on my bed, staring up at the canopy for a second before sitting up.

"I'm okay." I said to the worried faces that were now staring me down.

The angel – sorry, Gatlin – stepped closer to me, looking concerned. "He had no right to say that shit, Ria." He said, practically growling the words out between clenched teeth.

"We're all pretty fucking pissed at him right now." Rafe chimed in, his beautifully tan face hard with anger. The room filled with varying sounds of agreement.

This was getting out of hand. These guys barely knew me and had no reason to be putting my feelings above their own brother (friend?).

"Guys, I think it's super sweet that you're all mad on my behalf, but don't be." I said, raising my hand to silence the argumentative sounds that sprang up from the group. "I'll be out of your hair as soon as I can come up with a game plan." Gatlin looked downright furious, Rafe looked annoyed, Gray just looked sad, Beck looked like he was in denial, and Kellan looked confused. It was all super endearing, but I really didn't like being anywhere that I wasn't wanted; I had an insatiable need to be wanted, and I absolutely did know that it was insane. I was already probably insane anyway.

"You're not going anywhere, Little Star." A borderline annoying voice stated from my bedroom door.

I threw my hands up in the air. "Doesn't anybody ever fucking knock?" I shouted in exasperation. I rubbed my temples to ease some of the tension headache that was starting to form.

Clove ignored me completely and strode between the men that towered over her to sit beside me on the bed. "Eliam, that dear boy, he's very sorry for what he said. He doesn't always say what he means." She started rubbing small circles on my back, and Kellan handed me the two asprin that were still sitting on my bedside table. I gave him a grateful smile before swallowing the tablets quickly.

Rafe looked completely taken aback. "E *apologized?*" He asked, completely bewildered.

Clove snorted. "Of course not. That boy has more pride than all of the Sahara." She said while shaking her head with an amused chuckle. "No, but he made it very clear that he would like me to come clear up any misunderstandings, which I think is as close as we might get to an apology from him."

I looked at her warily, while she stared on at the boys with a small smile. "What misunderstandings?"

She turned back to face me. "Well, dear, it's come to my attention that I neglected to introduce you all, and that's only partially my fault." She stated, now shooting glares at the guys. "They were supposed to be out of town, but they evidently came back early. I could swear that I told you there were other residents, though." She mused.

I looked at her like she had grown a second and third head while the guys looked at me in confusion. "What? When?" I asked. I know for sure that if she had mentioned six guys that were too attractive to possibly exist in this reality, I would have remembered it.

She tapped her chin thoughtfully. "I believe it was when I was giving you the tour." She said, nodding in agreement with her own statement.

Okay, maybe I wouldn't remember it. I was a little obsessed with looking at the house, and I knew she had said a few things, but they mostly sounded trivial. *Oops.* "I don't recall." I admitted.

The old woman patted my back gently. "No, no, it's likely

my old memory. I tend to be very forgetful when it comes to this lot, as you can imagine." She whispered the last sentence with a wink and I nearly laughed. How anyone could forget these guys was beyond me. Maybe forgetting things around them, but not forgetting *about* them.

"Anyway," Clove continued on while standing and stretching like she had been lounging on a couch all day. "I really must be going. The very best to you all." She gave a short little wave and disappeared through the open doorway.

I stared after her as silence descended on my bedroom, the awkwardness threatening to completely overtake me.

My inner self was glaring me down as though she couldn't be more disappointed in me if she tried. I obviously stared questioningly back at her, since it wasn't my fault that the house was too pretty not to admire or that I had an insane panic attack on the bathroom floor.

She dressed herself in a slinky outfit and strutted around in it, striking poses as she went. I rolled my eyes at her – mentally, of course. She indicated herself and then me. Which was still me, but you get the idea.

There she was, a regal seductress with the power to captivate.

And there I was, pathetic, heartbroken, and way more weak-willed than I had ever been.

I understood what she was trying to say, but it was hard to channel her when I felt like the very fabric of my world had been burned to shreds, leaving nothing but ash and sadness where my light had once been.

She stomped around while equipping herself with an outfit that was well suited for a midnight rendezvous with the mafia or something, all black leather and badassery.

Her message was loud and clear.

*Kick some ass.*

I knew that I was better than this sad, mopey shell I had become, but I just got dumped and wasn't in the mood to be awesome, despite how much my inner self insisted that I should be. What did she know, anyway?

Before L – He-Who-Must-Not-Be-Named showed up, I was fine. Hell, I was way more than fine. It sucked to come home to an empty house every night, but I was still happy with the way my life was.

I put my own happiness in someone else's hands and I couldn't stand myself for it.

There, the truth was out.

He hurt me because I gave him the power to hurt me, and I wasn't so much upset about the way things ended as I was that I let things get so bad, that I didn't wear my heart on my sleeve, but handed it over along with a hammer.

The only reason I got hurt was because I was selfish and stupid to think that he was my perfect match. And that made me pretty fucking pissed off at myself.

Progress, right?

Someone cleared their throat, but I wasn't paying attention in all my internal seething and berating. "I'm not really sure how many looks just crossed her face, but pissed isn't a good sign, is it?" The throat clearer asked.

A familiar, clean and crisp scent washed over me as I stared angrily at my bedspread, like it was the root of my deep-seated issues. "I think she's just mentally talking herself up. It's easier to do it inside than out, right?" He directed that last part at me, but I was really interested in how the red, satiny fabric beneath me had wronged me. "It's all perfectly normal as long as you're not answering yourself." He said with a chuckled that he didn't know was ironic.

I snorted and straightened, jumping up from the bed. I shot Gray what I hoped was a thankful glance, because I wasn't sure I could trust my face to do my actual bidding after he just unknowingly reassured me that I am, in fact, crazy.

"Okay, here's what's going to happen." I stated while standing a little taller, my eyes raking over each of the five faces around me. "I'm staying, and I'm doing it because I want to. Not a single one of you has the power to make me leave, and I'm not giving you any. Eliam can shove that stick up his ass a little deeper, because I'm not about to get pushed around by some prissy nobody." I finished, crossing my arms to look a little more commanding than my smallish stature insinuated.

A slow clap sounded at my door way, and my eyes shot to the lean figure that was propped against the frame. "Delightful sentiment. Delivery could use a little work." Eliam drawled.

I was about to *deliver* a good kick to his crown jewels, and even opened my mouth to tell him so, when another voice interrupted.

"Look, we're all obviously on edge, but it's way too damn early in the day for this shit." Rafe said. I heard a dull metal *thunk* as he spoke and made a mental note to observe for a tongue piercing later. "My time is valuable, and I'd really rather not waste it on keeping you two from jumping each other's bones out of pure 'hatred'."

"In his dreams!" I practically screeched as Eliam echoed the sentiment simultaneously. Obviously with different pronouns, because if that bastard had called me a *he* I would have lost my shit for real.

I could practically see the loathing radiating from my own skin as the other guys nodded their agreement with Rafe and began leaving the room, each calling out some version of "see you later".

I didn't take my eyes off Eliam once and he stared back with frightening intensity. Not that I was frightened, because I could have beaten this asswipe black and blue if his brothers hadn't just been so kind.

Eliam was the first to break eye contact, but it was only a nanosecond before his eyes were raking over my entire body, somewhat appreciatively.

Then he smirked as he pushed away from his perch. "Things just got very interesting." He said as he turned his back and strode from my room, leaving me alone

I PACED ANGRILY IN MY ROOM FOR THE NEXT TWENTY minutes or so, considering all the possible ways that I could feasible murder a certain giant, sexy, blonde pile of flesh. Seriously, fuck that guy. Who did he think he was? And the way he was eavesdropping was creepy, not to mention stalkerish.

Ew.

I decided to shower and dress for the day, since I had hours of sunlight at my disposal. Stepping into the bathroom, I searched quickly for a towel and nodded as I found one, grabbing shampoo, conditioner, and body wash from the little shopping bag tucked into my suitcase.

I adjusted the temperature and nearly moaned when the water turned hot almost instantly. Being the badass freak of the night that I was, I liked my water to come straight from the fiery pits of hell.

Peeling myself out of my clothes, I stepped into the stream of disturbingly hot water and relaxed almost instantly. I sat down in the basin of the tub and just let the water do its magical thing, releasing the tension and knots in my muscles that I didn't know were there.

Two fucking days.

All it took was two fucking days for me to be brought to the edge of completely losing it. The amount of hot – and do I ever mean *hot* – and cold that I'd endured in such a short amount of time was overwhelming, not to mention exhausting and completely mind-fucking.

My mind tried to recap everything since the night I left my house, but I wasn't having any of that shit. I just started getting back to myself. I leaned back in the tub and forced myself to focus on the present. Not much better.

I sat there thinking about the six incredibly yummy guys that literally barged into my life and could help the fact that this shower just got a whole lot steamier.

*No. No, no, no. Just no.*

I shook my head until I could feel my eardrums being dislodged. This was me time, not sexy roommate time. The last thing I needed to do was send my poor ovaries into overdrive by thinking about guys – much less *those* guys – when I was naked and alone. My poor sex-addicted reproductive organs couldn't take it and I needed to respect that.

I groaned and slid further under the hot spray of water, laying almost completely on my back as I closed my eyes tight and tried to think of rainbows, unicorns, and other frilly non-sexy things. Only, it took a really bad turn because the unicorn horn made me think of a penis, and that made me think about multiple penises. I really didn't need to be thinking about penises when my head was already so jumbled up.

*So, think about vaginas.* My ever-helpful inner self supplied. It wasn't a bad idea in theory, but as soon as my inner thoughts reached my metaphorical ears, I caught my hand straying to my no-no squares. Yeah, I just said that. Thought that. Whatever.

I could mentally argue with myself (or my inner self?) all day, but even I could admit that a little stress *relief* would be nice for a change of pace.

Feeling relaxed and soothed by the steam that was rapidly filling the room, I allowed my slender fingers to roam over my suddenly hyper-sensitive flesh, lingering for longer moments over my breasts and inner thighs. The third or so time that my fingers lightly brushed my hardening buds, I succumbed to the desire that was rapidly pooling in my belly. I gave both nipples a small flick with my thumbs and shivered in delight.

My other hand slowly found its way to my already throbbing clit and began rubbing small, gentle circles around the sensitive area. My breath hitched at the change of pace and I felt rather than heard a small moan escape my lips. I bit down hard on the inside of my cheek to contain the sound, whimpering at the unexpected mixture of both pain and pleasure.

I continued to tease one nipple with my free hand, feeling as though my heart was beating low in my groin, rather than in my chest. I was never one for getting off on clitoral stimulation alone when I was with someone, but by myself was a different story all on its own.

As I increased both my pace and intensity, I could feel that bittersweet sensation of building, the one that is nearly impossible to describe without sounding like you're in actual pain. I propped a leg up on the side of the tub and the sudden jet of hot water on my tender sweet spot almost instantly pushed me up an over the edge and I felt the tension and release explode out of me.

Gasping and moaning at my impromptu little sexcapade, I stretched slowly and rode out the waves of my lingering orgasms.

I smiled to myself and then frowned. I wasn't thinking about any of the guys while I was off in sex land, was I? I tried to think back and came up empty, my thoughts too muddled to clearly recall. When pleasure's involved the brain just doesn't work the way it should.

I shouldn't have to beat myself up over it anyway, because the math was painfully simple.

Ria = hot.

Male roommates = hot.

Ria + male roommates = natural, instinctual attraction.

Plus, they smelled good, and that did hurt nor help – depending on how you look at the entire situation. I had read somewhere once that humans weren't designed to be monogamous anyway, that we were designed to be attracted to multiple people for hormone and reproductive reasons. I'd also heard that people only smelled super good to those that were genetically perfect matches.

But didn't Cardboard Eyes smell good? I tried to think back and couldn't recall anything about his natural scent. I mean, it was probably super weird to be thinking about how good people smell anyway, so there's that.

Unless it's just further proof that we weren't meant to be. But that would imply that I was meant to be with at least five of these shlongs, which is a fantasy that most women won't admit to having, but still not a fantasy that I would like to turn into reality with people I'm living with.

Clearing away my thoughts, I scrubbed myself down and groaned loudly when my soapy sponge brushed over my still sensitive sex. As I did, I heard a loud banging sound outside the door and nearly jumped straight out of my very attached skin.

I rinsed quickly and folded a towel around myself before stepping out into my bedroom to find a very sheepish looking Gatlin standing by my bed, rubbing the back of his neck as his eyes landed on my barely covered body.

I just stood there, arms crossed and tapping my foot like an impatient old lady. "Um, excuse you?" I was a little bewildered that Gatlin, of all the guys, was standing alone with me in my bedroom. I mean, I was about ninety percent certain he hated me.

He cleared his throat and glanced at me, then to the floor. "Uh, I can come back when you're dressed." He said gruffly. His embarrassment would be adorable if it wasn't for the fact that he was so intimidating. Even still, it was kinda cute.

I chuckled lightly and padded across the cool floor to my suitcase that was just to the right of my unexpected guest. "I'll just get dressed, then." I replied, turning my head away so he couldn't see my smirk.

I bent forward at the hips as I rummaged through my suitcase for something comfortable and cute, and heard the satisfying sound of Gatlin's sharp intake of breath. I finally settled on my green washed skinny jeans and a black off-the-shoulder top with neon blue, pink, and yellow paint splatters on it, feeling like going and scouting out some new towns and clubs later in the afternoon.

I stripped off my towel – like a pro, I might add – and shimmied into my clothes with painful slowness. When I turned around to face the sexy elephant in the room, his face made my procrastination oh so worth it; his eyes were dilated, his breathing noticeably heavy, and his fists clenched at his sides. I could see his jaw working and had to pour every last ounce of my will into not laughing at a guy that could rip me in two and make me enjoy it.

"Don't tell me you're one of those guys who's nervous around naked women." I teased while rolling my eyes. I didn't actually think that, because he *so* didn't seem the type. But hey, looks can be deceiving, so what do I know?

He cleared his throat again and it drew my attention to his bobbing adam's apple, which drew my attention to his throat... And his shoulders... And *man those biceps!*

"I wanted to come and talk to you about something, but I didn't realize you were... Ah... Busy." He hesitated, rubbing the back of his neck once more.

*Fuck!*

I panicked a little knowing that he had definitely heard the sounds of pleasure that I had apparently been showcasing for the entire house. Wait, no. It was probably just him. He was in my room, so the most plausible reasoning is that he was the only one that heard.

"Gray came up with me, but he didn't want to stay for the, ah, conversation."

Recital. Gray didn't want to stay for my Porn Stars of Tiny Towns recital. *Fuck.*

Oh well. No use in worrying about it now. The literal deed was done. "So what did you want to talk about, then?" I queried, sitting on the edge of my bed to throw my fluffiest socks and some converse on.

Gatlin sat down on the bed beside me and looked down at his hands clasped together on his knees. "The other night," He began, taking a deep breath. "I'm sorry if I hurt you. I was so caught off guard and I wasn't thinking."

To say I was stunned was an understatement. Kicking me out? Expected. Telling me to back off his bros? Expected.

Giving me *the talk?* Still more expected than what just sounded to my ears like a genuine apology.

He still hadn't looked at me and I was gaping at him like a retarded fish or something. What did one say to a guy easily twice their size who had given such a heartfelt apology? I wasn't even sure what I was feeling at that particular moment in time.

"Thanks." I blurted with overwhelming intelligence and wit.

Shame. I was feeling shame.

My inner self was doubled over laughing and dabbing little tears from the corners of her eyes. But she couldn't just do it normally, *noooo*; she was dressed in a regal gown straight out of a fairy tale and dabbing away with a little embroidered handkerchief.

*That bitch.* I once again thought to myself, about myself. She wasn't even really me anymore, she was gaining a mind of her own and I didn't appreciate it one little bit.

Gatlin stared at me quizzically, as though I had sprouted an additional head and webbed feet. But hey, at least he was looking at me. As I stared stupidly into his depthless grey eyes, I found myself wanting to get lost in them. And then I wondered why I wanted him to look at me in the first place. Sexy eyes were distracting as hell, man.

I stumbled about in my mind to find something much more meaningful to say than "thanks". *Thanks?* What the actual fuck was wrong with me?

"I mean, I appreciate your apology, but it's not really necessary." I amended, praising myself for delivering such a sophisticated response. "I was going to hit you with a vase, so I think we're pretty even."

I was rewarded with a small grin and he leaned toward me. "That little trinket wouldn't have hurt me." I gave him a look that scolded him for implying that I was weak, which also obviously implied that it was because I was a woman.

The look he gave me set a little fire burning low in my belly, his eyes striking the match right before my own. It was becoming impossible to think, to breathe. We were so close that I could taste his breath, and I just knew that I was going to be the one to do something stupid. I was impulsive like that, which was definitely a flaw, but it had taken me so far already. Maybe I could just wing it? Maybe...

No. I needed to clear my head and not give in to that gorgeous meld of golden-bronze hair and perfect silvery eyes. I especially needed to not give in to those strong, sharp jaws, ridiculously full lips, arms with cords of rippling muscles...

Before I could snap myself out of my little space-out moment, my lips were being crushed against another set. I couldn't control the massive release of air the forced itself from my lungs or the way my arms threaded up and around Gatlin's massive shoulders. They were solid and warm, but not bulky.

When his hands encircled my waist and turned my body fully toward his, I allowed my fingers to wind themselves into his messy, beautiful hair and I sighed; it felt as good as I had totally not imagined. Because that would be weird.

*Weirder than kissing your roommate?* My inner self chimed with a sneer.

I tried to jerk away, but Gatlin's grip on my waist was too strong – and it totally had nothing to do with the fact that I really didn't want to jump apart like a couple of guilty teenagers. I was in heaven, which is funny considering that I had called him an angel before. Two days before.

Crap. I needed to stop.

Shit. I really needed to stop.

Fuck. I *really*... Didn't want or have to.

Consenting adults and whatnot.

I crushed myself tightly against him, nearly flinging him onto his back, not that he seemed to mind much at all, because he was pushing back against my body with a fervor that left me feeling wanton. His grip on the delicate flesh at my waist tightened significantly and a breathy moan pushed past my lips to be swallowed by his own.

That little sound seemed to ignite something inside him and he pushed me until my back was flat against the bed and he was hovering above me, suspending himself on his forearms. Something about this position was turning that tiny little fire from earlier into a smouldering inferno, making me feel like I was burning up and near catching fire any moment.

I released my hands from his beautiful hair and lightly raked my nails over his back, eliciting a groan of approval from the beautiful man atop me. I slid my hands under his shirt, and applied a little more pressure with my nails than before, feeling goosebumps rise under the heels of my hands. I sucked his bottom lip between my teeth and nipped lightly, causing him to shiver and groan once more.

I was feeling a sick sense of pleasure and accomplishment at his reactions, and I wanted *more*. I was halfway prepared to draw some more pretty red lines down his lightly tanned skin when he tensed and drew his mouth back from mine.

He opened his mouth, and after the last couple of days that I'd had, I wasn't ready to hear the rejection I knew was coming. So, I did what any woman would do in my very naughty position, and I cut him off. I gripped the front of his shirt and pulled his face back to mine as I claimed his mouth hungrily.

His hands slid up and under my shirt, cupping both supple breasts in his large hands. I whimpered pitifully at the contact, but I wholeheartedly meant it as encouragement. I guess he picked up on my subtle cues, because the glorious torture to my nipples was suddenly stimulating every single little nerve ending in my entire body, lighting up the inside of my eyelids like the Fourth of July. I sensed rather than felt his own arousal growing, and I was fighting hard against my own morality.

I angrily shoved my conscience to go sit with my inner self and decided to go bold or go home.

With ever ounce of nerve that I could muster, I slid both hands into the waistband of his jeans and heard the satisfying groan that encouraged me further. As I slid both hands around to his front, he lifted just enough to give me some play room and I took full advantage of the opportunity by expertly popping the button and sliding the zipper down ever so slowly.

My libido was a raging lust fueled monster that knew no boundaries, and I found myself reaching deeper to grip him and gasped around his insistent lips. It wasn't the kind of big that seems like it would hurt, but it was certainly impressive. *Very* impressive. I held him tightly, my fingers not even meeting around his shaft.

"Fuck." He growled as he broke the kiss, leaning into my neck and planting little kisses from the base of my ear to my collarbone. I shivered, trying to commit the tingling sensations to memory while I gently toyed with him, my fingers trailing sweetly along his length before dragging my nails softly down the other direction.

He was practically vibrating with arousal and pleasure, and I was nanoseconds away from tearing the clothes from both of our bodies when he slowly sat up on his elbows.

I can't even imagine what my face looked like, but I hoped it didn't look as stupidly confused as I was afraid it did.

He grinned at me and straightened my shirt down, leaning in and giving me another kiss, this time soft and brief. "Later." He whispered. He suddenly looked so gentle, so kind. He looked like I had thought he'd looked the first time I saw him, and it was positively breathtaking.

I cocked my head curiously, my still damp hair tickling my back where my shirt hadn't been straightened.

He nodded at the door and held his hand out to me. "You've got company." He chuckled, helping me to my feet. I wouldn't admit it, but I was genuinely confused as fuck. Why would I have company? Who would company be? Ugh.

He held my hand all the way to the door before I pulled him up short and pointed silently to his jeans. I didn't trust my words at that moment, feeling shaken as I did. I'm pretty sure I would be a lot less confused and shaken if I was kidnapped.

What just actually happened? Did they make cones of shame for hos?

Gatlin full on laughed and tidied up his clothing situation before gallantly opening my bedroom door and gesturing for me to go first. Who said chivalry was dead? I made my way down the stairs and tried to sort out both my thoughts and my ovaries, feeling more than a little overwhelmed by all the sorting that was to be done.

Climbing down the stairs to the bottom floor, I could hear voices to the left, in the direction of the sitting room. Once I reached the bottom, I could see three of the guys, and they were all laughing and howling. Basically, they were being guys.

I rounded cautiously around the corner to find Rafe and Beck on the sofa with controllers in their hands.

At a second glance, I could see that they were all watching intently and cheering loudly as the two players raced around a curving mountainside in an arcade-style racing game.

"What are you playing?" I asked curiously.

Five faces swiveled to stare at me and then Rafe started cursing a colourful slew of words in a growling rage.

Beck groaned and the other guys laughed. Guys? Wait.

One, two, three, four... five?

"Way to go Ria, you made them fall behind!" Drea whined. She grumbled as she turned to Gray and passed him a bill. "I had good money on a tie!"

Beck levelled a frosty stare on me. "Yeah, thanks Ria." He complained as he rubbed a hand over his face.

I shrugged half-assedly. "Can't you just restart?" I suggested like the apparent noob that I am.

Drea approached me and gripped both of my hands in her own. "It's a multiplayer match, so no." She answered. She started dragging me from the sitting room and to the kitchen, passing a grinning Gatlin as we went. "Let's get you out of there before the mob starts in on you with their pitchforks and torches."

I giggled as she pulled me about and indicated for me to sit on one of the barstools. "How was I supposed to know? I was busy upstairs." I pointed out as she rummaged in the cupboards for what I assumed was a food source.

She glanced at me over her shoulder and wiggled her eyebrows suggestively. "Oh, I bet you were." She teased. She grabbed a loaf of weird looking bread and made a beeline for the fridge.

I gasped dramatically and covered my mouth as though I were offended at the implications. "I do declare!" I feigned fainting over the breakfast bar and Drea giggled. "But really, it wasn't anything like that." I was lying, and we both knew it.

"Uh-huh." She volleyed with a raised eyebrow. Holy fuck, she could do that? I wish I could raise one eyebrow at a time. "You and G-man all alone upstairs with a particularly steamy shower?" She hinted. "Of *course* nothing happened." She fell into a little fit of giggles and I couldn't help but giggle along with her.

I waved my hand dismissively. "'Think whatever you want." I said, not willing to admit defeat. "What are you making?"

Eyeing her spread of foods, I would think grilled cheese, but this looked more like a bread and cheese buffet.

She turned an excited grin on me as she said, "grilled cheese, duh." Sure, like it was totally obvious with what appeared to be eight or nine different kinds of cheese, weirdly shiny looking bread, and an array of seasonings and fresh herbs.

"What *kind* grilled cheese?" I asked suspiciously.

She started cackling like the witch from *Hansel and Gretel*, making me feel like she was about to shove me in a cage to fatten me up before she baked me into a pie. Joke was on her though, because I didn't fatten up. Perks of being near-perfect.

"A special recipe from yours truly. I'm a pretty fantastic cook, you know." She bragged while continuing to prep the food.

I snorted. "Actually, I didn't know, seeing as I've only known you two days and hardly know a thing about you."

She glared at me like my honesty was some sort of cruel joke. "Well, now you know." She said with a sniff. "And my last name is Edmont, so now you know something else, too." She smirked.

Ugh. I was really starting to despise that word.

"Good to know." I answered flatly, daring her to take my seemingly uninterested demeanor as bait. I would say absolutely nothing else, I'd just let her fret over why I didn't seem over the moon at learning more about her.

I was actually really and truly excited to learn more because it made me feel like one of the gang, and that was a damn cool feeling.

Did making out with a town citizen count as me becoming one of the group? If so, I was solid as a rock. A regular townie.

I watched as she continued on in her grilled cheese making task, her face dropping into a concentrated frown, inch by tiny inch.

I was trying really fucking hard not to laugh, okay? When someone falls into such a simply set trap, it's probably one of the most pleasing things in the world. Well, for sadists like me, I guess.

I needed some serious help.

Her face was about to break, I just knew it. No one's face could go into a deeper frown for any longer than she had held this one. Maybe she was onto me.

Ridiculous. Of course she wasn't onto me. I was a skilled, mastermind manipulator. Hell, I manipulated the mastermind manipulators. I was that good.

She wasn't gonna crack. She was just gonna stew in her own curiosity forever. Maybe she just needed a little *push*, and it just so happened that I had the perfect push as a failsafe.

All it took was a small feigned yawn, and she snapped like a rubber band stretched too far. "You know, if you didn't care, that's all you had to say." She chided, wielding her spatula like a magic wand that could smite me where I stood. Her eyes were wide and wild, her hair hanging in her eyes so that she looked like a sea witch or *The Grudge*.

I snickered, not even bothering to hide my mirth. "I really do care. I just wanted to see your face." I grinned at her. "Really, I'd love to get to know you better since I think we're almost friends or something." I added with a wink, folding my hands under my chin as though I was the poster child for heaven's greatest.

She just glared at me in response, possibly contemplating my very untimely and ultimately hideous demise. "You're impossible." She groaned, wiping a hand over her face as though I was seriously draining her mental capacity for the day. Maybe I was? It could be my superpower. In the books, every new person in weird towns had a superpower, so maybe mine was draining people.

I gave her my cheekiest of grins. "I *looove* you." I told her sweetly.

She rolled her eyes and started grumbling under her breath as she returned to her melted cheese sandwiches.

"I'm sorry, what was that?" I practically cooed at her, like she was an adorable toddler learning to speak a full and coherent sentence for the very first time.

"I said," she grumbled louder. "I love you, too. Newbie."

My grin took on a growth spurt of Cheshire proportions. "I won't be a newbie forever, you know. I'll be a regular member of small town society in no time at all." I spread my arms wide for a nice dramatic presence.

She went quiet and bent her head over her suddenly very focus-consuming task. Uh-oh.

"Drea, honey?" I coaxed gently. I got up from my place at the breakfast bar and walked around to my new friend. "What's wrong?"

She didn't even look up at me, but she did poke the poor grilled cheese with the spatula. She didn't seem sad exactly, more upset. But we were fine, right? What even happened?

When she finally peeked up at me through her mess of bushy hair, she looked hurt. Why would she be hurt? What did I do? "What if you don't like it here?" She asked quietly, avoiding eye contact again.

I was *actually* stunned, as though someone had *actually* hit me in the face with an *actual* frying pan – which I'm sure hurt like hell. "Drea?" I whispered to her, placing my hand on her back. Jesus, this girl was petite as they came. I felt like she might break from the small contact alone.

But she didn't break, she just glanced at me sideways,

unblinking. "I don't really have friends." She whispered back, as though the air in the room was tangible and fragile.

I smiled sadly back at her and rubbed small circles into her spine. "I know, honey." Wow, I was already *really* attached. Weird. "I don't have any plans on going anywhere any time soon, if at all. I like it here. It's cozy and friendly..."

She gave me a small smile and nodded once.

"And you're here. You're my friend and I wouldn't just abandon you if I did want to leave." I gave her a very pointed look. Stern, almost. I think. I just wanted to make her understand, because she was so sensitive and lonely, and I honestly cared a lot. "If I wanted to leave, I'd ask you to come with me. Then if you said no, I'd chloroform you and stuff you in my trunk with lotion and a bucket."

That did her in.

She was doubling over, clutching the spatula to her midsection as she howled with laughter. Little tears were springing up in her eyes, and mine weren't exactly desert-dry.

"Seriously, I like it here so far. I haven't really gotten the chance to explore or meet many people, but I plan on staying based on what I know so far." I told her.

She started to right herself, wiping her eyes clean, when her head caught the handle of the pan she was cooking with. The pan nearly flipped over on her head, and I knew that superhuman speed was doubtless not one of my superpowers.

And then the pan was gone, suspended above the stovetop in a neatly manicured male hand.

I swear my heart was drilling its way into my throat as I clutched my chest and waited for the breath to return to my lungs.

"What have I said about horsing about in the kitchen? You almost went and got yourself scalded, love." Eliam chided gently, setting the pan on a back burner.

Drea stood completely and brushed her hair from her face before turning to her saviour with a thoroughly guilty demeanor. "Sorry, E. I didn't mean to, Ria's just a real stand up act." She hooked her thumb over her shoulder at me and I rolled my eyes.

*Sure, blame the pariah.* I thought to myself.

Eliam seemed to feel the same way, as he arched a damn near perfect brow and slowly – painfully slowly – slid his gaze to my own. "I'm sure she is." He drawled. He turned back to Drea and tilted her chin up with his index finger. "Be more careful, love. Kel would have the head of the person," he shot his gaze to me again, "who let you get hurt."

"Duly noted." I muttered as he stalked from the room, not a farewell in sight.

Drea snickered as she turned off the burners and started hunting around for plates. "Don't mind E, he's harmless." She told me a little too gleefully.

That was a lie. He was about as far from harmless as they came, I'm sure, what with the whole threatened exile and nasty attitude. I hadn't even mentioned that I took off my clothes for money yet and I was already a leper in the eyes of the great Eliam. Yay me. So yeah, I was suddenly super positive that Eliam wasn't in the running for the world's biggest asshole, but was actual warmer, fuzzier, and more loving than a teddy bear. *Not.*

I just shrugged my shoulders in response to avoid any kind of potential argument over my sour roommate. Drea directed me back to my stool and placed the cheesiest of grilled cheeses before me, dramatically licking her lips as though she wasn't already holding her own cholesterol sandwich.

"Dig in!" She insisted.

I took a big bite – and I mean a really big bite, because I don't do anything by halves as well as just being overall a food lover. And holy fucking gods above and below, this was most definitely the best grilled cheese I'd ever had in my entire life. It was gooey and soft, but not sticky, and with so many conflicting flavours that it should have been disgusting. Not disgusting, by the way. In case I wasn't clear.

Drea was still staring at me while I inhaled my masterpiece, waiting for a response as though the aforementioned inhaling wasn't enough of a sign. "It's amazing, Drea!" I praised around a mouthful of bread and cheese.

Her face lit up like the Fourth of July, eyes beaming and smile dazzling. She threw her dainty arms around me and nearly sent my bite down the wrong pipe. "Sorry, sorry!" She apologized, not sounding the least bit apologetic. "I knew you'd love it!" She was in seventh heaven and I was just so glad that I could make her that happy.

And happy about the copious amounts of cheese that I'm sure would be fueling my bloodstream in no time at all.

"So, what are your plans for the day?" I asked my marvelous chef of a friend. Sure, it was just grilled cheese, but it was like six star restaurant grilled cheese. And yes, I know that's not a thing.

Blotting the crumbs from her mouth, Drea said, "honestly, not much of anything. I like to chill with the guys on my days off." She shrugged.

"Do you guys just sit around and watch or play games all day?" I asked.

Drea had opened her mouth to respond when Beck came in the open entryway.

"Dude!" He exclaimed, looking a little bit hurt as he stared down the last bite of grilled cheese in my hand. "Where's mine, Little D?" He was legitimately pouting.

My friend rolled her eyes as she stood and collected our plates. "You've already eaten five times today and the sun's barely in the sky." She told him with a pointed look. "You're gonna get fat, Big B."

Beck turned his eyes on my face and winked. "I'll never be fat."

Drea sighed. "I'm not making you food, end of story." Beck opened his mouth to say something else, but my elfish friend cut him off with her palm facing him. "And no, you're not gonna starve to death."

I was trying really, *really* hard not to laugh at the little exchange because new people were rarely allowed to have opinions in situations like these, but it was really funny.

"Drea, wanna go hit up some local small cities later?" I inquired thoughtlessly. Fuck. Fuck, fuck, *fuck*.

Stupid brain asking stupid questions without consulting stupid me first.

However, my friend's pretty hazel eyes grew the size of dinner plates and she started bobbing her head in a nod that made me wonder how securely her neck was fastened to her actual head. "Sure! What's the game plan?" She bubbled enthusiastically.

Oh boy. This was going to get me into a shit tonne of trouble, I just knew it. It was too late to back out, too, because my stupid mouth was in cahoots with my stupid brain. Maybe the truth would get a negative enough reaction that she wouldn't want to go, but also a positive enough refusal that we would still be friends. It was worth a shot, right?

I took a deep breath and beamed at her. "Ever been to a strip club before?"

"*A strip club?*" Drea asked for what seemed like the tenth time in a two minute time span.

Beck was doubled - no, *tripled* - over laughing, his arms crossed and clutching at his middle while tears streamed from his eyes. The second the words were out of my mouth, my fuzzy-haired, fun-sized friend had dropped her jaw all the way to China, her eyes practically bulging out of her head. The reaction was comical, for sure, but I was sort of at the butt of the joke here, even if Drea was the target.

I sighed and rubbed my temples to buy myself some time and patience. "Drea, forget it. It was just a suggestion. I had planned on going and thought it would be fun." I told her.

Her mouth opened and closed for a second or two longer before she managed to find the ability to speak again. "I mean, it was just so... Random! I'd love to go. I mean, I don't know that I'd *love* to, but I've never been, so it doesn't hurt to see, right?" Oh, the babbling.

Beck seemed to feel the same way I did about the incessant flow of sounds coming from her because he straightened and stopped laughing as he placed a hand over her mouth. People kept doing that to her, so it has to be some kind of muscle memory or instinct at this point.

"Little D." Beck said quietly. "It's a bunch of naked chicks. It's your zone, dude."

Drea gave a quick nod and said something that came out a mumbled jumble of miscellaneous sounds. In short, I had no clue what she just said.

Beck removed his hand from her mouth cautiously, as though concerned that she might start rambling again. "I was saying," she shot a *look* at the hunky skater boy, "what if we all go?" She suggested uncertainly.

Cue Ria's mental freak out.

All? All of us? Unless she was calling me fat, I'm pretty sure she meant us two girls and the six guys. I mean, it wouldn't be too awkward under normal circumstances, but these weren't normal circumstances or normal guys; they were not only freakishly attractive, but they were my roommates. I was going to look for *work*, not a good time, and I was totally cool with Drea knowing, but the guys I lived with? Sure, I couldn't see any possible way that this could go wrong. Testosterone and boobs and all.

I was fumbling for a good, sound reason to decline and change the direction this thing was going in. I wondered how quickly I could possibly contract food poisoning or the black plague. The odds were not in my favour.

I was literally two nanoseconds away from opening my mouth and blurting the first excuse that came out, brain approval not required, when our beloved pierced pal opened his trap and ruined any chance at escape that may have been previously available to me.

"Sounds fun." Beck replied nonchalantly. "Let me get the guys, we know where to find the best spots." And the dick strode from the room without a backwards glance.

I could hear him announce the plan to the guys, which was followed by a chorus of raucous cheers. Joy to the fucking world.

Drea looked positively giddy, so I supposed now was as good a time as any to let her in on my little secret. "Honey, come up to my room with me?" I suggested, gesturing for her to follow me as I made my way from the kitchen and up the stairs.

We made it all the way to my bedroom and I closed the door so hastily that anyone might think I had just robbed a bank. Which, in short, means that Drea was giving me a bemused look.

"Okay, so I'm actually going to look for work." I told her bluntly. Okay, right out there in the open. Always the best course of action.

She just shrugged and plopped onto my oversized bed. Or maybe it just looked oversized because she was so small? "I get it, not only do waitresses and bartenders make a killing in strip clubs, but the pay in outlying areas is probably so much better than here, yanno?" Oh boy. She didn't get it.

"No, I'm a dancer. It's what I did back home, and I kinda need money before I drain my reserves." I said it simply, very matter-of-fact. Nothing brings on worse reactions than beating around the bush, trust me.

And take that with a grain of salt, because Drea's face turned the alarming colour of fuchsia as she lay there on my bed, silent as a grave.

"Drea...?" I coaxed.

She made a little coughing and squeaking sound that I couldn't properly identify without some kind of special certification. "Uh, well. Explains a lot, I guess." She commented vaguely.

*Wait, what?* My inner self and I happened to think the exact same thing at the exact same time. *Explains what? Can you jinx yourself?* Probably only if you're certifiably insane, and I'm pretty positive I was getting damn close.

"What does it explain?" I queried.

Drea sat up on her elbows and stared intently at me. "All of," she gestured to my general personage, "you." Way to articulate, *Andrea*. "You're just like nine kinds of gorgeous, and it just seems like it fits; you have that whole confidence and poise and sexuality thing about you." She clarified.

See? I oozed sexuality, just like I said.

I chortled under my breath. "Glad to know I fit the bill." I shot back playfully.

She rolled her eyes at me and stood. "So, what do you need?" She asked, apparently over her little mini-panic attack.

I shook my head and smiled. "All of my things are in the backseat of my car." I told her, opening my door to head back downstairs. "Think you're up for trying something new tonight?" I was mostly teasing, but I also was under the firm belief that anyone who envied a dancer's confidence should try dancing at least once. It could be liberating and gratifying, or it could be humbling – the experience totally depended on the factors involved and the person.

The flying squid looking head shake was answer enough, despite her sinful looking grin. Oh, I was totally corrupting her.

We headed back downstairs to find the guys by the door – yes, including the dreaded Eliam, who wasn't meeting my eyes – looking snazzy and ready for an evening out. It was only about two in the afternoon, but I had no idea how close the nearest club was and probably wouldn't until I got somewhere with better cell service.

"Ready to go?" Beck called out. He wasn't looking in the direction of the stairs, so he had no idea that we were standing right behind him, which meant there was zero need for outside voices. Rafe smacked him on the shoulder and he turned. "Oh, that was quick." He amended.

I was so happy for a chance to roll my own eyes that I may have overdone it a little bit. "We're women, we don't need to make ourselves up to be walking sex magnets." I joked.

Gatlin caught my eye and I saw his lips curve up slightly. *Isn't that the truth.* His eyes seemed to say. He would know, since he accosted me in my private quarters not very long ago. Oh, and he was enjoying our dirty little secret. I was too, but I wasn't going to dwell on that at the moment, simply for the sake of both my sanity and dryness of my underwear.

"We're all set. How do we wanna do the car thing?" I asked as Kellan held open the front door.

Beck headed out first. "Whoever doesn't fit in my jeep can ride with you, if that works." He suggested.

I nodded to Kellan as I passed through the doorway. "Thanks, Mongo." I teased. He only snorted in response, yet another nickname sticking the landing. "Yeah, that sounds good." I replied to Beck as I opened my car door, my car already started and warming up.

"Wow!" Drea mused. "This is one hell of a car, Ria." She was in complete awe, climbing into the passenger seat gingerly, as though she might mar its beauty just by touching it.

I shot her a wink as I reached behind me and situated my bags in the floorboard behind my seat to make room for any other passengers. "Perks of the job, homegirl."

I saw Gatlin already making his way to my car and I audibly gulped.

*Calm, cool, collected, aloof, nonchalant, chill, relaxed.*

I repeated these adjectives in my head like a mantra to remind myself of what I should be at that particular moment in time.

Thankfully, my internal panic was momentarily doused by the sight of Kellan, Rafe, and Gray – *Gray?* – playing *rock, paper, scissors* outside of Beck's sleek black Jeep. I begged and pleaded in my own mind with the powers that be that they weren't arguing over what I thought they were arguing over.

Alas, Eliam's irritated scowl said it all.

The winner appeared to be Rafe, as he was walking toward my car with a cat-ate-mouse grin and Kellan was glaring him down like the mouse was his to catch. Did that make me the mouse?

*Don't pretend you don't love it.* My inner self purred. The harlot. I kind of did love it, but what can I say? I'm only human.

Gatlin slid into the back seat with ease while Rafe climbed in after him, their massive bulk taking up more space in the tiny vehicle than I had even considered. Oops.

After everyone was situated, I pulled out of the driveway behind Beck and we hit the road.

◆ ◆ ◆

WE HAD BEEN DRIVING for about twenty minutes, bantering back and forth, playing hot potato with DJ rights, and talking about some fun facts about the small, historic town of Willow Tree.

"And," Drea continued. "Father Augustus Belvieu is a complete and total loon."

There were two chorusing sounds of wholehearted agreement from the backseat.

Gatlin leaned forward and propped his elbow on my center console for the millionth time already. "He's one of those old-timey church leaders that stands on street corners and hollers about the end being near." He interjected.

"And how we're all sinners." Rafe added, snickering behind his heavily tattooed hand.

Sounded all too familiar to me, if I was being completely honest. "Like in *Little Nicky*?" Incidentally, one of my favourite movies of all time. The whole idea of Hell not being what my parents always made it out to be? Sign me up for a viewing every day until I die and can see it for myself.

This time, Rafe howled with laughter. "Yeah, just like that. He's got the hat and everything." I caught him grinning in the rearview mirror. He was a total goofball.

We swapped some more stories and whatnot while I followed Beck through some more tiny towns, less maintained and lively than our own. The drive was astoundingly relaxing, getting to spend some one-on-one time with some of the gang.

"Uh, Ria?" Gatlin's voice was strained, like he was trying not to break out in laughter, hives, song, or tears – I wasn't one hundred percent.

*Until* I looked in my rearview mirror and caught the now-imprinted image of him holding the garter skirt that went with my sexy maid outfit. I was opening my mouth to tell him to put it back when Rafe snatched it from his hands and held it up to the window like he was checking a counterfeit bill.

"Looks like a certain little bird likes to play." He purred. Oh, for the love of –

I gave Drea a quick look and she immediately reached behind her to yank the scrap of fabric from the man's hands.

Gatlin was smirking. "I think Ria has a story to tell." He said, sounding kind of sing-song. "So, come on. What's the down and dirty here?" I bet he had so much trouble keeping his face straight for that one.

I leveled my face into an expressionless mask as I stared straight ahead at the road before me. "I'm a dancer." I admitted, forcing some relaxation into my voice. They were gonna figure it out at some point on this trip, right? "Is there a problem with that?" Aloof. I was so fucking aloof right now.

Rafe shook his head. "Not at all. I admire your tenacity. It's not a very easy job from what I've heard, but I'm sure it can be very rewarding." He responded, gesturing to my car as he finished the sentence.

I'll admit that I was a little surprised, though not shocked. It wasn't very often, but it also wasn't uncommon for men to feel that they could relate or sympathize. "How would you feel if your girlfriend was dancing?" I asked. It usually told me how much of a pig a guy actually was. Now that I think about it, that's how I lost my last three boyfriends before Cardboard Eyes.

He sat back in his seat and crossed his arms firmly over his chest that was heavily emphasized by his black, fitted Under Armour shirt. "If she's mine, she's mine. She can do what she wants, as long as she's mine only." He seemed to think about it for a second before looking at Gatlin quizzically. "Would dancing make her not mine?"

Gatlin chuckled at Rafe's frowning expression. "No, she would still be yours until she kissed or screwed someone else." He assured his friend (brother?).

Rafe nodded his assent. "Then I wouldn't have an issue with it."

I felt a small sense of pride swell in my chest. Looks like I drew a pretty lucky card as far as male roommates go.

"So, you're looking for work?" Gatlin clarified, nodding his head in the direction of my bags behind my seat.

I nodded and then corrected myself. "Well, kinda. I'm just kind of scouting out the area right now and seeing what the surrounding places have to offer." I told him truthfully.

The lull in conversation couldn't have come at a better time, because Beck was pulling into a parking lot that housed a two story building with a neatly maintained exterior and decently full parking lot for only being about three in the afternoon.

The sign out front read: STARS GALA CABARET.

What was it with me and stars? It must – literally – be a sign.

I climbed out of my little car and stood, stretching my muscles that were cramped from the ride.

"Ria!" Drea snapped. "You're not even wearing shoes!"

I couldn't help it, I snorted out the most unladylike laugh that would make Miss Manners roll over in her grave. "I've got heels in my bags, but six inch platforms aren't exactly soothing to drive in." I explained as I pulled open the rear driver's side door. I rummaged for a second and came up with two pairs of stilettos. "Hot pink or classic black?" I asked.

Drea was slightly flushed. "Oh, sorry. Depends on the size." She told me.

Huh? What did the size have to do with anything? "Uh, seven?" I phrased it like a question out of confusion.

My friend lit up and said, "hot pink, and I'll take the black."

"Sneaky bitch." I marveled. She was catching on so quick. I tossed her the black heels and quickly fastened my pink ones around my ankles. I didn't wear strapless like some dancers because I never trusted that they wouldn't just go flying off during a trick.

Drea stuck her tongue out at me playfully and slipped into her own shoes. Once we were done, we headed to the Jeep where the guys had amassed.

"So, everyone ready?" Beck called to everyone, stretching out much the same way I had only moments ago. His deep blue shirt rode up just a tad, revealing his sculpted lower abs and a hint of his Adonis belt.

*Yummy.*

There was a chorus of "mm-hmm's" and "yeah's".

"Everyone have everything?" This time it was Eliam who spoke, casually leaning against the Jeep in his white button-up with the sleeves rolled to his elbows. He was yummy too, but the attitude made it a little harder to appreciate.

I was about to mention that I would have to head back out for my bags in a few when Gatlin moved in front of me, covertly putting a finger to his lips as his eyes sparkled with mischief.

Messing with Eliam? I was so down for this particular party.

I grabbed Drea and linked my arm with hers, heading into the club, feeling the teensiest bit giddy. "Are you guys regulars here?" I called out to our posse.

"We visit from time to time." Gray piped up. "It's not too far and they have happy hour every Thursday all day." I glanced back at him with a jokingly incredulous look and he just shrugged.

As we got to the door, it pushed open toward us and nearly knocked Drea and I on our pretty asses. The guy coming out was of slim build, with glasses and messy brown hair with eyes to match. At first glance, his eyes appeared waxy, indicating his level of inebriation, but that wasn't quite right; his eyes weren't exactly waxy, but just dull and flat. Lifeless.

"Richie!" Gray and Rafe called. Apparently, this was a friend.

The two guys surged forward to bro-hug the stranger. "How've you been, man?" Rafe asked, giving Richie a very masculine punch on the arm.

Richie barely reacted. "Fine." He said in an almost mechanical voice. The guys looked confused, so I'm gonna go out on a limb here and say that wasn't normal behavior for the dude.

"Hey, you alright?" Gray asked, his eyes furrowing.

The man – Richie – had still yet to meet anyone's eyes. "Fine." That was all he said before he started stumbling and practically zombie-walking away, leaving Gray and Rafe looking entirely perplexed.

I felt bad for their confusion and the way their friend had just blown them off. "Do you wanna go check on him?" I asked the two guys, genuinely concerned.

They both shook their heads and then offered their arms to Drea and I, so we all marched into the strip club for a night of fun, trying to ignore zombie-Richie just outside.

## 12 RIA

My first impression of the club? Not so great. My second impression? Pretty swanky. It almost had a prohibition-age feel that made my eyes water a little in awe.

Long chandeliers hung from a section of the ceiling that looked like the inside of a hollowed-out book, their crystal beading glistening in the ambient lighting of the faux candles around the steel frame. The bar was visible from the front door and was made prominent by the age-old brickwork that served as an almost grungy, vintage backdrop that somehow didn't look dirty or tacky against the rest of the décor. The walls were adorned with beautiful gold filigree against crimson panels, with sleek black armchairs lining the walls. There were decorative sconces spaced to perfection along the walls and the carpet mimicked old cobbled flooring in varying hues.

But the stage is what caught my eye.

It was shaped like a cross, with a gleaming brass pole in the very center and varying acrobatic apparatuses at each end of the stage. To the far left was a trapeze, hung by chains that had been wrapped in what looked like corded rope. To the right was a hoop – or lyra, as it was actually known. At the back, on either side of the entryway to the stage, were silks in a deep but vibrant green that changed shades in the pulsing lights. The front of the cross was likely left open for an unobstructed view of the stage, since it was facing the majority of the club's seating space.

I was completely in love. The place was strangely majestic and totally my taste.

I had managed to make it by the doorman without having to openly explain that I was looking for work by gesturing to my heels, then to the guys, and winking. Apparently, ladies kept these things from their guys all the time.

Not that they were *my* guys. One of them might be, but that was a bit of a fuzzy subject.

The only thing I didn't like was that the music was obnoxiously loud. I heard Eliam shout something that sounded annoyingly British and nodded, because I heard him say 'pint' and decided to roll with it.

We made our way over to a corner booth and took up two tables while a waitress wearing a black tutu with matching corset and heels took our drink orders. I noted that this club also had a kitchen, which was a ginormous plus in my book.

The girl on stage was pretty boring and basic, but I tried like hell to pay attention and see what kind of tips she got. Pro tip: if the girl on stage is terrible and gets hella cash, that's a bad sign for the venue. It means they're not paying for the show, but for... Let's say services rendered.

The guys were chatting up a storm beside me, hardly paying attention to the bony woman sitting doggy-style on the stage trying to make her ass pounce – not that she had an ass, because that was absent. As the song finished and her departure was announced, I excused myself to the guys and Drea, and made my way to the dressing room.

There was a pixie-like woman sitting behind a counter with one of those sliding glass windows that you see at doctor's offices. "Hi." I greeted warmly. "Can I speak to the floor manager, please?"

The pixie woman looked up from whatever she had been writing down, tucking her super short black hair behind her ears. "Yes, I'll call him now." She told me, her voice soft and tinkly as though she talked to little forest critters instead of manning a desk at a strip club. "He'll be back in a minute. What's your name?" She asked, grabbing up her pen and a sticky pad.

"Ria." I said. "I dance by Omen."

She wrote this down and beamed. "Great! I'm Lani, I'm the house mom." She held her hand out the little window as she introduced herself.

I shook it and smiled back. "Oh, great!" I felt like this place was a good fit already.

As I waited, I glanced around the dressing room, taking inventory of any pros and cons. The room was carpeted with a dark maroon coloured office carpet, short and easy to clean. The lockers ran in rows and were painted in a vanilla shade of white and decorated with their user's own personal touches, like stickers and magnets, and glitter. Lots of glitter. The counter was a large U shape, with bolted down barstools every couple of feet. It was a nice and clean looking set up.

I was perusing outfits and such from the window of a tiny boutique toward the back of the room when a voice cleared behind me. I turned slowly, meeting cold, flat, glassy blue eyes. He was about half a foot taller than me and obviously in his fifties or sixties, judging by his white hair and countless wrinkles, that is. But his eyes, man. They reminded me of how Richie's had looked just outside the club; no emotion, no life, no light.

I extended a hand in his direction and fought to keep my uneasiness from making me tremble. "Hi, I'm Ria. I was hoping you were hiring dancers." I said politely, my hand still extended but unmet.

The man glanced at my hand slowly and stuck his hands in his pockets. "Okay." He said flatly. Then, he turned and walked away, through a door leading to what I assumed was an office, without a backwards glance.

*Huh?*

That was eerie and creepy, and I couldn't shake the feeling of foreboding that settled over me.

"Alright, you can go check in with the DJ and we'll take care of the paperwork after you're dressed and ready, okay?" Lani chimed.

I nodded and set about my semi-regular routine of preparing for my shift.

---

MY HAIR WAS QUICKLY CURLED into immaculate loose spirals that hung in curtains down my back and over my shoulders. My startling eyes were boldened further by the smear of black liner around them and the golden glitter on my lids, highlighting the gold that was swirling in their depths. And my lips were emphasized by the natural pink lip gloss that I had chosen to create a more sultry than sexy appearance.

As I mentally approved my appearance and my inner self nodded her agreement, I rushed quickly to change, silently thanking whoever was looking out for me that Drea had come back to see if I needed anything. Gal pals were the absolute best.

Well, gal pals who didn't sleep with your fiance behind your back were the best. My inner self stated flatly, not a hint of mercy or sympathy in her tone. My tone.

No, no, no.

No thinking about that. If you're going to think devastating, think about some other devastating thing. Think about the crises around the globe, or the child loss epidemic in third world countries, or the resource scarcity in Venezuela. Just think about anything other than Cardboard Eyes and get your game face on.

Now that I was pushing my mind away from its topic of origin, I was actually pretty freaked by the glassy-eyed thing that seemed to be going on here. What if it was some sort of drug trafficking hub? In one of my educational classes for people in the adult entertainment business, I remember hearing that a lot of hubs liked to keep their proprietors drugged to keep them docile and quiet.

But the guys wouldn't bring me some place that seemed like a sex trafficking hub, I don't think. And even if they would have, they wouldn't have done that to Drea. Not sweet, beautiful, derpy Drea.

No, something else was definitely going on here, and I wasn't a detective, so I was staying out of it so long as my people were safe. Leave it to the authorities and hospital personnel to diagnose the whole situation.

I slapped my cheeks a couple of times to both snap myself from my thoughts and bring some natural colour to the surface. Blush sweated off way too easily. I took one last look at my appearance and attire and felt a sense of pride. Oh yeah, I was totally owning this place tonight.

I covered my skimpy leather ensembled with my t-shirt and jeans that I walked in wearing and made my way back to the clinical-feeling window where Lani waited. "Ready!" I chirped, my smile betraying my own excitement.

The house mom looked me over and smiled wide, clapping

her hands together. "I love your makeup, but you totally haven't changed, babe!" She chuckled, probably thinking I was a novice in disguise. Nuh-uh, not me.

"Sorry, I just have some friends with me and I'm sort of playing a trick on them with this because they don't know that I dance." I explained with a casual wink.

Lani nodded in understanding and grinned mischievously back at me before handing me a small number of papers. "I totally gotcha, girl. Just sign, date, and initial these and we'll take care of the tax forms if you decide to stay through the night, okay?" She instructed. I finished off the paperwork and then headed in the direction she had indicated to find the DJ.

Once everything was completely settled, I made my way back to the table where my friends awaited.

Well, not all friends, but mostly.

"Ria!" Beck shouted unnecessarily. It was loud in this club, but not that loud, and I was practically tight next to him. The dark-haired dancer on his lap seemed to think he was extraordinarily loud also, but, in his defense, loud did kinda seem to be his entire personality.

I smiled broadly and plopped myself down on the seat between him and Eliam, feeling a bit of sadistic pleasure as the British dick leaned ever-so-slightly away from me. Ha.

Beck was leaning around his companion to get a better look at me. "Where'd you go? Did you do your makeup?" He frowned. "We didn't want to buy any more drinks without you, but we were bored so we ordered another round for you, too." He said happily.

I beamed and glanced at the table, looking for a drink that looked like mine. Problem was, there were three drinks on the table that looked like mine, in addition to several shots. "Beck!" I whined. "Which one is mine?" They were all identical, and I totally didn't want a mouthful of whiskey when I was expecting rum. Try it sometime, you're guaranteed to gag.

Beck laughed and then gestured widely at the table. "All of them. The shots, too." He replied, halfway bending over in a mock bow. "What the lady wants, the lady shall have in excess."

I giggled like a schoolgirl. "Why, sir," I clutched at my heart dramatically. "Kindness is a virtue, indeed." I gasped dramatically as I grabbed a glass from the table.

"The excess of a virtue is a vice." Eliam goaded, smirking into his glass of, what I was thinking to be, scotch. He seemed like a scotch kinda guy.

Beck leaned around me and punched his brother (or friend? I really needed to get this figured out) on the shoulder while I rolled my eyes.

Not only was the tough masculinity think stupid to me, but Eliam was being an ass just because he could. Why couldn't he pick a half-naked girl like Beck and... Nope, just Beck.

Whatever, he could have a stick up his ass if he wanted to, it was no business of mine.

A balled-up napkin hit my cheek as another dancer was called to the stage and I turned to Drea who cocked her head to the side, then at the stage.

I shook my head at her and grinned. I had revealed to her

that I was a dancer, but I hadn't told her my stage name to keep it a surprise. I had already checked with the DJ and counted the number of girls ahead of me so that I would have enough time to excuse myself to the "bathroom" and then strip off - pun intended - my civilian clothes. I was a sucker for the wow factor.

Which is why I was practically knocked off my ass when I watched a man with a black uniform, white collar, and bible step through the door.

I get it, I really do; we're all sinners. But a priest? What?

I watched as he sat in a far corner, angled toward the stage. He was older, maybe in his sixties or seventies and looked worse for wear, his skin pale with a green tint that made him look half decayed. He was decrepit, but it was his eyes that startled me, being pale as the moon, but much more menacing. He set the holy book on his lap and folded his hands atop it, closing his eyes and going still, excluding the minute movement of his lips. And I was so stunned that I almost didn't realize that the dancer right before me was halfway through her set.

I quickly downed the rest of the drink I held and stood up, looking at the guys. "When a girl's gotta go..." I told them with a shrug.

Eliam was indifferent, Rafe and Gatlin shrugged back, Beck and Kellan looked disappointed, and Gray just smiled and made a shooing motion with his hand. Drea, however, was lit up like a Christmas tree and practically bouncing in her seat.

I shot her a quick glare to remind her to stay silent as a mime, then I took off for the curtained back of the beautiful cross-shaped stage. Now that I thought about it, maybe it was the stage that brought the priest here. Wouldn't that be funny?

With the song nearing its end, I swiftly shimmied out of my clothes and adjusted the leather straps that made up the entirety of my outfit, crisscrossing over my body as if they bound me together and kept me whole. It was a wonderful piece, and one of my all-time favourites.

The song faded out and I heard the first key notes of Florence and the Machine's "Bedroom Hymns" over the speakers before the DJ's voice boomed out.

"And now, let's welcome Omen to the stage for her first time at Star Cabaret!" He played a clapping sound effect that faded out into the music as I stepped out from behind the curtain.

My heart was hammering the way it did every time I was under those lights, feeling like this was my first time performing but thrilled and excited for the potential that I saw in myself and the experience. I slinked out down the stage, feeling the way my body naturally responded to the rhythm and beat of the music and my own heart. My body twisted and twirled of its own accord, desiring freedom and freeing its desire all at once, inviting the world to enter a fantasy with me. I continued to feel my way and let go of my thoughts, stopping just before the pole in the center.

It felt like it was waiting for me, like an old friend, and I dropped to my knees before it as though in prayer or worship. Before I knew it, it was in my hands once more, the cool metal igniting that spark that I held so near and dear to my heart, that passion, that lust for excitement. And then...

I was flying.

My body sailed through the air, the muscles in my arms burning pleasurably with the exertion and my core tightening in anticipation. The music was background noise, the people just paintings in my mind - nothing existed but my passion, my own little world.

I landed hard on the stage and I felt no pain, my legs positioned in a side split that I had long since mastered with relative ease - and I could faintly hear voices in the crowd roaring and cheering. I spun my body quickly in a move that should have been impossible to do in heels this large and pulled myself into a deadlift handstand which sent the cheers booming louder across the club.

I considered the other options on the stage, but I just wasn't feeling them call to me, tempt me. I had plenty experience with my other three options, but the pole is what called to me now, beckoning me away from my floorwork and back to it's seductive promises of thrill and adventure. And I allowed myself to be drawn back, pulling myself up it's cool steel and relishing it. I settled myself into a split against the pole, supporting my weight with the inside of my elbow, and then I curled myself into a tight ball, like I was huddling around the shining rod. And I dropped.

Catching myself at the very last second, I had timed it just well enough to catch the end of my song and the collective gasp that met my ears from the crowd around me.

The DJ was speaking again and I was grinning as I took a bow, sweat beading on my brow. "Wow, ladies and gentlemen, now THAT was a performance I would pay to see! But I'm getting paid to see it and you're not, so show our girl, Omen, some love up in here!" Cue fake applause and real applause combined.

I bowed again and collected my tips from the stage. As I started toward the curtain I entered through, the priest caught my eye and a chill ran up my spine like ice. He was staring intently and angrily, a fire burning in those pale depths that left me feeling a little terrified. But I was safe here and he couldn't hurt me if he tried.

I was safe.

I HADN'T EVEN MADE IT COMPLETELY OFF THE STAGE before I was surrounded by men. But these were my men, so that was okay. Again, not that they were *my* men. They were just men that I somehow didn't mind picking me up and spinning me around like we were in some happily ever after in a romantic comedy.

I laughed heartily, the sound full and untouched by the hurt that had been haunting me over the past few days. I pushed back to see who was holding me captive and found myself gaping at Kellan.

"Put me down, Beanstalk!" I scolded as I swatted playfully at his shoulder.

The giant of a man set me on my feet, grinning like an idiot the whole time. "'That was amazing, Ria." He said in awe. "Where did you learn to do all of that?"

I looked around at the other guys - surprisingly, including an impressed-looking Eliam - and figured I'd put them all out of their misery before any of them spontaneously combusted. "Ah, well, I've been dancing for four years." I told them. "Ever since I moved out of my parents' place." *Sore subject, abort! Abort, dammit!*

Luckily, Gray unwittingly saved my bacon. "But, I mean, I've never seen a stripper do anything like that - what you did, I mean. Mostly strippers are just supposed to be sexual objects." He froze then and turned a little pale. "I'm sorry, was that offensive? Fuck, that was offensive, I'm so sorry." He muttered, his cheeks reddening as he tried to look everywhere but at me.

The other guys looked about ready to drop to the floor laughing and I was trying so hard not to join them. "No, honey, it's fine. I'm not about those stigmas. It is what it is, and I know what I am." I soothed, smiling nicely (as opposed to smiling with repressed humour). He smiled back, apparently relieved that he hadn't caught a bad case of foot-in-mouth syndrome.

"But really," Gatlin interjected. "That's not normal stripper shit you were doing up there. You were like an acrobat."

The other guys nodded their agreement.

About to explain my talents, my breath caught in my throat when I remembered how I learned to do the things that everyone else considered a show. What most people didn't know is that the things I learned to do, I learned out of self-defense. I learned to protect myself. I learned to keep myself safe.

*I was safe.*

*I was safe.*

*I was SAFE.*

Cue stereotypical traumatic past experience highlight reel:

WHEN I WAS NINETEEN, I wasn't of legal age to drink. That, however, didn't stop my customers from drinking themselves under the table while I pretended to drink an elaborate cocktail that I couldn't even remember the ingredients of (spoiler alert, it was always cranberry and Sprite with a hint of grenadine for alcoholic colour).

One night, I had one such customer, except he was pushy, insisting that the bar was watering down my drinks because I wasn't getting drunk enough. He didn't know it was a fake drink, so I could see how he would be enraged on my behalf, but he was also getting increasingly aggressive and handsy, refusing to take no for an answer. So, I did what any slightly intelligent woman would do, and I excused myself, never going back to his table. I was scared.

After I got off work that night, it was just like any other. I was the last one out because I liked to use the time during closing to practice and use YouTube tutorials to learn new tricks, and Rory never minded one bit, saying it was refreshing to see such bright spirit. After I was finished and sweating bullets, I walked out to my crappy old clunker that I had got off some guy on Craigslist with a dodgy-looking title. Only, when I got to my car and moved to unlock the doors, I found large hands wrapped around my throat, the aggressive customer's slurred voice in my ear.

He told me that he knew what I wanted because everyone who worked in this industry must want it. Why else wouldwe put our bodies on display? He told me that I was asking for everything he was about to do to me and called me some things that I wouldn't even call my worst enemy.

Who also happens to be the one who saved me that night. She had been staying late to catch up with her boyfriend, one of the newer bouncers, and when she saw this brute's hands around my throat, my feet off the ground, legs flailing, eyes rolling back in my head, and hands clawing at his arm feebly, she sprang into action. She dispatched him with ease and called the cops immediately, and she was also just as quickly my best friend. When the cops arrived, they were kind enough to warn me that, should I continue in this profession, I needed to learn self-defense.

And they were right. Mercedes had learned karate as a child and reserved her skills for life-threatening moments. So, I did some digging and found a class that I knew would benefit me in more ways than one. It took me nearly a year to get good, but once I did, I knew that I would never be unsafe again. Not with my badass skills and my best friend.

I was unstoppable.

I was safe.

"EARTH TO RIA." Someone was saying in our loose circle.

I snapped out of my reminiscing. "Oh, uh, parkour. I learned most of it through parkour." I responded distractedly. "Where's Drea?" I couldn't see my bushy-haired friend anywhere and it had me worried, given my recent trip down memory lane.

One of the guys grabbed my hand and started leading me back to the table while I squinted across the club.

"She's at the table." Gray told me, pulling my arm gently to lead me in the right direction. Even being the second shortest in the group, he was freakishly tall. "You know parkour?" His eyes were wide in amazement and awe, which was a look that was echoed across the faces of the rest of our group.

We arrived at the table amid the guys' buzzing chatter and I plopped down on the leathery seat behind my adorable friend who was sipping on her drink and staring off into the mass of bodies. My sweat-slicked skin clung to the seats and made me cringe as it made a squelching sound as I moved.

I waved my hand in front of Drea's face. "Anybody home in there?" I teased.

She turned back toward me with a frown. Unease settled low in my belly at the grim expression in her eyes.

Eliam took notice and reached across to grab her free hand before receiving a threatening growl from Kellan. "What's wrong, love?" He queried, his brows drawn in concern. It was kind of bizarre to see this concerned, gently, non-dickish side of him. Drea seemed to be a weak spot for all of them.

Drea shook her bushy curls and smiled tightly at the two of us. "It's fine. I just saw Mayor Holden over there yelling at a guy." She explained, looking sad and worried.

I started looking around for Mayor Holden, trying to catch a glimpse of his... Brown hair? Red hair? Purple polka-dotted hair? Green fire hair with pink highlights? Who was I kidding, I had no clue what the fuck the guy looked like.

I started to open my mouth before my inner self forced me to shut it again. If she was howling with laughter, there was a good chance that any one of the six sick bastards around me would probably do the exact same thing. Only, times six. And sexier.

Eliam was scanning the area as well, his striking violet eyes narrowed in concentration. After a moment he stopped and wiped his face clean of any thought or emotion that might be flitting through his mind. "I see him. I think we should go." His voice rang with a barely contained rage. He gently, oh so gently, pulled Drea up and dropped a few bills on the table before heading toward the door.

I cleared my throat awkwardly. "Uh, I'm still working." I stated with wavering uncertainty and determination. All six guys and a poofy head of curls turned back in my direction.

"Then stay, but we're getting out of here." Eliam replied dryly. He turned, with my friend in tow, and exited the building.

*Dick.*

I looked to the other guys with a question in my eyes, and they all looked terribly undecided. They glanced at each other and seemed to have their own private conversation. Gatlin looked straight up pissed at whatever the other guys were saying - or not saying. Rafe was probably the only other person who didn't look too pleased about their brother/friend's executive decision.

As their silent debate continued on for what felt like an eternity, I grew increasingly agitated and anxious. The urge to chew my neatly manicured nails was so overwhelmingly strong.

"Whatever." I finally said, throwing my hands up as I turned to storm off. There was money to make and I wasn't going to let half-developed feelings get in my way.

I scanned the tables searching for one of the barely-noticed faces that had tipped me on the stage. Finally, I saw one sitting off in the corner nearest the stage, right below a television displaying a sports game that I really had no interest in whatsoever.

I was mid-stride, heading straight for the customer when a firm arm wrapped around my elbow and pulled me up short. Whipping around, other elbow ready, I smashed it straight into the face of my assailant.

"*OW!*" Rafe cried, clutching the side of his face. He looked shocked at first, then pissed as all hell, but then his expression melted into one of confusion. "Ow?" He asked curiously. He turned stormy brown eyes on me, narrowing them to questioning slits.

I didn't budge an inch, looking pointedly at his hand still wrapped around the crook of my elbow. He released his grip on me immediately, lifting both hands into the air in what I assume to be a peaceful gesture before once again rubbing his stubbled jaw. "How much would you have made tonight?" He finally asked.

I shrugged my shoulders and took a cursory glance around the building. "I haven't gotten a feel for the clientele yet, but probably about eight." I replied, eyeing a gentleman in a pressed suit and no company in sight.

Kellan was completely taken aback, if his expression was anything to go by. "Eight dollars?" He gasped in outrage.

I leveled him with a glare that clearly said: "are you stupid or just pretending?"

"Eight hundred, you mammoth." I sniffed, totally offended by his low ideas about me. My inner self was glowering in a no-nonsense sort of way, like a teacher would look while scolding a misbehaving child. See? She wasn't pleased, either.

Beck let loose a round of guffaws as he patted Kellan roughly on the shoulder. "Bro, you really need to get that foot out of your mouth. It's not a good look on you."

Kellan only glared back at him in response, resuming his tight-lipped demeanor.

I turned to look at Gatlin again, but he and Rafe had vanished. *WTF?*

I was about to storm off in the direction of the dressing room when I saw a mess of blond hair heading back our way.

*I'm going to pretend you didn't just audibly sigh in relief, you floozy.* My inner self was so strong-willed and independent, it was a wonder she was actually a part of me at all. And a floozy I might be, but I really wanted to believe that the heavenly, astonishingly gorgeous blonde angel and I had a little something going on - and no one could say that make out sesh wasn't steamy as all hell.

Gatlin arrived in front of me and handed me a wad of bills. "Here. You said eight, right?" He confirmed.

I nodded before realizing what just happened. "I can't take your money!" I exclaimed indignantly. I could feel the heat rising to my cheeks in complete outrage. "I'm here to make my *own* money." What was it with guys and not understanding that, as independent women, we ladies liked to actually earn our way through life?

Gatlin glowered down at me, standing at least a foot-and-then-some above me. "You danced, you earned it. Consider it a tip." His patient tone highly disagreed with the anger on his face. What the hell was with these guys?

I seriously contemplated throwing the bills in his face, but I knew that I couldn't make any of the guys stay against their will. Not only that, but the novelty of shocking them had already worn off and I was bored with my little game.

"Fine." I hissed as I snatched the money from his hand. "Let me go get dressed." I didn't wait for a response before storming off to the dressing room.

I was hunting through my bag that I had stashed under one of the counters when I heard someone approach me. I was focusing on ignoring them. I didn't want to talk, I just wanted to get the hell out of there and go curl up in my bed with some Netflix and my hitachi. My inner self drooled at the very idea and I had to wholeheartedly agree with her. Hitachis make everything better in the world. The presence behind me shifted and made me a little anxious, but I continued to pull out my street clothes and wiggle into them quickly.

I was just pulling on my top, sans bra, when a sweaty hand clapped down on my shoulder. I whipped around and opened my mouth to tell the person a good long story about personal space and what happens to the people who violate it, then I realized who it was and nausea roiled in my belly.

It was the priest.

"What do you want?" I snapped angrily. I'd been approached by people of faith multiple times in my career, thus far, but none made me so uncomfortable as the sallow, decrepit man before me.

He was even worse up close than he had been under the lights of the floor, and when he sneered at me I couldn't do anything to suppress the shiver that wracked its way down my spine. "You're the worst kind of sinner." He announced, his voice raspy and cracking with the effort it must have taken to even breathe, much less speak. "You are wrought with lust and covered in the vile slime of the remaining sins."

His breath was reaching my nose and I had to fight like a lion at meal time to keep from visibly gagging at the stench. He smelled like he was *decaying*. "I've heard it all before, old man. Go find a different place to preach your hypocritical virtues." I told him, subtly taking a step back under the ruse of adjusting my stance. "God made me the way I am, so I'm pretty sure the big guy knows what's up."

And with that, I spun on my heel and set about once again retrieving my things. Before I fully realized what was happening, the man's sweaty palm was cupped over my mouth, effectively gagging me as I shouted and tried to spin to confront him.

Only, he was a lot stronger than he should have been for a man that brittle-looking. He held one of my arms tightly behind me and started dragging me along with him, my normal strength hindered by the effort it took not to vomit from his horrible stench.

He pushed through the exit door and into the backside of the parking lot. I screamed and clawed at the hand over my mouth with the sharp nails on my unrestrained hand and pitched what could be seen as the world's biggest hissy fit.

Fear was coursing through my veins in place of blood and I could hear my heart in my ears, struggling to pump the thick substance through my body. It was irrational. I had the capacity to fight back, I had the skills and strength to take down this shell of a man. But, between my fear and memories of the last time I was helpless, and that *awful fucking smell*, I couldn't make my body snap out of it's sluggish state.

Where was he taking me? What was he going to do with me? This couldn't possibly be happening. I was supposed to be safe now.

My mind went rampant, imagining all the scenarios, all the ways that this could end badly, trying to remind my own brain why it was so important to fight, to hold my own against any would-be assailant. There was of course, every woman's worst fear in these situations, the reason most traveled in herds and didn't go out at night to walk the streets. Then there was the reason that cults were illegal – and I really wasn't keen on being sacrificed. All the blood, and off-key chanting, and robes. Nope, I'm good. Sacrifices aren't my thing.

But the one that scared me the most was the one that took me back into the mind of a blonde-haired, green eyed eight year old girl. She sat in the cellar, white dress stained red and brown and black from the weeping wounds slashed across her back. Shallow enough that the scars would likely go unnoticed, but bad enough to leave the girl sobbing and fading into unconsciousness in a puddle of her blood.

The words surrounded me once more in my mind, threatening to drag me under, to pull me into their dark and sinister hold. *Sin runs through your veins. We must purge the wicked stain on your soul.* Her father said that to her every time the whip cracked and split her flesh, every time that little girl cried out in pain. *The pain is the devil fighting back! Embrace it and eradicate this scourge on the earth.* She would beg and plead for him to stop, but he did only after her body began to disagree with the lack of blood.

I couldn't stop seeing the memory on repeat in my mind. It was taunting me and pulling my mind to pieces, leaving it as defenseless as my body was to my captor. Tears of despair started to stream down my cheeks as I continued clawing away.

"Let her go, *NOW!*"

I turned my head just enough to spot all of my roommates running full steam ahead, Gatlin in the lead and Eliam hot on his heels, Rafe, Beck, Kellan, and Gray looked angry than I had seen and were barreling right behind them.

Fresh tears sprung hot from my eyes at the scene before me.

My heroes had arrived.

## 14 RIA

I never thought I'd be so happy to see a hoard of guys running toward me that I'd known for all of about forty-eight hours, but I definitely was. I wasn't sure, however, if I'd ever be able to look any of them in the eyes after this.

"I said let her go!" Gatlin growled. His beautiful silver eyes were filled with raging flames, lighting them up and making him appear a hundred times more dangerous than I could have ever imagined. He seemed almost deadly, a force of nature that not even a skilled assassin would consider going up against.

Eliam strolled up to Gatlin's side once they were near and crossed his arms leisurely, a stark contrast to the fury that mimicked my angel. "I think he means *now.*" He drawled, reiterating Gatlin's previous demand.

The priest removed his hand from my mouth slowly, allowing me access to much needed fresh air, but maintaining his grip on my arm. "This creature is sin itself!" He spat at the guys.

Every single one of them looked at one another, seeming like they were mere seconds away from-

They all doubled over, holding their guts, tears streaming down their faces... Laughing. *Laughing?!* Are these idiots for fucking real? No, don't mind me, I was just in the middle of being *kidnapped!* I couldn't believe that I thought for one second that they were actually concerned enough to come to my rescue.

Kellan was the first to compose himself crossing his arms in a way that was much more menacing than Eliam's casual ease. "Okay, so she's sin incarnate, manifested here on earth." He humoured. "What, exactly, had you planned on *doing* about it?"

A huge lump formed in my throat as my own mind threatened to swallow me up in my childhood memories. I could easily imagine what he had planed on doing about it.

The man didn't respond, only tugged at his collar with his

free hand.

"Preacher Belvieu, let her go, or you're really going to regret it." Gray said cooly, lazily. As furious as he looked, he also looked bizarrely relaxed.

Preacher Belvieu let out an animalistic, sickening sound. "No!" He screeched. He began jerking his finger at the sky. "Sin must be cleansed or the devil shall claim us all!" He was hysterical, the very definition of a person who's lost every single one of their marbles. He was shaking and wavering slightly, and I could only hope his age caught up to him.

Sensing my opportunity as the brittle and decrepit man wheezed painfully, I jerked my arm free and into his jaw. As he howled in pain, I took off running for the guys, who seemed like they were about half a football field away in my distress. Just as I was about to stop and kick off my super unreasonable - but adorable - shoes, something slammed into my back, leaving a sharp, burning sort of pain radiating down my spine.

"NO!" One of the guys boomed. I turned my head to find the preacher straddling my back, his milky eyes full of mirth as he grinned a rotted smile down at me. I tried to stand, but the pain in my back wracked through me like an avalanche, crushing my bones. I screamed out pitifully.

I turned my head to sea a stream of wispy red light slamming into Belvieu's chest full force, casting the man backwards and off of my body.

Despite the fact that an impact such as that should have broken several bones, he got right up to his feet and wailed shrilly before taking off around the building.

"I'll go get him." I heard Eliam say to the others.

Gatlin growled low in his throat, the sound more desperate than menacing. "No, we need to get her out of here." He said sharply. "Gray, Beck, get her shit in the car, we need to go."

The two guys muttered their assent and were gone.

I closed my eyes against the pain that was radiating through my back and seeping into every bone. I couldn't focus and was beginning to find it difficult to breathe. What was happening to me? What had that maniac done? The questions were starting to grow fuzzier as I tried harder to think about them.

I could distantly feel a hand on my back and relaxed into it, instinctively. "Stay with me, Ria." The voice attached to the hand said softly. I couldn't even make out who it was in my blurry state of mind.

Seconds later, I was floating and voices were crowding around me, pounding against a sheet of ice that had started to form over my mind. Arguing. Shouting. Doors slamming. Silence.

As the ice thickened, I could feel my conscious mental processes slowing at a terrifying pace and I could see my inner self beating on the ice in an attempt to shatter it, to no avail. I wanted to push back against it, thaw it with the sheer force of my will, but it just didn't respond. I was trapped in my own mind and losing the strength to struggle.

So, I let the darkness take me.

*"I'M SORRY, DADDY!" I cried as my father drug me through the house and towards the cellar, as he did every time he saw the devil in me. It was a routine, a cycle, but this time was different. I didn't want to go and bleed the evil from my body because I had done nothing wrong. The devil wasn't inside me, Mrs. Crimshaw even said so!*

*But my father wouldn't listen, and my mother did nothing but sit on the far side of the couch, focusing on her needlework.*

*We had reached the door to the cellar and paused while my father unlocked all seven locks. He always said it was one lock for each day God worked to create the world, but I always thought it was one for each of the deadly sins. "The wickedness of the devil is reaching out of your soul and affecting the faithful. It must be purged before any more innocents can be infected by your carelessness, Ria!" He scolded me, as if this were a normal punishment for a normal misdeed. I had no control over how others thought, and it was beyond me how my own father could think I was so horrible.*

*I fought to pull my wrist from his hand, digging my bare heels into the rough and splintered wood of the old steps. "No daddy, I'm not evil, I promise! I pray every night with all my heart and I do everything right." I sobbed. "Please don't hurt me anymore." That last part was said on a choked whisper that reached no ears but my own.*

*He ignored me and led me further into the darkened stone room, setting me on my knees before the altar that he had erected there. While I sat obediently on my knees, sobbing uncontrollably, my father took to the closet, where I knew the whip was stored.*

*I screamed out and scrambled back, putting as much distance between the leather corded weapon and myself as possible. "Please, daddy, no! It hurts!" I screamed as loud as I could, thinking that the louder I was, the more likely he was to actually hear and listen to me.*

*"The pain is the devil fighting back! Embrace it and eradicate this scourge on the earth." He told me simply, completely void of any emotion toward his only daughter.*

*"No!" I screamed. And I kept screaming the word over and over as he closed in on me, each step of his booted foot clapping against the hard concrete and echoing violently around us.*

*Before I had a chance to react, I was face down on the cold rock, once again before the dreaded altar. My father reminded me to begin reciting The Lord's Prayer, and I did so with the shakiest voice I'd ever heard.*

CRACK

*The leather came down on my skin hard, burning a line from one shoulder to the opposite hip. I cried out in pain and stopped my recital to catch my breath and reign in my tears. "Daddy, why are you doing this?" I choked out weakly. I wasn't sure how I spoke, but I did.*

*"Sin runs through your veins. We must purge the wicked stain on your soul." He replied, this time sounding angry. "Begone, devil! Remove your vile claws from the soul of this child of God!"*

CRACK

*CRACK*

*CRACK*

"Can't you go any faster?" Gatlin snapped at me from the backseat, where he cradled an unconscious Ria. I could see the lines of worry around his eyes, the tension he carried in his shoulders, and the concern that I could visibly see radiating from him.

I glared at him in the rearview mirror. "I'm bloody trying." I practically shouted back at him. I'd wanted the annoying girl gone, sure, but I had never wished any physical harm upon her. Whatever that insane preacher had done to her, whatever he used on her, it wasn't something that I knew humans had access to. I had seen him talking to Mayor Holden right before I insisted that we leave, knowing that the powerful man was suspect for the strange bouts of comas that had been occurring all over town. It wasn't a far cry to assume that he had a big part to play in the whole ordeal.

Gatlin shifted in the back, laying Ria a little further out and lifting her head. "You're not fucking trying hard enough." He insisted. I knew it wasn't really my brother talking, it was desire, but it still stung. We'd never not had the fullest confidence in one another. We'd always trusted each other implicitly, it was our dynamic - the one I had been concerned about Ria ruining from the moment I laid eyes on her. I knew she'd cause trouble.

I opted to say nothing in response, but pressed harder on the gas, almost shoving it through the metal frame of the easily-destroyed car that she insisted on driving. The foreign little thing would never hold up in a serious accident. Before too long, we were pulling down the long driveway up to the house and Ria was extremely pale, her small freckles becoming very prominent in contrast.

The moment we were stopped, Gatlin was out of the car, carrying her the porch and into the house, the rest of our brothers right behind him, similar looks of worry and fear etched on their faces. The entire thing was ridiculous, their feelings toward her. We'd only known her a couple of days and they were acting like she was an irreplaceable member of our group, like she was one of us. But all of us knew that she wasn't, and never could be, anything like us. She would never completely fit and it would drive her mad.

I don't know how long I sat in her car, gripping the steering wheel a little too tightly, my knuckles white. Eventually, I calmed myself down enough to release the steering wheel and make my way to the house, noting that the door had been broken open despite the fact that it was never locked. Once inside, I made my way up the stairs, trudging along slowly for a reason unbeknownst to me.

I made it to her bedroom and froze in the door frame, watching in shock as my brothers gathered around the petite blonde and stripped her down. "What in the bloody hell do you think you are doing?" I demanded, schooling my face in an expression of nonchalance. It was a face I hadn't worn in a long time, not since... Regardless, I seemed to have no choice but to wear it consistently around Ria, a girl who's last name I didn't even know, but couldn't seem to be unaffected by.

None of my brothers so much as glanced toward me, focusing instead on their task at hand. "We need access to the wound to see if we can figure out what it is and how to extract it." Gray said simply, always the voice of reason and cool as a cucumber. Everything was always so methodical with him.

I didn't bother responding, knowing they were all completely focused on the girl, the deathly pale, unmoving, barely-breathing girl. If I was completely honest with everyone involved, I was completely focused on her, too. It was my fault that she had gotten hurt because my own Sin had prevented me from seeing clearly. I was too prideful to consider that the crazy old preacher might try to attack a woman of her profession, much less one that so obviously enjoyed what she did. I was too stupid to put aside my pettiness for a few moments to just hang out and keep my eyes on the suspects.

That wasn't the worst of it, though. It was pure coincidence that she turned out to be a stripper. We had already planned on going and staking out the club that Jonas Holden liked to frequent, the place where we were sure he picked up most of his victims. As if the things he did to his own stepdaughters weren't bad enough, we were pretty positive that he had gotten his slimy hands on something that he shouldn't have. That he was causing these tragedies and tearing families asunder.

I tried my damnedest not to feel the guilt that was creeping up my spine like a snake, slithering its way into my conscience. But it was there, nonetheless. Watching the way my brothers frantically assessed and evaluated her, they way they looked both helpless and determined in the face of losing this stranger who had only just flounced into our lives, it almost ripped me completely in two.

I stood straight and rolled my shoulders back, taking determined strides toward the bed where Ria was now laying on her stomach, black tendrils inking out under her fair skin from a relatively small wound. At least the knife had not been very large or penetrated deeply. "Back up." I commanded, pushing through the circle the five of them had formed around her.

Rafe got right up in my face, his own darkened with a fury I had only ever seen on Gatlin. "I'm not going to let you let her die, E. Over my own dead body." Rafe was slimmer than

I in stature, but I had invested much more time and effort into my fighting skills over the course of my long life. I could take him down in a heartbeat if that was my wish.

"Get out of my way, Greed." I hissed. "No one is dying today." I shoved him aside, not caring to make sure he didn't fall into anything. He would live. Ria, on the other hand, would not, unless I did something fast. I had only seen this poison at work once that I could recall, and it was so far in the past that I wasn't sure I would be able to remember exactly what the treatment was. The black lines were spreading too fast for my comfort, spurred on by the presence of our Sins. "Get out. You're all making this worse." I hissed, searching my mind for the method that would remedy the troublemaker's ailment.

The guys all hesitated, seeming unsure of whether they could trust me, once again sending a wave of hurt through me. They could trust me, that was one thing I knew for absolute certain. Finally, they all seemed to come to that same conclusion and filed out of the room, one by one.

Once I had room to think and the darkness had significantly slowed its rapid spread, I delved into my memories, searching for a particular one. There was a girl, dressed in all purple, laying on the ground, a warrior standing above her with a blade that dripped with her blood and poison.

The memory started to fade and I pressed my fists into my temples, fighting to keep the images in my mind. Time did horrible things to the mind. I dispatched the warrior quickly and ran to the woman's side. I distinctly remembered thinking she was the most beautiful woman I had seen in my entire existence. Black vein-like tendrils spread out from a deep wound in her chest.

*"Suck the poison out, like a serpent's venom, then heat the wound."* The woman had said. It sounded too simple, too easy. I remembered thinking the woman was completely mad. *"Make my heart beat faster, to push it all out. I shall heal then."*

I shuddered a bit at the memory, realizing what I was going to have to do. "I'm so sorry, Ria." I whispered to her, knowing full well that she would not be able to hear me. I pushed her her hair away from the side of her face that wasn't on the bed.

I WAS PRACTICALLY dead on my feet, completely knackered by the time I reached the bottom of the stairs. As soon as my foot touched the floor, my brothers were there, matching expressions of fear and anticipation etched into their eyes themselves. I felt horrible for what I was about to have to tell them, for how I had to save the girl that they were all so infatuated with. They'd forgive me, sure, but the implications of what had to be done were absolutely horrifying.

"She is going to be fine." I told them.

They all breathed a heavy sigh of relief, one they must have been holding in for the hours it took to accomplish what I needed to do. The girl would be fine, and so would they.

Gatlin stepped forward first, looking like he had aged ten

years, which was impossible. "How did you... Fix it?" He hesitated, searching my face for a sign that might explain it all to him.

Breathing in deeply, feeling too tired to move at all and just sat on the floor at the base of the stairs, leaning my head and back on the banister. "I had to take her Sin. All of it." I admitted quietly, feeling the crushing guilt hit me like a speeding train.

I swear that I could see a mirror shatter in my brother's silver eyes. "You... What?" He whispered, his voice wavering between fury and fear. I had anticipated this. I knew what I had to do was risky.

"I had to make her Sinless, then give it all back, then take it again. I had to keep her heart rate high enough and long enough for her body to push out any lingering traces of the poison. And for her to heal faster." I added the last part to reassure them all that she was going to be okay, and quickly.

That wasn't completely true, and I knew my brothers could see right through the hole in my explaination. The truth was that the poison only responded to magic, so I had to take it all away to nullify its effect. But you can't give magic back in the exact amounts in which it's taken. If I had given too little, her lifespan would have been significantly shorter. If I gave too much, she lived much longer than any mortal ever would. And I gave too much

When I saw each one of them slowly deflate, I knew they had processed everything enough to forgive me. They all seemed to realize the same thing simultaneously and each turned their tired eyes on me.

"How much Sin did you give, E?" Kellan was the one to ask

what they were all thinking and I could hear the strain in his voice, the barely subdued anger. Who was I kidding? Of course Kellan would be the most affected by the issue at hand. He had seen me give too much before.

I closed my eyes against the curious and concerned stares that my brothers were giving me. "Enough. If we tell her everything else, we can't tell her what saved her life. If she looks too hard, it could do a lot of damage," I explained staring at the faint light coming through my eyelids. "To more than just her." We all knew the same thing, and it infuriated me just the slightest bit.

She wasn't going anywhere for a while.

"Ria?" I heard someone say. They sounded close, but muffled and distant. I knew their voice sounded familiar but couldn't seem to put a name or face to the sound. I could definitely smell, though, and the heavenly aroma of something deep and woody mixed with the rich, unmistakable scent of coffee filled me with absolute bliss.

Wait. Coffee?

My eyes flew open painfully, and I almost jerked upright before Eliam's hand came crashing down on my chest to hold me still.

I stared at him warily, his blonde hair messy and violet eyes dark with the bags to match. "What just happened?" I asked cautiously, trying to subtly adjust the position I was in. I felt like I'd been asleep for a week.

Eliam snorted a laugh and gave me a sideways glance. "*Just?*" He repeated. "Love, you've been out for nearly a week now."

I actually gasped. Out loud. For real. "Are you fucking serious?" I sputtered. My head whipped around as I looked for any sign at all that he was lying. Literally anything would do. "There's no way in hell." I mean, there actually was. After all, hadn't I just remarked on how my body was feeling that very way?

Eliam just shook his head in bemusement. Not irritation? Huh. "Just over five days, only by a few hours, though." He elaborated. It may as well have been 2064, because I just lost a whole business week.

"So, then what happened just over five days ago?" I asked, my eyes narrowed at him in a way that I hoped conveyed my suspicion. Of course, I remembered the whole ordeal from my own perspective, but I also remembered the pain and not knowing where it came from.

He took a deep breath and let it out before finally replying. "Belvieu... He stabbed you." He said, staring at me with those fathomless eyes of his. They really were beautiful.

I snorted. "Yeah, I got that much, Einstein." I rolled my eyes at him. I mean, really. It was easy enough to deduce, even though I hadn't been one hundred percent positive. "But, I'm still breathing and obviously well enough to be at home, so what gives?"

He just raised a perfect brow at me. "Well, you appear to have all the answers, so I'll let you figure it all out." The bastard was smirking at me. I was really starting to hate that expression.

"Fine." I snapped at him. Then I settled my face into a smirk of my own and added, "but could you get your hand off my boob, first?"

His brows drew together in confusion as his eyes drifted down to where his hand still lay pressed against my chest. More specifically, my breast. Still looking like he didn't quite understand, he looked up at me. Then he grinned and gave it a quick squeeze before removing the offending limb while I looked on in complete shock, my jaw hanging so low that it dangled by a mere thread.

*What the hell?*

"Why did you even come to help? I thought you wanted me gone." I puzzled, crossing my arms over my chest and lifting my chin.

Eliam's face dropped into one of such sadness that I had trouble processing the image. A face like that, so full of raw confidence and ferocity, wasn't a face that an expression like that belonged on. "Ria," he said solemnly. "I may have wanted you gone - I still do - but I'd never want you dead."

I was take completely by surprise. Of course, I never even

thought that he would want me dead, but that spurred on a bigger question. "You thought he was going to kill me? What makes you so sure?" I asked. My mouth was suddenly dry, my throat itchy, and my limbs heavy. I could have died.

"You can't reason with a madman, love. And Augustus Belvieu is as barmy as barmy comes." He explained, surprisingly gently considering the last several conversations we'd had. I was having a hard time wrapping my head around everything.

I had lived in this town for a total of two days and so much crazy had already happened. First Clove, who definitely counts as crazy, then the guys, then that psychopath preacher trying to *kill me*. That was all a little much for my brain to take in. I would have rather dealt with a cheating ex and the heartache of it all than face potential death. It was probably in my best interest to get the hell out of dodge, but I'm an honest-to-God liar. That's because I actually would do just about anything to avoid ever seeing those cardboard brown eyes ever again, much less those soft teardrop blue ones that I had trusted, foolishly, for so damn long.

Unfortunately for me, "just about anything" included sticking around this already whacked off town.

Eliam was still staring at me patiently, as though he understood that I was talking myself through inner turmoil. "So..." I started. "If he stabbed me, why am I okay?" I thought back to when Belvieu was launched into the air by the wispy red stuff. I hadn't seen where it had come from, but I also didn't give it much thought. It seemed familiar, somehow.

"He didn't get you very well, but the blade was sharp and coated in a mild toxin." He answered. "If the dagger hadn't ended up in one of those scars, the toxin would have traveled faster than we could have done anything." He looked grim, and whether it was from the whole knife thing or the scar thing, I couldn't tell.

Trying to think of something to say, I decided I'd rather think about almost being murdered rather than about my childhood. "What kind of toxin was it?" I asked quietly.

Eliam, the asshole, gave me a bemused look that also seemed to ask if the blade had actually landed in my skull instead of my back. "The killing kind, Ria." He deadpanned.

"So helpful, Eliam. You should be a professor with that skill of yours." I said dryly with another roll of my eyes.

He turned to look out my large window and said, "I was, once."

*Wait, wha-*

"Ria!" A voice screeched from the doorway. I turned my head just in time to briefly spot a bushy brown blur racing toward me at a dizzying speed. "You're awake, OMG, you're awake!" Drea cried into my hair. Ew, my hair. Pretty sure I hadn't been bathed. Ew.

I laughed softly and patted my friend's back. "I'm awake. Down girl." I chuckled as she drew back and wrinkled her nose at me. "Yeah, I know, I stink." I told her, frowning.

Drea glared at me. "No, you talked to me like a dog. Rude, much!"

"More like a puppy."

"That's supposed to make it any better?"

"Yes, because they're cute and amazing snugglers."

"I am a pretty fantastic snuggler..."

"Well, there you go." I patted her head playfully and she stuck her tongue out back at me.

"Where are the rest of the guys?" I asked, noting that it was Eliam of all people that I woke up to.

Drea smiled a knowing smile. "They had to do a job. They'll probably be back sometime tomorrow morning." She told me. Her eyes darted to Eliam, back to me, then back to him. "E, can she get up?" She asked him.

Eliam turned back to me, leaning back in his chair that he had pulled up to the bed and crossing his arms. "If she can walk seven steps without getting dizzy, she's good." He said with smug looking grin on his stupid face.

Seven steps would be a piece of cake,

I flung the covers off and was shocked to see that I was in a pair of black capri yoga pants and a red tank top. "Who changed me?" I asked with eyes narrowed in Eliam's direction.

He only shrugged in response. What a dick.

I shook off my irritation for the time being and focused on sitting up without outwardly wincing. I'll give the asshole that much, sitting up wasn't exactly pleasant, so probably not the wisest decision I'd ever made. Certainly not the stupidest, thought. So there's that.

Once I was sat up, I allowed myself a few seconds to adjust

to the feeling, and for the sting and burn of my too-tight muscles to fade. Once I was sure I wouldn't get a charlie horse the second I moved, I stood and stayed still. No dizziness. I took two steps with no issue and was pretty happy. Another two steps. Almost there...

I took two more successful steps, but as I put my foot out for the last one, I felt a shift in the air that seemed to intentionally bump me just enough to make me wobble.

"Oh dear." Eliam clucked. "Looks like you got dizzy after all."

*Get that stupid fucking smirk off your fucking face before I fucking smash it in.*

"I didn't get dizzy." I ground out between clenched teeth. "Something pushed me."

The infuriating Adonis of a man - wait, what? Not what I meant at all. The infuriating man chuckled. "What could have pushed you? Neither of us were near enough." He said, reminding me too much of Dr. Evil.

"Eliam!" Drea admonished. "Stop that right now, you prideful ass." Drea grabbed my arm and started leading me to the door. "Come one, let's go eat." She said to me, making my stomach agree loudly.

"The phrase is *pompous* ass!" Eliam called, having not moved a single inch.

Drea threw a dismissive wave over her shoulder as we crossed through the doorway. "Not when it comes to you!" She hollered back, shooting me a light, friendly grin. I knew there was a reason I kept her around.

We took the stairs slowly, because I still wasn't convinced that I wasn't going to get hit with a wave of dizziness strong enough to flip an elephant. Once we reached the bottom, I let out a breath that I didn't realize I'd been holding. Never had I been so afraid of stairs. And in this day and age, no one at a hospital would believe for a second that I actually fell down the stairs. (Thanks a lot, assholes.)

We walked into the kitchen and I immediately plopped my ass down on the floor, my back leaning against the cabinets.

"What's on the menu, chef?" I asked as Drea watched me with amusement.

She tapped her chin thoughtfully and grabbed a plate off the counter above me. "Grilled cheese?"

My mouth watered and my stomach threw a party at just the thought. I snatched one off the plate and stuffed my face in the most unladylike way possible. Don't care. Need food. "Can you make anything other than this amazing grilled cheese?" I asked around a very large, cheesy bite.

My friend laughed and sat on the floor next me, setting the plate of grilled cheesy goodness between us. "What, sick of it already?" She asked. Something in my horrified expression must have been hilarious, because she said, "kidding! I'm a pretty good cook. I feel like if I didn't cook for these guys, they'd live off boxed pizza and chicken nuggets for the rest of their lives.

I laughed out loud at her certainty, causing a few crumbs to tumble from my mouth. Oops.

We talked, we laughed, we gossiped, and we ate grilled cheese until we were full to bursting. It was a nice little dose of normalcy and I felt absolutely shitty for possibly ruining the mood.

"Drea?"

"Mhmm." She replied around her own mouthful.

I carefully weighed my question before asking it out loud. "What are those guys?"

DREA CHOKED ON HER GRILLED CHEESE, SENDING HER into a coughing fit that had her tripled over. I sat patiently while she used her fist to pat her chest. Such dramatics.

But, I mean, I had just asked her what the guys were, so it was safe to assume that the question would take anyone by surprise that way.

"What?" Drea asked incredulously. Her eyes were bugging out of her head and she was rubbing her chest where she had been hitting herself.

I raised a brow at her. "You know what I'm talking about." I said. "What are they? I saw that red stuff at the club and I know Eliam did something with the air." I just knew he had to have done something, I knew that she knew what the hell was going on. There's no way she was so close to these guys that she cooked for them on a regular basis and didn't know their secrets.

Her cheeks flushed with pink and I knew I was right. "It's not my place to talk about..." She mumbled, staring intently at a stain on the white tiled floor.

"Oh bull." I scolded. "Spill. I live here and deserve to know what mess I just got myself into."

"They're... Not normal."

"No shit, Sherlock."

She finally turned to look at me, glaring at me with those big, innocent eyes of her. Translation: it wasn't even a little scary. "I mean, they're not like physically normal. Like, human and stuff." She finally said.

Not human? How could they not be human? Then again, those muscles certainly weren't worldly. I mean, damn. I'd give up all my Louboutins just to catch a glimpse of a towel falling off and revealing a nice, hard-

"Girl talk, I presume?" Eliam drawled as he strolled into the kitchen, looking down at us plopped on the floor with a plate full of crumbs between us. "Love, your sister is waiting outside." He told Drea with a tight smile.

My friend frowned harder than I'd ever seen a person frown. "We'll talk later, okay? I've gotta go..." She hesitated, eyes flashing with hurt. "Home." She finally said through clenched teeth. She gave me a tiny peck on the forehead and scurried out the door, blowing Eliam a kiss on her way.

Eliam propped his hip up against the counter and stared down at me, his mouth quirked up in a lopsided, smile. "How's the back?" He asked casually.

"It's fine, actually. When I don't move." I admitted. Boy, did that one hurt my ego.

His smile didn't waver as he moved to pick up the plate from the floor and put it in the sink. He turned back around to look at me and crossed his arms over his chest in what was becoming his signature pose. "Want to go back up to your room?" He asked politely. Where was this civility coming from? He'd been so hostile and aloof toward me just a few days earlier. What changed while I was dead - no pun intended - to the world?

I shook my head and smiled my thanks. "No, I've been there for five days. And honestly, those stairs are probably going to haunt my nightmares for the next few decades." I joked, hoping that this newfound lightness would last a little longer. "I'd kill for a shower right about now, though."

He stared at me, unblinking, with a wry smile. "Delightful choice of words you've chosen there." He said sardonically.

"I'm nothing if not an optimist." I replied cheerily.

Eliam shook his head and offered me his hand, but I vehemently refused. "Nope. The whole moving thing, remember?"

He shot me a grin that offered nothing but mischief and just as promptly, he blanked. What did that even mean? Did I even want to know? I so didn't want to know, not when Eliam of all people had that look on his face. It was something akin to the look of a cat who's owner just bought a new canary. That canary was about to get eaten, and I personally wasn't down for being the canary. "Fine." He said, the line becoming a trademark staple for any conversation we ever had.

"Fine? What do you me-" I squealed loudly as he reached down and plucked me from my seat on the floor like I was nothing more than an errant pencil that had made its way to the ground. "What are you doing?" I tried to yell. It came out more like a breathy whisper, because my heart was suddenly pounding in my ears and it wasn't from fear.

I analyzed his features and my racing heart almost stopped. I had noted what a beautiful man he was from the first time I had seen him, but my distaste for him from his initial introduction had blinded me. His jaw was angular and sharp, giving him a very authoritative appearance, and his lips were full and completely free of dryness. I wondered briefly if they would feel as soft as they looked. And his eyes would never fail to baffle me, their rich purple hue noticeable from even a fair distance, so expressive, and full of something dark that said he was an old soul. What I wouldn't give to have those eyes staring... Right back at me. No really, he was staring at me.

His mouth kicked up into that cocky fucking smile again and I quickly looked at the collar of his shirt. That's what I'd been looking at, if he asked. "Something you like?" He teased. Teased! I wanted to keep this side of the moody, rude Brit.

"I like your shirt. Excellent design." I muttered, still staring at the fabric.

He only snorted in response as he walked through the doorway into my bedroom. I was expecting him to deposit me on the bed against my desire, but he bypassed the bed and made for the bathroom door on the opposite wall.

If I were standing, I would have dug my heels into the ground, but I wasn't. So I settled for shouting indignantly, "what are you doing?" There was a time when certainly lines could be crossed, but two days of conscious interaction wasn't it.

Gatlin already saw you naked. My inner self snarked at me. Don't go acting pure now. I blushed furiously at my inner self's scolding. She - I - was right, after all. I wasn't what you'd call modest in any way. Though, I preferred the term "sex connoisseur" to the more derogatory titles, I wasn't ashamed to admit that I was a pretty big slut sometimes. Not always, but sometimes.

"You said you wanted a shower and that stairs are evil, so here's your solution." He explained curtly. He set me down on my feet and turned to walk from the small room, but just before he was through the doorway, he turned back with a smirk. "Unless you need help bathing, too."

I wasn't sure if the blood drained from my face or rushed to it. "No!" I yelped. I walked painfully to the door and started pushing it closed against Eliam's bizarrely strong frame.

He just laughed and said, "just shout when you're ready to

come back down." As I slammed the door, just barely missing his nose, I could hear him chuckling still from the other side.

What. A. Dick.

ONCE OUT OF the shower and into some very comfy pajamas that were covered in unicorns (don't judge me, 'kay?) I was feeling much more like an actual person again. I stretched up and winced at the pain in my back but was glad that it wasn't as bad as it had been earlier. I seriously debated whether or not I should just curl up in bed and go to sleep, but my mind and body were both far from tired. I would guess that's what five days of sleep would do to a girl.

I gathered my hair into a ponytail and trudged down the stairs, looking around for any sign of the asshole that was masquerading as a nice person. When I deemed the coast was clear, I made a break for the kitchen, only to find the man himself moseying about, with skillets and cutting boards and pots.

He looked up as I gaped and smiled broadly. "Hungry?" He inquired.

I bobbed my head up and down. Those grilled cheeses of Drea's were bomb as fuck, but not really proper sustenance. "Definitely."

He gestured toward the pot he was stirring with a ladle.

"Then get to cooking. You're going to have to work for your meal." He commanded with a chuckle.

I visibly shrunk back and was seriously thinking about bolting. I ended up on one of the barstools because the food just smelled too delicious to pass up.

His eyes turned instantly mocking and I hated him for it. God, it felt amazing to feel that familiar sense of loathing return. "What is it, then? Can the minx not cook?" He taunted.

I was instantly taken aback and straightened up to my full height in indignation. "I can cook very well, asshole." I snapped. "I just... Choose not to." Oh, this was humiliating. Cooking in private? No problem. Cooking in front of others... Ah, not the wisest decision.

"And why is that, exactly? Perhaps because you can't cook?" He was baiting me and I knew it.

I ground my teeth together as hard as I could without breaking them all. "No, I just... Accidentally get hurt a lot. Burns, cuts, you name it." I admitted without an ounce of visible regret. How humiliated could a person be before they passed away from sheer embarrassment? It took about eight hours for a Sim to die from it, I was pretty sure.

Eliam's jaw dropped like a sack of bricks, sheer astonishment coating his handsome fingers like a Sheen of sweat. "You're saying you can do all of-" he waved and twirled his hand around in huge gestures that I assumed were meant to indicate my dancing "-in heels almost as tall as Well, but you can't cook without hurting yourself?" His eyes were bugging out a little and he seemed completely shocked by this.

I folded my arms protectively across my chest and stared down my nose at him. "Yeah, don't rub it in." I sniffed. "I usually cook when no one is looking, to preserve my dignity."

"Love," Eliam started with a swift assessment of me. "Your dignity fled the country the moment you put those on." He indicated my unicorn pajamas.

I scowled and lifted my chin indignantly. "Don't judge me, English boy."

"Boy!" He threw back his head and laughed, a full-bodied, hearty sound that thawed my heart against my will. "Sweet Ria, I'm much older than you think."

I smirked and him. "Well then, how old are you?" Finally, some details.

He just threw me a wink and turned back to his task of stirring. "An Englishman never reveals his age." He teased. "Now get over here and earn your dinner by washing these vegetables, and don't touch anything sharp." He wagged the ladle at me and I could only roll my eyes at him.

I got up from my stool and started toward the sink. "It's ladies that never tell their age." I muttered as I passed him. I grabbed a carrot and turned the water on, setting it to a lukewarm temperature before starting my task.

Once the vegetables were all rinsed and scrubbed clean, I jumped up to perch on the counter across from Eliam. I wanted so badly to ask about his very sudden shift in personality, why he suddenly felt compelled to sit by my bedside and wait for me to wake up. I wanted to, but I didn't, because I felt that if I brought it up, he would immediately turn back into the complete asswad that I had first met. So, all I ended up doing was sitting there and staring at him while his long, graceful fingers worked their magic over the stovetop.

I did need to say something, though, because just staring at a guy for long periods of time was probably not the most well-received method of getting a guy to like you. "Where did you learn to cook?" I asked, seeing it as a pretty harmless question to ask.

He didn't even look up from his task. "I've picked most of it up over the years, but a lot of it I just taught myself." He explained to me. I don't know why, but it felt somewhat like a secret confession, like it wasn't something that a lot of people knew.

"Wait."

This time he did turn toward me, one brow arched. "Yes?"

I propped my chin on my fist and narrowed my eyes slightly. "If you can cook like this, why does Drea think you'd all basically starve to death without her?" I was pretty sure that the answer was something along the lines of having an excuse to have her over more. Judging my her sullen expression before she left, my guess was that she didn't mind the excuse in the least.

Eliam chuckled at me, as though he found my mild outrage amusing as all hell. "There are two parts to that answer. The first is that my brothers are all possessive in their own little ways. If you do one thing for them, they'll expect it forever - even from one of their own." He explained before wagging his spatula in my direction. "Which you'd do well to remember." He warned.

Shit, he was probably talking about that hella hot makeout session with Gatlin... *Mmmm... Gatlin.*

"The second," he continued, stirring the pot of whatever the heavenly smell was originiating from. "Is that Drea doesn't care for her home life much at all. It works well because the guys and I quite enjoy having the little pixie around."

*Called it!*

"That's very noble of all of you." I compliment.

Eliam snorted slightly, throwing me off for a moment. "Don't get me wrong, Ria." He said, his voice lowering in pitch and taking on an almost growling sound. "We don't do things that don't benefit us, first and foremost. There is nothing noble in how we live." He was stalking dangerously close, leaving his precious concoction behind him on the blue and yellow flames. "Anything we want, we take." He finished once he was close enough for me to stick out my tongue and lick the tip of his long, angular nose.

I shiver ran through me, but I was having a hard time deciphering the nature of my reaction. I consider myself to be a pretty honest person, and I could openly admit to myself that I was seriously attracted to Eliam, despite his dickishness before. Being honest, I was really damn attracted to all of the guys. As much as I wanted to jump every last one of their bones, I was a relationship addict. Sex was fun and amazing with the right partner, but the romance aspect was what I loved the most.

I just stared at the sexy blonde specimen in front of me, who hadn't moved a single inch. Que the mental war. Pros: super sexy, can cook, great style, heavenly accent. Cons: major ass, and... Yeah, that was about it. I really couldn't come up with any more cons? Huh. That answered that, then.

So, I went for it. I leaned my body forward just those few short inches between us, my heart hammering in my chest, my mouth going dry. I could hear his own breathing pick up just a notch and see as his lips parted ever-so-slightly.

Then I licked his nose.

Eliam backed up several more inches and stared at me, violet eyes full of surprise. "Did you just... Just *lick me?*" He asked, astonished. I could see the wheels turning in his head, trying to make sense of what just happened.

I laughed out loud, throwing my head back as my mirth shook my entire frame. Little tears were welling up in the corners of my eyes and I wiped them away with a finger. "What?" I choked out between bursts of laughter. His face still showed his confusion and it was almost too much for me to handle. "Were you expecting something else?"

His eyes were reduced to slits as he finally shook himself from his surprised stupor and he glared. "Well, yes, actually."

"I guess you don't always get what you want then, hmm?" I taunted. Oh, this was grand. Unfortunately for me, I didn't see my demise coming until it was too late.

He rushed forward, wrapping a strong, warm hand around the back of my neck as he drew my to him so quickly that I didn't even have time to gasp properly. Before I knew it, my lips were crushed against his and I made a sound that was nearing animalistic, a sound that I can't recall ever making before that moment.

He teased at my lips with his tongue and they seemed to part of their own accord, pulling a sigh from me as they did. My tongue danced with his, scraping teeth and tangling together until I was sure that they would form a knot.

I gave up my pride on this one, finally wrapping my arms around his neck and running my fingers through the hair at his nape, which felt so much silkier than I had imagined. Not that I had imagined it. Again, that's just weird. I pulled him further in me and he responded immediately, drawing me in as close as physics would let us. The suddenness and surprise of it all had my mind spinning and turning upside down.

Where did this even come from?

In a swift and firm movement, Eliam's hands were under my thighs and lifting me from the counter, making me break the kiss with a gasp. Could I do this? We hadn't exactly gotten a gold star for our very short track record.

*War makes for some strange bedfellows.* My inner self laughed at me. Yeah, yeah, I got the message loud and clear... And I didn't care.

I pressed our lips together once more, savouring the heat that rose through my entire body and into my core. Wait. Heat. "Stove. Food." I gasped as I broke the kiss once more. It was delightful to know that I was as eloquent with my spoken words as I was with the unspoken ones.

Eliam made a growling sound deep in his chest, which everything from my breasts down was pressed against. The sound and vibration did some strange things to my body, so it was really no surprise that when he made to put me down, I clamped my teeth down hard on the side of his neck, just below his ear.

The growling sound intensified as he clutched my body tight against his, my devious plan already working well. He moved again and did something - probably turned off the stove - and started making a relatively rushed assent into the upper floors of the house. Which featured all the bedrooms, by the way. Which, by association means bed. My heart rate spiked again at the thought, and I couldn't help the wanton way my body was responding.

I released my vampire death grip and licked the spot gently, awarding me a light shiver from the body against my own. Only further urged on, I trailed my tongue lightly up his neck until I found his earlobe. I bit down on it delicately, pulling ever-so-slightly, and reveled in the involuntary shivers and shakes from the prideful man that held me.

I was *this close* just throwing myself completely over the side of the wagon right where we stood when I was suddenly sailing through the air and landing without a sound on my bright red covers.

Eliam stood over me at the edge of the bed, looking down at me with the hunger of a lion who's spotted a particularly plump-looking antelope. However, the only thing especially plump about me was my set of nicely-sized breasts that were rising and falling heavily with heavy breaths brought on by barely suppressed desire.

I was way in over my head and had no honest clue what the hell I was thinking – this was *fucking Eliam* for God's sake! I found it hard to keep that annoying little thought in the front of my mind when he was standing there, smirking triumphantly down at me. The feminist in me was screaming in outrage. He began unbuttoning his pressed light blue shirt and I almost screamed, too, torn between wanting him to hurry the hell up and also but the damn thing back on. Once it was off, though, all bets were right behind it.

His chest and abdomen were mapped out in perfect dips and rises, like the Willamette mountains. It was almost as if he had been carved from some foreign, perfect stone. My eyes traced down from his well-defined pecs to his golden, tanned Adonis belt, pausing there as my breath hitched and caught in my throat. He just stood there leisurely, enjoying my appreciative gaze.

He seemed to have decided he'd had enough after what felt like several hours of near-unblinking staring and he leaned onto the bed, crawling over me and supporting his weight on his elbows. He didn't say a word as he dipped down and pressed his lips firmly against mine again, this time with a more seductive, slow rhythm than our frenzied attack in the kitchen.

As we continued, he pushed his body against mine, his hardness pressing against my core and making me squirm desperately. I was a big ball of ignited nerves and white-hot flames; the more accurate way of putting it is that I was hella hot and bothered. I mean, *fuck.*

Eliam pulled away slightly, breaking our kiss and my heart a little bit, too. He seemed to be searching for something as he stared into my luminous green eyes with his own multi-hued purple ones.

"Yes." I whispered breathlessly, nodding as I did so.

That seemed to be what he was looking for, because we were suddenly back to our previously frenzied state, and my mind went a little blank in the moment, desire taking over, all the way to my bones, and making me feel feral and unchained.

His hands slid down from my shoulders to my breasts, resting there as he teased my nipples with his thumb. I arched into him, soft moans escaping from low in my throat as pleasure swept through me in violent waves. He continued down his self-made path, sliding his hands to my sensitive waist and squeezing slightly as they stayed there.

Finally, he reached my hips and hooked his thumbs into the waistband of my pajama pants and I was suddenly alert. I had had an ex who loved to literally rip clothes off. I lost half my wardrobe to the asshole. I broke the kiss this time to tell him, "these are my favourite. Don't mess them up." I narrowed my eyes in a warning glare to emphasize my point.

He chuckled back at my his, voice sounding deeper than usual. "I wouldn't dream of ruining your adorable unicorns, love." He told me. I wasn't convinced and wouldn't be able to relax until my *adorable unicorns* were safely on the ground, bed, window, ceiling fan – anywhere in one piece.

Eliam slid them down my hips and over my thighs without moving an inch away from my face, his lips still hovering just above mine. I couldn't decide whether it was skill or just long arms, but I honestly couldn't care less. Once they were to my knees, I kicked them off before he could change his mind about destroying my pretties.

Once off, the fire that was raging through my entire body

seemed to congregate low in my belly, making me core pulse with need. As if he could sense it himself, he brought his fingers down, down, down, all the way to my slick entranced. He grinned pressed his lips to mine once more while his finger explored in little circles over my clit. I bucked from the unexpected pleasure and shuddered when his finger slipped over my entrance. "Oh my God, *yessss.*" I hissed, tossing my head back.

I could feel his own arousal through his jeans where he was pressed against my inner thigh and it drove me a little wild, causing my instincts alone to take over as my hand reached for his zipper of its own accord. He shivered slightly, which made my grin against his lips.

Once he was free, I sucked in a gasp and bit down lightly on his lower lip, eliciting a groan from him. He pulled back and glanced down at my hand wrapped around him.

"Fuck." He growled, watching my hand move in small twisting motions, gathering precum to lubricate his shaft as I went. His own hand never faltered, teasing small circles around my clit and periodically flicking it ever-so-slightly, making arch into him over and over again with strangled sounds of pleasure.

He was suddenly moving, rolling until I was atop him and gasping for breath. His exotic eyes told me exactly what he was waiting for and I was more than happy to oblige, no words needed to convey the need we were both experiencing. I moved position myself just over him, desperate for my release after his relentless teasing and playing.

I was *this* close to sitting my ass right the hell down when I heard the distinct sound of the front door opening and closing.

"E?" I heard Rafe call. The two of us froze in place like idiots, waiting for the sound of footsteps on the stairs. Maybe we had imagined it. Paranoia was a huge issue in this day and age.

We heard steps on the ground floor, but none coming up. "Is she up yet?" Rafe shouted out, louder than before.

"Fuck." Eliam growled again, this time without the strain of arousal behind the words.

"Don't go anywhere." Eliam commanded, looking a little confused. I nodded furiously, completely okay with not moving from my spot. He got up and adjusted himself quickly, tugging his shirt back on and making quick work of the buttons, much to my dismay. He shot me a cocky grin that said he knew exactly what was running through my mind. He started walking toward my bedroom door, then stopped, turning around and staring quizzically at me. Right before he turned back to the door, I could have swore he looked... Angry? He shook his head and then left, closing the door behind him a tad aggressively.

I was a little bit worried about getting found out, but only a very little bit; I was a grown woman and could do as I pleased. What was more concerning to me was that I was currently laying in my bed, half undressed, waiting for a man to come back that I was still pretty sure hated me. I had no clue what had been going through my mind or had possessed me to suddenly want to jump the brit's bones, but I was here all the same. I had never been a real big fan of hate sex, but what had just developed between Eliam and I didn't feel much like hate sex. It felt like unbridled, newly freed passion.

I stretched up and across the bed to snag one of my pillows and crushed it over my face, making random, unintelligible sounds out of frustration. My inner self seemed to be just as baffled as I was, just as confounded. She paced back and forth across a (faux) fur rug in my mind, alternately rubbing her temples and making wild gestures with her hands as though having an intense conversation with herself.

Says an awful lot when even the voices are hearing voices and talking to themselves, too.

Somewhere between the pillow screaming and myself talking to herself – myself's self? – I seemed to come to my senses, or what was left of them after the past few days I'd had. I jumped to my feet and started the hunt for my pajamas, finding them, surprisingly, laying in a peaceful little heap right beside my bed. I sighed out in relief that even though he was a huge douchecanaoe, he wasn't a wardrobe destroyer.

By the time my cute pajamas were neatly back in place and my hair was combed through with my fingers, Eliam still hadn't come back, which was irritating if I was being totally honest. *Time isn't free, buddy.* I thought, shaking my head. It was a damn good thing I came to and decided not to wait after all.

I padded over to my bedroom door and cracked it open, peering through the small sliver of space and listening for anyone hanging around. When I confirmed the coast was clear, I did one last comb through my doubtlessly messy and still damp hair and stepped out of the relative safety of my bedroom.

Once I made my way down the stairs, I could hear all the guys in the kitchen and braced myself, not really knowing what to expect. Waking up to a house full of guys, while not at all unpleasant to look at, was still unchartered territory for me, and these definitely weren't normal guys. The thought made me stop and wonder for a moment about what Drea had been about to explain to me before she took off so abruptly.

After I rounded the corner into the kitchen and dining space, I was a little surprised to see all the guys just scattered about with beers in their hands and huge, goofy grins on their faces. When they saw me in the doorway, they all noticeably brightened; not in the sense that they were happier, but they actually seemed *bright*, like they had this ethereal glow around them all as if they were standing in the moonlight.

I cleared my throat a little, standing in the doorway a bit awkwardly. "Hey guys." I greeted softly, wary of whatever greeting I was going to receive.

Beck set his beer down on the counter and strode over to me quickly, immediately wrapping me in a huge hug that knocked the breath right out of me. "I'm glad you're up, Ria." He whispered, the sentiment contrasting against his normal aloofness. "I'm so happy you're okay."

He had barely gotten the last words out before he was suddenly no longer attached and flying across the foyer behind me, skidding on the polished wood floors. I whipped my head around to see what the hell had just actually happened when I found myself being crushed once again, this time by huge muscles that smelled so familiar and hypnotizing, like smoke and cinnamon, like rage and passion. I was astounded my how safe I felt in Gatlin's arms and how pleased I felt that he wanted me there. *Down, ovaries.*

"I'll kill him." Gatlin growled, the rumble doing many confusing things to my exhausted body.

I wriggled around to extract one squished hand and rubbed up and down his arm – for his comfort, of course. "It's fine, Angel. I'm a-okay." I reassured gently. He noticeably relaxed little by little, in time with my petting.

"I want a hug, too." I heard Kellan grumble. I tried to peek around the wall of muscle that was holding me, but ultimately failed and settled for crooking my finger in the general direction of his deep, thunder-like voice. The next thing I knew, I was sandwhiched between the two biggest guys in the room, and not in the sexy way that I'd fantasized abou... That I'd never fantasized about before.

I huffed out a laugh, the air literally being pressed from my lungs. "Good to see you, Mountain Man." I managed. All I got was a grunt in response, but that was good enough for me.

I don't know how long we'd been like that when I felt another body press in on my right. It felt like I was suffocating, but with concern. I was pretty sure the new addition was Gray, judging by his silent demeanor and slighter figure than his brothers. I didn't complain. I just leaned into him and sighed out loud, reveling in the peace of the moment.

I heard a grumble from nearby and could easily guess who it was. "If you want in on this, you better get over here before these guys realize they're being cuddly." I teased, earning a resounding growl from my human cage.

"I want my *own* hug." Rafe complained, sounding indignant and irritated. *Aww, he feels left out.*

I really didn't want to leave my cozy nest of muscles and testosterone, but I really did feel like Rafe would explode if I didn't do something; I'd never seen a person explode before and I wasn't signing up to see it now. So, I extracted myself from the others and wobbled a little when I realized how much good oxygen I had been missing out on.

When I looked over to Rafe, he was pouting – like honest to god, *pouting*, arms crossed, looking down at his feet with his lips pursed. It was, without a doubt, the single most adorable thing I had seen since the first time I was introduced to Grumpy Cat. Not that I would ever tell him that in a million years, because I really liked this whole living gig. It was working out pretty well for me so far.

I walked over to him and gave him a firm poke in the belly button, trying not to smile as I did so. He peered up at me through his ridiculously long, dark lashes. I smiled tentatively and opened my arms a little in invitation, making the first move. He stared at me for a long moment more before moving so quickly that I barely had time to blink, wrapping me up in his arms and buring his face in my hair. I could have swore he actually sniffed it. On second thought, he probably did sniff it. These guys were weird as hell. And sinfully sexy, but that much was obvious.

I nuzzled my face into his chest – the highest point on his body that I could reach – and was rewarded with a warm humming sound. "It's good to see you, Rafe." I told him with as much sincerity as I could muster. He just hugged me tighter and I felt all warm and fuzzy inside.

"I want another hug!" I heard Beck whine from somewhere behind me. I tried really, really, *really* hard not to laugh. I was way too close to biting my own tongue off with the effort it took to keep my mirth contained. My inner self had no such qualms, giggling uncontrollably because we – I? – totally knew that Beck wasn't going to be satisfied with a single, short-lived hug.

Rafe growled against me, the sound traveling from his chest and into my little pleasure palace. Yes, she has a title. Get over it. "Then get one from Kel, this is *my* hug and it will last as long as I want." He snapped, my stomach deciding to contradict him with a protest of its own. "It will last as long as Ria's stomach wants." He amended. I appreciated that, as did my insatiably ravenous stomach.

I peeked up to sweep my eyes over the kitchen, spotting Eliam back at the stove, stirring away like nothing had ever happened. He didn't even look up at me. I, however, turned as red as the sauce in the pan closest to me, whether from shame, anger, or attraction, I wasn't sure. All three emotions were sitting pretty closely on the couch in my mind, so it was hard to tell which was which.

I poked Rafe in the side and he looked down at me. "I'm *hungry*, Seymour." I whined at him, batting my eyelashes in what I knew to be a very flattering way. Not just anyone could pull it off, but I was most definitely not just anyone. I was Ria freaking Grimm, and I was a sexy beast.

I heard Kellan snort and I turned my head around, watching him cover his mouth. I narrowed my eyes at him in a mocking sort of glare. "*Feed me*." I directed that one at the giant of a man who dared to laugh at my totally hilarious use of a classic line.

At that point, every one in the room laughed.

Excluding Eliam, of course, who turned around and wagged his spoon in my direction. "I thought you were more mature than that, love." He scolded, making us all crack up even harder.

"You know nothing, Jon Snow." I quoted, burying my face in Rafe's chest again as I shook with laughter.

Eliam scowled and shook the spoon, sending red sauce splattering across the floor like paint. Or blood. "You misquoted it, too!" He pointed out.

"Quote, shmote. It was funny." I shot back, grinning like a damn fool. I looked around at all the guys. "Right?"

They all agreed in their own way, but they all unanimously agreed. "Six against one, pretty boy." I beamed.

"Humph." Eliam turned back to his task, shaking his head and shooting the guys glares out of the corner of his eye. "Traitors."

We lost it all over again, leaning on one another to stay upright as we all shook. Poor guy, he didn't stand a chance. It was nice, however, to see him being sociable with me around. I wondered what changed. It was a novel idea to consider that my near death experience had somehow changed the fact that he viewed me as a threat to the whole family dynamic or some shit, but I highly doubted that was the case at all. More likely, he wanted to let me fade into the blackness and cut his losses, but the others wouldn't let him. They were probably threatening him within an inch of his life to play nice and not be such a massive dick. Which I wholly appreciated., even if they didn't know it.

I thought back to my first night in this house and how horribly everything had started off. Not an experience that I would ever – not in a million years – want to repeat, but one that I was strangely thankful for. Looking around at our odd little gathering, and noting the great and subtle differences in each one of us, I couldn't help but thank the stars above for the terrible events that had brought me here.

Without looking back at us, Eliam lifted a hand and made a shooing motion. "Go entertain yourselves elsewhere and wait for dinner, you lot of heathens." He said dismissively, but with a light, amused note to his tone.

It only made us laugh harder, but we did as he demanded and filed out of the kitchen, leaning on one another as we continued to shake with mirth so that we didn't tumble across the foyer floor. It really was a great thing to be a part of, this sense of family that was all too foreign to me.

I eventually found myself sandwiched between Gatlin and Kellan on the small, floral sofa that must have been Clove's doing. And, of course, it would be the two largest and beefiest guys that would decide to deprive me of my right to my share of the world's oxygen. Rafe was at my feet, Gray was lounging on the arm of the sofa, and Beck was sprawled out on the rug with his head under the coffee table, wiggling his eyebrows at me suggestively.

"I hope you hit your head." I tell him without an ounce of sympathy.

He mockingly pouts back at me, doing a horrible job imitating the puppy dog face that I could win awards with. "That's not very nice, *Omen*." He objects.

I struggle to grab one of the decorative pillows out from under Kellan's absurdly heavy ass. "Don't be a dick." I say as Kellan releases my weapon of choice with a sigh and I chuck it at Beck's head.

"Aw, but I'm *the* dick, remember?" He said in a smooth-as-butter drawl.

I froze in the middle of trying to free another pillow from under Gatlin's admittedly gorgeous ass. "What?" I asked slowly. "What is that even supposed to mean?"

Beck grins at me and folds his arms underneath his head,

lounging around like the cat who ate the fucking annoying canary. "When you were out, you talked."

"A lot." Gray chimed in. I shot him a glare that could cook a turkey in seconds.

Beck continued, obviously enjoying the awkward position that I had found myself in. I'd never talked in my sleep my entire life. "It was like you were planning out characters in a book or something." He points to his own self. "Beck: the dick."

"Gray: sweet, Russian or something." Gray added.

"Kellan: insert giant joke here." The man in question supplied, all too happily for my taste.

"Rafe: punk with tats." Rafe snorted.

I turned to Gatlin, both knowing and dreading what he was about to say and his answering smirk was all the confirmation I needed. "Gatlin: angel." He said slowly, sadistically, enjoying the mortifying shade of red that my face was undoubtedly turning.

I buried my face in my hands. "Why me?" I whined.

The guys broke out into rounds of snickers at my misery, which only made my cheeks flame hotter. Give me a room of fifty or so old guys who were constantly judging me and deciding the fate of my financial status, I'd be fine. Give me six super hot male roommates who set my nerve endings on fire, I was a goner.

AFTER ABOUT FIFTEEN MORE MINUTES OF INCESSANT teasing and taunting from who I now deemed a whole lot of assholes, we all finally had settled down and started in on the shooting game that Beck and Rafe had chosen as a joint effort. They probably thought to humiliate me, but it turned out that I was surprisingly great at the first person shooter game. I didn't have to compete against the guys in this game, which probably had a lot to do with it, and they even made me my own profile which they infuriatingly named *DeadlyOmen7*. The humour was not lost on me, but I wouldn't ever let them know that.

In the game, I could play solo, which meant by myself, in pairs, which they called duos, or in a squad that consisted of four people. The goal was to survive by outrunning the deadly storm that came in circles and by killing other players as the circle got smaller. My eyesight was always pretty great and the screen didn't seem to really impair it at all, so I always managed to kill the other players pretty quickly. I ran into another player once who survived an entire game by hiding as a bush, which was a legendary item that you could pick up. No one ever saw them, and I was very impressed.

After another very solid victory for me, which had made about six in a row, one of the guys reached around me and plucked the controller from my fingers. I heard a collective sigh of relief from all the guys.

"Hey!" I exclaimed, turning on the culprit. It was Eliam, of fucking course. "Give it back!" Who would have thought I'd be whining like a petulant ten year old boy over a video game controller?

Eliam smirked that annoying and sexy smirk at me and I bristled a bit. He only smirked when he was being a cocky prick. "Dinner is ready and my brothers are just about tired of seeing you win. Isn't winning their hearts enough?" He chastised, shaking his head in mock disappointment.

My jaw dropped through the floor like an anime character or something and my inner self was reacting equally for once. My face seemed to say it all, and with one last smirk and a wink - a fucking *wink*? - in my direction, he sauntered back to the kitchen, presumably to let me stew in my now frazzled thoughts. It was like all basic operations had ceased to focus as I mulled over it all.

Their hearts? I won their hearts?

My own heart felt full to bursting and I almost felt as though I might cry. I had said it before and I was more than willing to say it again and again: I was a total relationship ho. That entire statement made the butterflies flutter around in my belly. Did that mean that they really cared about me? Or more? It had only been about a week, so it couldn't be *love*, but holy fuck was I game for these guys.

Wait.

Six of them.

One of me.

*Holy shit.*

It was like I had my own little harem. I wasn't complaining, but wow. It was a lot to take in.

I forced myself to zone back in on the world around me and saw the guys all sitting around with smirks that matched Eliam's own. Well, except Gray, who was smiling kindly at me, because he was sweet and not dick like the rest of these heathens.

"Take a picture." I snapped halfheartedly as I got up and strode into the kitchen with as much dignity as I could manage while they all snickered behind my back. I tried as hard as I possibly could to convince myself that they were amused by my magical pajamas, but even my own brain wasn't buying it. So smooth.

I nearly jumped up onto the counter like I had earlier once I reached the kitchen, but memories of that steamy encounter with Eliam just wouldn't allow it. Looking at him, he seemed to be thinking the same thing I was and I gulped hard.

Instead, I reached around him to stick my finger in the red sauce and licked it as un-sexily as I could. Which, you know, totally backfired.

Eliam laid a hot palm on my hip, holding me in place as his face dipped close to mine. His lips were dangerously close to my sensitive skin and I wasn't entirely sure I trusted my own self control. "I thought I told you to stay put?" He whispered into my ear, his hot breath dancing over my ear and neck, making me shiver.

"I'm not yours to control." I whispered back, looking him dead in his gorgeous, hypnotizing eyes. Another mistake. His eyes flashed briefly and then he smiled dangerously, heating me up from my core.

"We'll see about that." He breathed, his eyes still locked onto mine and making me tremble all over with both the threat and challenge laid out before me. The drastic change was still dizzying, and I wasn't even sure that he knew exactly what had changed.

A throat clearing from the doorway drew our attention and I flushed a very unappealing shade of read. I knew because my face was hotter than hell itself.

"If you two are done here," Beck drawled, a strange kind of

heat in his eyes that made me think that the idea of Eliam and I being together was a huge turn on for him. Kinky bastard. Not that I had much room to talk, either. "I would like to *eat.*" The way he said those words made it very clear that I was probably right.

I tried to keep a straight face as I stepped away from Eliam and his hand fell from my hip. "You ate five bags of chips already." I reminded him in exasperation.

"And? I'm still hungry." He shrugged.

I threw my arms up in the air. "Where the fuck does it all go?" I demanded, gesturing to his very trim physique. There was, no joke, not an ounce of fat on that man's body, and I swear he never stopped eating. Ever.

Beck stepped uncomfortably close to me, his arms folded over his chest as he towered over me. "I can show you, if you'd like." He purred, leaning his face down toward mine.

*Oh hell no. Wait. Why not? Oh, yeah. Brothers. Near. Oh God.*

I lifted my hands to Beck's chest and I practically felt him vibrating. Like, actually vibrating. It's like his veins were humming on some weird frequency. "Don't be a dick." I laughed as I gave him a little shove to send him a step or two back, just enough to make my great escape.

Or, I thought it was a little shove.

At my so-called "small" push, Beck went flying backward, landing on the floor and back against the refrigerator. My eyes were as wide as dinner plates as he rubbed the back of his head and looked around in confusion. I looked over at Eliam who was standing off to the side and rubbing his stubbled chin in thought. He didn't look the least bit concerned by what had just happened, just curious.

"Oh. My. God." I dashed over to Beck as quick as I could and knelt down beside him, my hands fluttering over him as I looked for major injuries. "I am so, so sorry! Are you okay?" I asked, my voice cracking a little from panic.

Beck rubbed the back of his head again and then looked at me as if contemplating something. "I think I'm a little hurt. A kiss might make it better." He said with a wink and puckered his lips.

I felt like pulling my hair out in frustration. Was this man ever serious for a single second? I smacked him on the shoulder, not even caring if it hurt him this time.

"Ow. You've got some serious guns there, hot stuff." He commented.

I looked around at the guys who had gathered around us where we sat on the kitchen floor. "What the fuck just happened?" I asked them all, looking from one set of eyes to another and feeling more anxious than scared, even though I knew that I should have been terrified.

Eliam was the one to make the first move, stepping forward with a sigh and extending a hand to help me up. "Come love, we need to have a chat." He said as I gazed warily at his offered hand.

"Um." I said eloquently. "I don't think so." I shook my head furiously and batted his hand away. The pushing incident was weird as hell, but an Eliam wanting to talk was way more fucking weird than just about anything else in the world. The unicorns could have leaped right off my pajamas at that moment and Eliam needing to talk would still be weirder.

He made an exasperated sound and ran his hands through his beautiful hair as I watched with more fascination than was probably acceptable. "Ria, this is bloody important. Be serious." He scolded.

"I am. The answer is no."

"You're being unreasonable."

"Literally everything about you is unreasonable."

"Focus, you infuriating woman!"

"No! I mean, I am focused!"

"Then let me help you, dammit."

"I don't need your help!"

Eliam made a primal growling noise in the back of his throat that was equal parts sexy as hell and terrifying. I looked around at the others for help, but they were all just watching our verbal sparring match with rapt fascination and amusement. Fucking bastards. When I turned back to look at Eliam, he was reaching for me with both hands as if to help me up by force, which was a serious oxymoron, I know.

I threw my hands up at him, as if my palms could ward him off. And to my complete and total shock, they did. I watched as Eliam drew closer as if in slow motion, and crimson smoke-like light burst forth from my hands, sending the Brit soaring backward and into the kitchen sink.

I couldn't help the manic laughter that bubbled up in my

throat and spilled out of me. Eliam looked on with fury and indignation in his eyes that only made me laugh harder than before. Before I knew it, I was joined on the ground by four other guys - not counting Beck, because he was still sitting there - all clutching our midsections as we shook and trembled with laughter.

Eliam extracted himself from the sink and adjusted his sleeves as though it was a nervous habit, which it probably was. "Don't you want to know what just happened?" He exclaimed loudly in an attempt to be heard over our vociferous amusement.

I wiped a tear away from the corner of my eye as I was laughing so hard that it actually hurt. "I don't even care anymore, I'm probably dead anyway." I managed on another burst of guffaws. It was all honestly a lot to handle. Not that I couldn't handle it, but it was a lot, and I really didn't deal with too much stress very well. Not the part of myself that I had ever been the most proud of, but a part of me, nonetheless. I had either died of a heart attack when I'd witnessed *his* betrayal, or I had died when I was stabbed in the damn back - literally - by a psychopath preacher-zombie. Neither were how I had imagined myself going out, but such is life. Or death? Such is death? Was that right?

Eliam stormed right on up to me and knelt down to put his face so close to mine that all I could taste was the chocolate-like sweetness of his breath. "Oh, you are very much alive, love." He said in a deep, seductive tone. "And you're alive because of me." His last words were on a whisper that sent chills of fear skittering down my spine and caused my hairs to stand on end. If it hadn't been for the horror-moviesque nature of his words, it would have been hotter than hellfire.

His eyes caught mine as they lit up, like *actually* lit up, and I balked. My laughter stopped almost immediately in my state of shock and I backed up until my back was pressed against the cupboards, the sharp corners of the wood digging into my spine with the amount of force I was using to press into them. If I was particularly luck, I would fall backward and into Narnia – something much more normal and realistic than the hell I felt as thought I was now in.

"What the actual fuck?" I gasped. I really was fucking dead. And if I was in heaven, Eliam the great asshole would definitely not have been with me. So, it must have been hell. I was finally paying for my sins.

I heard all the guys groan collectively, but I couldn't look away from the familiar and strange man in front of me.

"Did you do the glowing eye thing, E?" Gatlin demanded rhetorically. Oh, lovely, so they were all in on it. My roommates were fucking aliens.

"Are you ready to talk with us yet, Ria?" Eliam purred like the predator he obviously was.

I rubbed both hands over my face and buried them in my hair, having a little internal freak out. "Did you turn me into an alien, too?" I asked softly, hardly daring to breathe lest my new alien self kept on living. I wouldn't live as an alien. That wasn't fucking happening.

Eliam looked at me in complete shock for a moment before he and the guys burst into their own rounds of laughter, this time with me as the subject of their amusement. Once he had calmed down enough to look into my doubtlessly terrified eyes with his own determined ones, which had turned back to their normal, non-luminescent violet, he straightened his face as best he could and tried not to look as amused as I could tell he was. "We didn't turn you into an alien, Ria. My god, do you also think the moon is a spaceship?"

I didn't bother telling him that yes, I did in fact think the moon was a spaceship. It fucking *rings*. Non-hollow objects don't *ring*, okay? Besides, those astronauts looked like they had seen some serious shit, and a giant hunk of rock wasn't going to do that to someone. Just saying.

"Then what the hell did you do to me?" I challenged.

Eliam rolled his eyes at me and then grinned like the cat who ate the damn mouse. (Me. I was the cursed mouse.)

"You're a Sin now, just like us."

I felt like I was going to hurl. My head was spinning with my father's words ringing in my ears from when I was just a little girl, telling me that there was so much sin in me that I was nothing but sin. Telling me that I was evil. Telling me I was a demon or devil. Telling me that there was no redemption for my soul.

"No." I choked out, the tears in my eyes filling my vision completely.

I wanted nothing more than to run from the room and into the middle of some busy road somewhere, but the nausea wasn't letting me move a single inch. The memories, the trauma, I couldn't keep living with it all in my mind where it could follow me wherever I went. I even swore that I had heard Eliam say those words to me, validating my nightmares and darkest fears.

I felt as thought I was teeter precariously on the edge of insanity and reality, not really sure what was happening but living it all the same.

Or, at least, it seemed like I was?

I could sense, rather than see or hear, people moving about. I could feel the tension in the air and it was smothering, overwhelming, suffocating. I felt something boiling in me, hot and agitated, pushing at the seams and boundaries of my very being. I tried to make my senses catch up with the world around me, fighting off the sense of vertigo that seemed to be attacking my brain.

"Ria, calm down!" Someone shouted.

"Make her stop!" Another voice yelled, hurting my ears through the fogginess.

The hot feeling was starting to push outward, making my skin feel warm and uncomfortable. The world around me was blurry and unfocused, but I could sense that something was very wrong. I also got the feeling that whatever was happening was my own doing, and I couldn't even make my eyes focus, let alone stop whatever mayhem was taking place.

I felt myself being moved and my vision was suddenly overtaken by a violet haze of smoke, or maybe it was fog, I had no clue. It felt as though the cloud was charged with an electric current that was swimming through my veins, paralyzing me. I tried to scream, but I couldn't seem to find the right way to make sound come out. My brain was scrambling. Through the fog came a bright light, and I knew what was coming next, so I braced myself.

Instead of being the light at the end of the tunnel that I completely expected, I found myself staring at my own face, my own self, storming toward me with fury blazing hot in my own eyes. It was my inner self, but it was like I was seeing her - me? - in 3D for the first time, instead of just in my mind; my actual eyes could see me - her? - as though corporeally manifested, like actually right fucking there.

My inner self marched right up to me until we were face to face, and my own was likely frozen in utter shock. I was prepared for the end-of-life speech, words of wisdom, my fate being decided and announced to me. I was not prepared for what happened next, like at all.

"Snap the fuck out of it and get a damn grip!" My inner self snapped at me. And then she slapped me hard across the face.

I had always sort of laughed at the people who would talk about out of body experiences and the sensation of being slammed back into your body, like a cord was yanked by a crazy body builder, but that's what it felt like. I felt myself falling at a dangerous speed - down, up, backward, forward, sideways, I had no clue. It just felt like I was being sucked into a dangerous vortex or a whirlpool, not that I knew what either of those things felt like at all.

I snapped my eyes open and gasped, sucking in air as though I had been stuck underwater for too long. I was sitting in the kitchen still, but the guys were scattered all around me, holding their heads or their midsections. The kitchen was completely destroyed, with the cupboard doors hanging precariously, the sink faucet was apparently a fountain now (I'd always wanted a fountain), and all of the decorative knickknacks were in varying states of destruction and disarray. More saddening than that was the pots and pans of food that had just been prepared stuck through the walls or on the floors.

And worse still, was that I was being cradled in Eliam's arms, with him hunched over me as though protecting me from a natural disaster.

I tried to scramble up and was amazed at my lack of dizziness or nausea. I actually felt pretty fucking great. You know, except for the fact that Eliam's arms might as well have been solid steel bands wrapped around my body.

"Are you gonna buy me dinner first, or...?" I asked, directing the question to the man-cage. I couldn't even turn my head toward him because of the angle at which he was bent around me. It seriously could not have been very comfortable, but what did I know? Guys are fucking weird.

He lifted his head at the same time five others did the exact same thing. I wasn't going to ask what happened, because I was feeling great and honest to goodness did not want to know. Bizarre shit wasn't my forte. "Are you back to normal now?" Eliam asked warily, adjusting his position to better accommodate my very mobile form.

When I craned my neck to turn and look at him, he looked fucking terrible. I mean, he was still sexy as sin, but he looked exhausted and completely drained. The rising sun peeking through the large bay windows shocked me half to death and I had a hard time deciding which thing most concerned me: the state the guys were in or the fact that an entire night had passed in a matter of minutes - if that.

"Er... I guess so? Was I not normal?" Okay, that was a trick question. Most of society didn't consider strippers people at all, let alone *normal* people.

All six guys turned to face each other simultaneously, looking like they were having some sort of silent, telepathic conversation amongst themselves. Hell, they probably were. I was about to open my mouth to say something snarky about being *right fucking there* when I heard something.

*...Sin is just like* hers...

My mouth dropped open and I gaped at the six of them like a fish, probably the least attractive I had ever looked in my entire life. And that was really saying something, considering that one time in Vegas...

"I knew you guys were talking in your heads!" I shouted accusingly. I whipped around to face Eliam again, but way too fast, because I accidentally knocked my head against his chin and it hurt like a motherfucker. "Owwww!" I rubbed my head, knowing that it was about to give me one hell of a headache. The stupidly attractive Brit, on the other hand, didn't look at all phased, and that bugged the shit out of me.

They all turned slowly to look at me with wide eyes. Apparently, I was right and not hallucinating again, if their expressions alone were anything to go by. And if I deduced correctly, which I was positive I had, I was also not supposed to know this. Just a week of living with a bunch of guys and I was already ready to punch each one of them in their stupidly incredible jaws bones.

Eliam started to move me off his lap and out of his arms. I opened my mouth to protest, but he shushed me with just a look. *Damn that rat bastard.* Once I was sitting on the, admittedly cold, tile floor by myself, Eliam stood and turned to his brothers, his face set into a cold, hard mask, as though he was made of pure stone. "We need to talk." He ground out between clenched teeth. His eyes darted over to me briefly. "Alone." He clarified.

Each of the guys nodded in agreement but said nothing, causing my heart to contract painfully. The men who once defended me, stood up for me, rescued me from a psychopath preacher, they were all freezing me out, and I didn't want to admit that I could audibly hear the sound of my heart crumbling all over again.

As all six of them stood and filed out of the room without so much as glancing in my direction, I fought to hold back the tears that were threatening to spill down my cheeks with no indication of ever stopping. Once they were all out and I heard a door close behind them, however, all bets were off. The tears flowed freely and silently, making me wonder where they were actually coming from. I was a really ugly crier, that much I could admit.

Did that mean the wound was too deep? Too sharp? Like a

cut from a sharp piece of glass that takes awhile to bleed because your body doesn't realize it's been injured?

A small sound escaped me that sounded something akin to a small, wounded animal and I clamped a hand over my mouth as quickly as I could. I needed to get the hell out of the stupid house that had turned my life on its head. I stood quickly and was impressed once again by the lack of vertigo I was expecting to experience. As I grabbed my keys from the counter and sprinted through the open front door - "open" is a relative term, it was actually blown clean off, but semantics - and made a mad dash for my car, I couldn't help feeling like I felt different.

*Well, duh, you just leveled an entire house. How about an award, Einstein?* Ah, there was the inner self that I loved so much (she thought sarcastically). Her sudden appearance did make me take pause though, as I was climbing into the driver's seat of my car. I tugged the collar of my pajama top up a little, protecting myself against the cold of the early morning. I didn't want to think about it, I didn't want to focus on it, I didn't want anything to do with it. And honestly, I was seriously starting to doubt exactly how worth it the Severin brothers actually were.

*You didn't do any of this for a bunch of guys and you know it.* My inner self chastised.

Okay, that was true. I was only in this town to begin with because I was a coward who ran when things got hard or scary, but my sense of self preservation had kept me going strong thus far. It had kept me safe, secure, and confident.

So, the way I saw it, I had two choices: I could stay and fight my gut, which had never led me astray, or I could trust myself to do what I needed to. There were equally hefty pros and cons to each side of my own ultimatum, and I knew that choosing would be almost impossible.

Before I even knew what I was doing, my car was in drive and peeling out in a circle over the gravel driveway, no clear destination in mind and no idea what I was going to do when I got wherever I was heading.

I ENDED up right at the beginning, where this whole mess of an adventure had started in the first place. I pulled into the parking area behind the coffee shop and put my car in park. I sat there for a completely undetermined amount of time, trying to get my brain to play catch up with my actions. I had no idea why I came to the coffee shop, but there I was, nonetheless.

I decided, finally, that I had two options now.

I could sit in my car forever in a state of numbness and confusion, much the same way I felt the first time I arrived here.

Or I could put on some damn normal clothes and go get some fuel for the day. And by fuel, I mean coffee.

Deciding on the latter, I climbed into my backseat and rummaged through my emergency bag, which held several spare sets of clothes, toilet paper, breath mints, bar soap, and bobby pins. It was a remnant from my days after leaving home, when I had nothing at all but the bag on my back. I swore then, that I would always be prepared, and I haven't regretted it since. The pajama predicament was a very good example of why.

I finally selected an old red checked flannel that had the sleeves cut off, a pair of boyfriend jeans with studs on the back pockets, and a pair of my old, worn out, black combat-style boots. If it works, it works, right?

After shimmying into my clothes using a trick I had learned when I was homeless, I got out of the warmth of my car and ran my fingers through my absurdly messy hair. When something pricked my finger, I pulled my hand away and looked at it, seeing tiny little shards of glass.

Another reminder of whatever had just happened overnight at the Severin house.

I shook myself, refusing to think on it, and started trudging my way around to the front of the building. Once I had made it inside, it was like I could breathe again - nevermind, I was just unintentionally inhaling the coffee fumes like the nutcase that I was.

I spotted Drea's messy brown hair below the counter, so I walked up and pulled myself up on top of it, right next to the display case with all the yummy pastries in it. A display case which I opened and kidnapped a poor, defenseless blueberry muffin from. It never stood a chance.

Drea chose the moment that I moaned around a bite of the berry-goodness of the muffin to poke her head up. "You could have just asked, you heathen!" She said, exasperated. She gave me a pointed look and I only shrugged in response.

"It was right there, ripe for the taking." I told her without an ounce of regret. Who could regret a muffin this good anyway?

She rolled her eyes and leaned a hip against the counter, obviously deciding that my antics weren't worth the fight. "I'm glad to see you feeling better." She said in a softer tone. A slight tremble in her voice betrayed how worried she really was about me after the incident at the club and my heart melted a little.

How could I leave her? In such a very, very short amount of time, Drea had become one of the best friends I could have ever asked for or dreamed of. She was kind, loving, understanding, funny, and grounded. I could never imagine her betraying me or trying to hurt me. I also never felt like I couldn't open up to her. "Better is a relative term." I mumbled, staring down at the muffin that had looked so appetizing just moments ago.

I glanced over at Drea, her eyes filled with concern. "What happened, Ria?" I felt like she knew exactly what had happened. Well, maybe not *exactly*, but pretty damn close.

"Do you have alcohol right now?" I asked her, feeling suddenly exhausted. Drea nodded and reached under the counter, revealing to me a bottle of beautiful, beautiful tequila. I wasn't really a day drinker, but it was a special occasion. After twisting off the top and taking a couple of huge, burning swigs, I turned to look back at my friend, concern etched into her gorgeous face.

I looked around at the small clusters of people gathered around the mismatched tables. There weren't many people here, but enough that I took pause at discussing the events of the night. I spotted an infuriatingly familiar face and tried to keep my blood from boiling.

It was the pushy red-headed guy from before and he looked more terrible than before, if that was even possible; his eyes were huge and puffy, his chubby cheeks stained red and snot was pouring, disgustingly, out of his nose.

"Whats wrong with him?" I asked Drea out of curiosity. Not because I cared, but because I was a nosey bitch sometimes. Okay, all the time.

"His mom is in the hospital. She has that illness thats going around and is in a coma." She whispers back to me. "Sanya isn't a very nice person. She likes to con people out of their money and leave them to the wolves."

I couldn't say I felt too bad, given my own family issues and lack of empathy toward the slimeball of a boy. Knowing his mom was just as shitty explained a lot, though.

"Tell me about the illness while I see how long it takes to finish this bottle." I told my best friend, holding up the bottle as if in victory. I was already feeling the effects of the harsh liquor, and that made me feel a bit better. It made me start to forget a little.

## 21 KELLAN

I FILED OUT OF THE KITCHEN AFTER MY BROTHERS, trying my best not to look at Ria and see the heartbreak in the striking emerald depths of her eyes. It fucked with me more than she knew, but what had just happened was too important to ignore. Too dangerous.

Once we had all made our way into the study on the

opposite side of the house and closed the door, Eliam turned on us all, his eyes blazing, but he wasn't the first to speak.

"What the fuck just happened?" Rafe all but growled. I had noticed his wooden sculpture had made a nice sized hole through the kitchen wall, so it was understandable that he would be upset. Well, understandable for Rafe.

Eliam turned his gaze on our brother, his eyes illuminating the way they did when his power was trying to seep through. "How the bloody hell am I supposed to know? I've never had to do what I did on a mortal and you know it."

"How are we going to explain any of this to her? She's in denial right now, and that can only be detrimental." Gray said from the corner of the room, where he lounged in an aged recliner chair.

I leaned back against the wall nearest me and examined the worn, stressed faces of my brothers. No one knew how to handle a situation like this in the first place, but our undeniable connection to the alluring blonde made things more complicated, along with the fact that she was our responsibility since Eliam saved her life with his own essence, his own Sin.

Eliam looked like he was only seconds away from ripping his own hair out, and I understood the feeling all too well. "She didn't even have to look, E." I told him. "She utilized her Sin without even knowing it was there. This isn't good."

"You think I don't know that already?" He shouted back at me, his vividly illuminated eyes all but shooting lasers at me. "She shouldn't have been able to do that, and I don't understand." Ah, there it was. He had tried for so long to contain his Sin, to not let it define or control him, but Ria seemed to have weakened his resolve in the short time she'd been near him.

I understood the feeling all too well.

We all sat in silence for far too long, each of us entangled with our own thoughts and fears. None of us had any idea what the situation meant for us, much less the poor woman that had been dropped into our world with no sign or warning with which to prepare herself with. But, on the other hand, I had known from the beginning that there was a certain kind of attraction that we all had to her, not specifically the romantic kind, but the celestial, magical kind.

"What should we tell her?" Beck asked while pacing a moat around the coffee table.

Gray sat up a bit straighter, the wheels in his head turning. "Before the kitchen incident? I believe she could have handled it." He pointed out. "But now, I don't think she'll cope very well with everything. She'll see herself as a freak."

All of our faces wrinkled in disgust at the same time. Gray had the most knowledge about these sort of things, seeing as he had married, and confided in, a mortal woman. The only one of us to go that far. We knew our fates, and as such, the fates of any mortal we let too close.

"She's different." Gatlin growled, spinning to face Gray.

"That may be so." Eliam interjected diplomatically. "But we still don't know how she's going to take any of it. It's a threat to us."

Gatling whirled on our purple-eyed brother, his fury

evident in the sharp, silver glow of his eyes. "What the fuck are you suggesting?" He snarled.

"I'm just suggesting that we find a way to fix this," Eliam defended. "With as few casualties as possible."

"And without chasing her off." I added before I could stop myself. Not that I really cared whether they knew how much I cared at that particular moment.

It looked like everyone had something to say all at once, and I was was ready to argue or agree, depending on what was said, when Gray sat straight up, eyes wide. "She's gone." He whispered those two words, but we all heard them clearly.

I hadn't really noticed all the white noise in my sixth sense until that moment, when everything suddenly cleared, and I cursed up a storm. I wasn't going to lose one of the only people outside of my family that meant anything to me, that made me *feel*.

"Gray, can you sense her? Where is she going?" Eliam snapped the question, perhaps being a bit too harsh, but I understood his concern.

Gray nodded. "Yes, she's heading toward town."

"Drea." I said as five sets of eyes swiveled in my direction. "She's going to the coffee shop, where Drea is." Ria was drawn to the sweet, curly-haired woman the same as me, feeling the same pull. She was like an anchor in a raging sea, keeping us from going under, being a point of safety and stability.

BY THE TIME we had made it into town, I was getting a sick knot in the pit of my stomach. I knew what the result would be if Ria didn't take the information well. I couldn't stand the thought of her being hurt, but I also couldn't tolerate the idea of the madness that could consume her or the destruction that could rain down on humanity if she lost control. I had learned long ago that control was not something that could easily be regained.

We all piled out of the Jeep and I walked around the back hatch to let Beck out. There were only five seats, and he had drawn the unlucky straw, as usual. He shot me a glare as he stumbled out and stretched dramatically. "Sucks to suck, dude." I smirked.

After delivering a mock punch to my shoulder, he took the lead and started inside the coffee shop. I could never say that I was prepared for the sight that awaited us inside, but it was certainly not the most surprising thing I had ever seen - no, that was topped by finding a half-naked woman in my kitchen in the middle of the night.

Ria was standing on one of the tables with a karaoke microphone in one hand and a bottle of clear liquor in her other. She was singing a song that I didn't know, and she was surpisingly not all that bad, just a little off-key, which I was sure was due to her inebriated condition.

"Ria!" Eliam thundered. It struck me then, that I had no idea what her full name was. Judging by my brothers' mirrored looks of confusion, they had just come to the same realization.

She turned and looked at us then, grinning hugely and waving her half-drank bottle in the air in greeting. "Hey guys! Look!" She called, spreading her arms wide in a gesture at the small crowd of people that were standing around and cheering at her. Only Ria could make a stage out of nothing. "I made some new friends!" Her words were slurring, but she still seemed mostly coherent. Just a little bit happier.

Gatlin stormed up to the table she was standing on and her eyes went wide. "Come on, we need to talk." He growled at her.

She shook her head, her long blonde locks flying. "Nope!" She said, popping the P at the end.

When she jumped off the table and tried to take off running, I was there in an instant, grabbing her around her waist and walking toward the back of the building. As she beat on my back halfheartedly from her upside-down position, I looked at Drea and inclined my head toward the storeroom. She nodded and went back to cleaning, acting like I wasn't carrying a grown woman over my should who was acting like a toddler.

Once in the storeroom, I set Ria on her feet. Well, I intended to set her on her feet. What actually ended up happening was I tried to set her down and forgot she was drunk for a moment, so she stumbled and then fell flat on her sexy ass.

"Owwwww!" She whined, glaring at me.

I only shrugged and stepped aside as Eliam walked toward her. "We need to have a chat, love."

## 22 RIA

To say I was pissed would be a massive understatement. I was pissed that the guys would just up and abandon me, I was pissed that they had the audacity to come and manhandle me, and I was pissed that I was way too fucking toasted to properly be pissed. As Kellan dropped me hard on my ass - the asswad - and all six guys converged in on me, I felt the rage I was feeling rise in my chest, like an angry beast rearing its head.

That was bad enough, but when Eliam stepped ahead of the rest while declaring our need to *chat*, self-proclaimed leader of the gang, the beast let out an angry roar. Okay, *I* let out an angry roar, which sounded a lot more like battle cry of a wounded mouse.

I took a swipe at him, intending to slap him hard across the face for the second time since we'd met, but I misjudged the distance and my sense of balance due wholly to my highly inebriated state. I tumbled over, and tried to catch myself, but ended up catching a large handful of someone's clothing.

Staring in abject horror, I looked up, up, up from the crotch that my hand had snagged, and I felt myself turning an angry shade of red - probably not my best look.

Beck grinned down at me as I removed my hand as quickly as I possibly could and cradled it to my chest, as though it had been harmed somehow. "I mean it, sweet thang, all you gotta do is ask." He winked at me and I felt nauseous - not because I wasn't like eighty-five percent totally game, but because my stomach was suddenly very displeased with my recent life choices.

By recent, I mean the last half hour or so.

Arms hauled me up from behind and my stomach lurched again in displeasure. I craned my neck and saw that it was none other than Gatlin. This situation was feeling all too familiar, but at least I was wearing more clothes than the previous time. "Ria, you need to sit down and try to listen." The angel growled at me, simultaneously igniting something low in my belly and feeding the troll in my head. He turned me to face him, and I honestly never knew why I did some of the things that I did - blame it on the alcohol - but I stuck out my tongue and blew a raspberry right in his face.

Gatlin stared at me in utter bewilderment. "Really? What are you, ten?" He asked in astonishment.

"Ten and *a half.*" I corrected.

I looked over my shoulder and saw that Rafe and Beck were leaning on one another, shaking with contained laughter. Kellan's face was twisted in a very grotesque sort of way that made me think he was trying especially hard not to crack a smile. Gray wasn't bothering to contain his grin, obviously amused by my drunken antics - I liked him so much more for it.

Eliam looked straight up pissed.

"So, we're back to being a snobby prick, huh?" I asked him while raising in eyebrow. I think I raised an eyebrow, anyway. Face things were hard.

The appalled expression that was planted on Eliam's annoyingly attractive face made everything worth it. *Everything.* "Ria, be serious." He scolded, wagging a finger at me. Did he really wag his finger? Like some eighty year old woman or something? "We all need to talk, and that means you need to focus right now." He came toward me as though to manhandle me himself and I snuggled into Gatlin's chest, feeling him still in response.

I stuck my tongue out at Eliam. "If you want me, you're

gonna have to come get me yourself." I taunted. "Instead of sending the Hulk after me, I mean."

Kellan's offended face was about halfway real and completely hilarious, and I assumed that was because of my inferring that the pompous Brit had sent him to grab me in the first place, as opposed to the nickname; I was pretty sure he was actually entertained by them.

I heard Rafe and Beck finally crack, breaking into howling fits of laughter.

"Hey, feeling a little *green*, buddy?" Rafe snickered, which only sent the two of them into more of a hysterical outburst.

Turning my head, I saw Kellan glare at his brothers. "Oh, can it you two, or do you want to spar again?" He asked with a smirk.

Both the guys mostly sobered, still grinning, but no longer laughing.

"I'm not *envious* of either of you at the moment." Gatlin's voice rumbled through his chest and into me, like rolling thunder. The low bass of it was soothing and comforting. I almost wanted to go to sleep right then and there.

Eliam's voice kept me from doing that, though. "All of you, just stop." He commanded, his voice booming in the small, enclosed space. He turned back to me, and I withered under his gaze. "Are you ready to talk, or are we going to be here all night?" He asked me, raising one perfectly arched brow at me.

I nodded before I knew what I was doing. I wasn't ready to talk at all. I wanted to go back to that little space in the back of my mind where everything was bright and happy, where my inner self wasn't nagging me to hear the guys out, and my brain wasn't struggling to wrap itself around what I had seen and experienced.

"Good." Eliam said as he sat on the floor, cross-legged.

The rest of us followed suit. Well, I just kinda hung in Gatlin's arms as he sat down and placed me effortlessly in his lap. I blushed furiously, realizing how awkward of a situation I was in - and how *hard* a situation I was on. I had almost slept with Gatlin, and then almost slept with Eliam. I didn't mind being a little bit of a slut sometimes, since I could do with my body as I pleased, but I was starting to understand the fear that Eliam had of me messing with the whole family dynamic.

As I rested against Gatlin's chest, sitting sideways in his lap, I waited for whatever the guys needed to say.

Eliam cleared his throat and looked pointedly at me. "Ria, I'm sure you've figured out by now that we're not quite normal, as far as normal people go." He said calmly, professionally, as though he were conducting an interview or training session.

I snorted at his statement and he looked at me curiously. Before I could stop the words from coming out of my mouth, I said, "uh, duh." Classy. Eloquent. That was me in a nutshell. As if I wasn't torturing myself enough, I gestured to all of the guys. "I mean, look at all of you. You're fucking smoking, and that's not natural." I explained.

Oh. My. God. It was about to get worse, wasn't it?

"Plus, there's no way all of you are actually brothers, none of you look anything like each other." I froze in thought for a moment, tapping my finger on my chin. "Except you two. You look close enough that you could pull it off." I indicated Kellan and Beck. Aside from the obvious stuff, like the tattoos and piercings, the two looked sort of similar, like they were of the same ancestral decent.

The two guys laughed, effectively making me wish my mouth was super glued shut.

"*Anyway*," Eliam interrupted. For once, I was grateful. "We're not mortal, we're not regular people, we're not even human. And neither are you, Ria." His blunt statement through me for a loop, and I was almost positive that I was incomprehensibly, undeniably still drunk off my ass. I was on my second bottle of tequila already by the time they had shown up, so it wouldn't come as a huge surprise to me.

"Oh god." I whispered, moving my hand to cover my mouth in shock. "This is like that book, *A Demon's Blade,* isn't it?"

The guys all looked at each other in confusion.

I rolled my eyes at them. "The main character finds out she's half demon and thought she was human her entire life." I explain to them, watching varying expressions of amusement cross their faces.

"No." Eliam said flatly. "We're Sins. The Seven Deadly Sins, to be precise."

My brow furrowed as I tried to make sense of what he was saying, and I was pretty damn impressed by my serious lack of freaking out. "So... You're demons." I fished, phrasing it like a sentence. I mean, the Seven Deadly Sins were bad, they were things you would go to hell for committing, so they weren't exactly fairies or anything light and happy.

Eliam rubbed the bridge of his nose as though I was giving him a major headache, and I secretly hoped that I had. It's the least the bastard deserved. "No, Ria, we are not demons. That's ridiculous." The patronizing tone to his voice made me bristle.

"How the fuck am I supposed to know what's ridiculous? I'm a stripper living with six hot guys - it sounds like a fucked up romance novel." I huffed. I fought back another bout of nausea and tried to focus on taking deep, steady breaths. He was talking about me being ridiculous, but the entire predicament I found myself in was bordering on unreal. Bordering? It *was* unreal.

Gatlin rubbed my back in soothing circles and I relaxed into him. "You're supposed to know by listening." He whispered, causing the little hairs on the back of my neck to stand on end. If only he knew the things he did to me by just being in the near proximity.

Stunned as I was by Gatlin's mere presence, I almost missed what Eliam was trying to tell me. "We've been around since before the demons and angels made their presence known. We were here when you humans built that ridiculous tower in an attempt to reach the heavens. How none of you realised that there is nothing but sky up there is beyond me, but such is the way of the mortal mind." He said with a shake of his head.

I chewed over what he was saying, thinking it over. If they were as old as mankind, they had to be really old, like thousands of years old. The thought made me cringe and put about an inch of space between Gatlin's warm chest and myself, much to my own chagrin, because I was comfortable. But the real question was still burning the back of my mind, and it pissed me off to no end that this was my huge concern at the moment. No more tequila for Ria, like ever.

"So," I began as every set of eyes in the room swiveled to my face. I gulped nervously. "If you're the Seven Deadly Sins, why are there only six of you?" I asked.

When everyone's faces scrunched up the same way, in identical, unreadable expressions, a thought struck me. "Holy shit. Am *I* the seventh Sin?" I gasped, pressing a hand to my heart as if that pressure alone could prevent it from beating straight out of my chest. It was just like the books. I wasn't ready for anything like this, and I knew it was so typical for me to do the whole "you have the wrong person" shindig, that was how I felt.

Everyone was silent, their expressions grave. The violet-eyed Brit, however looked straight up stormy, furious even as he pinned me with a glare that made me feel as small as an ant. "*No.*" He snarled at me. I was completely taken aback, not really sure where the hostility had come from.

Eliam rose from his place on the floor and stormed out through the door of the storeroom, slamming it so hard behind him that a little dust fell from the ceiling above us. I didn't get it. One second he was so insistent that we talk that he tracked me down and ambushed my in a dark storeroom - which, while kinky as hell, was not exactly my idea of a good time.

I don't even know how long I sat there in Gatlin's lap, silent but for the sound of my painfully throbbing heart. I didn't know what I said or what I was supposed to do in a situation like the one I was in.

"It's not your fault." I heard Gray say gently from my side. I jumped and turned to him, having no clue when he had gotten so close. He brushed a thumb across my cheeks, which were wet with tears. I hadn't even known I was crying. And now that I knew that I was, I had no idea *why* I was.

I sniffled a bit, grateful that I never snotted when I cried. I didn't want to be all teary-eyed and emotional, but my alcohol tolerance wasn't what it was even as little as a year before, since I stopped drinking as much at work in order to better be aware of my surroundings. "Then why?" I asked pitifully around a hiccup. Hiccups were the absolute fucking worst. I couldn't stand them, but then, I didn't really know anyone that enjoyed them.

Gatlin tightened his arms around me, effectively smothering me. I didn't mind though. "Our fellow Sin isn't around anymore, and she and Eliam were extremely close. They found each other first."

"Found each other?"

"We were spread out across the globe when we were first... Created, I suppose you could say." Gray's accent was soothing to me, reminding me of how he found me the last time I was in tears. "So it took us awhile to find each other. Kellan was the next to find them, very shortly after."

I separated my face from the soft material of Gatlin's shirt to gaze at Kellan. His expression was tight, almost pained, as though the memory was not a happy one. It made my heart contract hard and I struggled to free myself from my very attached position as I made my way over to Kellan on my hands and knees.

n

That was the moment I lost it, laughing so hard that my ribs hurt and more tears started pouring down my face I collapsed on the hard concrete ground, unable to hold myself up with all the shaking my body was doing, and hit my shoulder hard.

I winced in pain for a moment, though still couldn't stop laughing. "Can we go home to talk?" I asked the guys.

And through a mixture of expressions, ranging from concerned, to amused, to puzzled, all the guys nodded in agreement.

## 23 RIA

WHEN WE ARRIVED HOME, I WAS SURE THAT I WOULD
have a pounding headache and a waking hangover - one of
those hangovers that stays with you before you've gone to
sleep. I was pleasantly surprised to find that I felt fit as a
feather though, but considering how much alcohol it took
me to get drunk in the first place, I couldn't say I was
entirely shocked.

What did shock me, was that I clearly remembered everything that had happened in that storeroom, and I still wasn't feeling the need to freak out. What did it say about me that I was so willing to just roll with the punches and accept the things I was told as fact - no matter how bizarre and impossible.

After getting out of the car, I followed Eliam's lead into the house and noted absently that the door was still laying on the flat on the porch. He had been surly the entire drive home, but anyone could chock that up to Rafe and Beck complaining and bickering from the back of the Jeep, where the luggage usually goes.

Eliam made for kitchen and then seemed to think better of it as he turned abruptly and headed toward a part of the house I'd never been into. When I thought about it, I hadn't been in most of the house, not even to be nosy and poke around the brothers' bedrooms, which was extremely unusual for me. I supposed that I had just been too caught up in craziness to take the time to be my normal, prying self.

We ended up in a room that looked much like an old-timey study, but with odd bits of floral patterned furniture scattered about. This must have been Clove's husband's study when they still lived in the house together. The sudden thought of her being all alone in the cottage next door made my heart hurt.

Someone closed the door behind us and it made me jump, which also infuriated me, because I wasn't a skittish person by nature. I had no reason to be.

"So, do you have any questions?" Gray was the one to speak, which surprised me since he didn't really seem like the take-charge type - that was Eliam's role. I opened my mouth to speak and he stopped my by holding up a hand. "None about the seventh Sin, okay?"

Ah, that explained that. I nodded my agreement and sat down on the arm of a faded pink and white loveseat by the door. Quick escapes and all.

I thought hard about my questions, trying to think of the ones that would provide me with the most answers. "Okay... What Sins are all of you?" I asked cautiously. I thought I had them pegged, but I was prepared to be wrong.

Beck raised his hand as if he were in class. "Gluttony." He stated a little seductively with a lick of his lips that made me shiver inwardly. *Down, ovaries, down.*

"Sloth." Gray said from a lounging chair in the corner of the room. *When the fuck did he get there?*

I turned to look at Gatlin, feeling a little wary. "Wrath." He said darkly, the deep bass of his voice reverberating through me, despite the many feet that separated us. I swallowed hard and averted my gaze from his own heavy one. *So intense. Called that one, though.*

I looked pointedly at Rafe before he could say a single word and jabbed my finger in the air in his direction. "You're Greed." I said accusingly. He only shrugged and grinned in response, confirming my suspicion.

I looked at Kellan and thought back to our first real conversation, where he confessed that he loved Drea because she was one thing she could never have. He looked at me, steel in his gaze. "I'm Envy." He told me, as though he already knew that I had him pegged. Suddenly, I got Beck and Rafe's hilarious inside joke back at the coffee shop. I sent them a glare and they nearly fell into another fit, only stopped by Gatlin and Kellan's hard-as-steel glares, which were much more effective than my own.

I turned to the last man standing - literally; he was the only one standing - and I waited. There were only two of the Sins remaining, I was sure I already knew which one he was, but our steamy encounter in the kitchen, both times, made me waver on my decision a bit. Eliam was facing away from the rest of us and toward the large floor-to-ceiling windows that took up nearly the entire east wall, his hands folded behind his back. If I'd had any artistic talent at all, I'd have drawn him right then and there.

"Pride?" I hazarded a guess and a slight inclination of his head was all the confirmation I needed. It made a bit of sense if I thought about it.

In the kitchen, the first time, I had offered him a challenge by practically laughing off his advances. It made sense, but all that knowledge did was cause my heart to crack painfully in my chest. It wasn't logical for me to be hurt by it, but I was - I was nothing more than a challenge, not the object of his attraction. Not that I was an actual object, I was a human being with feelings, feelings that were pretty damn hurt.

Everyone was silent for a long time, the guys giving me time to mull it over, and me overthinking everything, which was wholly unlike me. "What happened back at the club?" I asked in a hushed whisper.

The guys all looked at each other and then at their self-proclaimed group leader. Eliam finally turned around and huffed out a breath while running a hand through his perfectly styled dark, dirty blonde hair. He finally met my eyes and I could see the exhaustion in them. "The small athame you were struck with was laced with a poison that is dangerous, crippling even, to Sins, but fatal to mortals." He explained, his expression stoic and neutral, despite the dark nature of his words.

"Why does a poison like that even exist?" I puzzled.

"In the world's youngest days, the Sins were not feared for the threat of being sent to hell, but for the otherworldly power that they possessed." Rafe explained, catching me off guard by his seriousness. "So the people of one village captured one of the Sins and experimented with different tonics and tinctures to see if anything could diminish their health."

My eyes were wide in shock and abject horror. How could anyone be that cruel? I mean, I had heard all about the cannibalistic serial killers in the news and in books, but I still found it hard to comprehend.

"And when nothing else worked, the begged the heavens for a way to accomplish their goals." Kellan said, jumping into the conversation. "Their calls were answered by winged men who descended from the sky, calling themselves angels. In reality, they were called andjinns, or just djinns as you call them now." He paused, looking like he was trying to keep his poker face in tact and struggling with the feat.

Eliam took a step forward with a pointed, sympathetic look at his ginormous brother. "The problem with djinns is that they will grant any wish, but with a heavy price." His expression was grave and made me shiver again, but not in the sexy, aroused way. "They granted the peoples' wish for a way to harm the Sins, but it would harm them in two different ways: it would stain and deteriorate their souls, and it would kill them. The only way to cure the poison's effects would be for a Sin to remove theirs and then burn it away with their own."

"So, the poison was the villagers' gift and curse?" I asked, completely bemused by the unexpected, twist on such prolific biblical lore.

They all nodded simultaneously.

"Yes." Eliam answered. "But there were still those who thought the price would be completely worth the prize." It was an interesting way to view things, especially since prizes were meant to be won, not bought.

I furrowed my brow in confusion. "So, why didn't the angels - I mean, djinns - just give them a poison that would kill the Sins?" I asked, needing clarification.

Gatlin laughed darkly and I turned to meet his equally dark gaze. "We are older than most things, Ria. There was no way they could have found or created a single thing to destroy us - balance doesn't allow for it."

"Okay, but don't you offset the balance?" I was trying to make sense of the new information I was gathering, and I was absorbing it all greedily.

"We were created to maintain the balance, babe. There would be no free will without sin, but too much sin can also corrupt. So we were created to balance it out by removing and placing sin as needed." Beck explained, looking completely at ease on the floor in front of the long couch in the middle of the room. "For instance, your sins were decided before you were even born."

That threw me for a loop right there. Did that mean I was always fated to be born into a family that didn't want me? That I was always meant to pursue a career that meant exposing my body to the public eye for sexual pleasure? I found it hard to believe that there was any force out there that wanted me to do what most would consider bad things, unsavoury things.

Something struck me then that I don't know why I didn't pay any attention to at first. "Wait a second." I turned slowly to full face Eliam. I got up from my perch and walked over to stand directly in front of him, and tried not to shake. "The remedy to saving mortals that were affected by the mortals, is that how you fixed me?" I asked slowly, terrified of the answer I would receive.

Eliam's hard gaze met mine and he nodded once, quickly. My whole body went cold at once. "You said that sins equal free will. Does that mean..." I trailed off, pleading with my eyes for him to fill in the gaps.

"I had to take away your sins and replace them with my own over a short period of time. You still have all of your sins, but you have some of my Sin as well." He told me, staring directly into my eyes with an intensity that I wasn't sure whether it was terrifying are extremely sexy.

Swallowing hard, I maintained eye contact. "What does that mean for me?" I whispered, unable to gather the strength needed to speak at a normal volume.

"It means," he said slowly. "That we're connected now and have a much longer lifespan than any human being."

"And...?" I pressed.

"And, you may have some residual side effects that include abilities that are similar to our own." He said it like a fact and not like it was super world-altering, life-changing news that he was delivering.

Turning my head to glance at the guys, I saw that they all wore similar tight smiles, obviously hoping for the best but expecting the worst.

I looked back at Eliam and shrugged my shoulders. "Okay." I said nonchalantly. I spun on my heel and made my way to the door, intending to head straight up to my bed room, get into some new pajamas, and enjoy the rest of my... Saturday? Wow. The realization of how much time I had lost caught up to me and I had to mentally shake my head to chase the thoughts off until much later.

I heard Eliam splutter behind me as I pulled the door open. "*Okay?*" He blurted, sounding astonished. "That's it?" I looked behind me to see his mouth hanging open wide enough to catch flies and had to keep myself from outright laughing.

"Uh, yeah. Were you expecting something else?" I asked in mock confusion.

He looked at me like I had grown a second and third head. "Where are you going, then?" His accent was especially thick when he was mad, and it was admittedly hot.

I pointed out the door way and raised one eyebrow. "I'm going to go change into something comfortable, then I'm gonna start cleaning up so I can relax." My tone made it sound like it was the most obvious thing in the world and I was highly enjoying watching his face turn multiple shades of red as I hurt his *pride*. Heh.

With that and without looking back at the six guys - no, the six *Sins* that were now laughing like I had never heard them laugh before, I made my way up the stairs, knowing that everything was changing.

But I knew I was strong enough to handle it.

I WIPED THE SWEAT OFF MY FOREHEAD WITH THE BACK of my hand and leaned my mop, admiring my handiwork. I would have to hire someone to come and fix the windows, but in three hours I had managed to patch the holes in the wall, temporarily fix the sink (I was sad to see the fountain go, but it wasn't very practical at all), put all the furniture back in it's place, and sweep and mop up all the debris. For three hours I'd worked my ass off, and though the guys offered to give me a hand, I took a lot of, well, pride in cleaning up a mess that I had created.

I had sorted through and worked out most of the more obvious blank spots in the tale the Severin brothers had told me, but there were still a few details that eluded me. I had just called for the guys, and they had only just started filing in as I stood and enjoyed their matching looks of admiration.

"You did all of this?" Gray asked in bemusement while he glanced around the kitchen and dining area.

I pushed a stray hair out of my face and smiled proudly. "Yeah. I need to call someone to fix the windows, we still need paint to cover the drywall putty, and I had to throw out some not so salvageable cookware, but it's done." I summarized.

I was so busy looking around to make sure I hadn't missed something that I didn't see Beck charging in my direction to sweep me up in a big hug that took my feet off the ground. "You're so fucking awesome, Ria!" He exclaimed.

My heart swelled with joy. "Like, I said, there's still work to be done." I reminded him.

"Who cares? This was an incredible feat." Gatlin commented, still looking a bit dazed.

I swatted Beck's hand playfully as a sign to put me down, which he did, but not before grabbing a nice handful of my ass. I shot him a sideways glare that he only shrugged in response to.

I moved to sit at one of the dining table chairs and gestured for everyone else to do the same as I folded my hands under my chin. I was secretly waiting for someone to notice that I had found another dining chair in basement, along with all of the supplies I needed to make my repairs.

Once everyone was seated, I waited a moment or two more before speaking. I really wanted someone to mention the fucking chair. "Okay, so I thought of another huge question." I watched their guards all go up at once, shutting me out in case I said something that would hurt them all. How had we all come to care so much about each other already? Well, except Eliam, but he was a dick.

"Calm your tits, it's nothing bad. Well, it's bad, but not like emotionally bad." I rambled.

Eliam waved is hand in a circular motion. "Get on with it, Ria." He wasn't harsh in the way he said it, which surprised me.

I put my hands up. "Okay, so how the hell did crazy preacher guy get his hands on a thousands of years old poison?" I just threw the question out there.

Several of the guys balked, but they all noticeably relaxed. Paranoid, much?

"Jonas Holden, the mayor, has been on our radar for quite a while now. He seems to be at the center of all the disappearances, deaths, and the sickness that's going around." Gray says without too much interest. Kellan's face tightened and scrunched in anger, but I pretended not to notice.

I remembered Drea telling me about the sickness. She mentioned that the doctors knew it was affecting the supramarginal gyrus and the frontal lobe somehow, and that it eventually caused rapid swelling of the brain, but couldn't quite isolate anything in particular that would or could cause the issues. The people affected by the sickness basically became mindless zombies until they fell into a coma and eventually died. No one had survived thus far, but everyone was hopeful.

"I know about the sickness, but tell me how the mayor fits in to my question." I urged.

Eliam was sitting at the opposite end from me, mimicking my posture. I hoped he had noticed the chair. When he glanced at the table in front of me and then back at my face, I knew it. He had totally noticed the chair. "Holden has been the last person to interact with every single person who has been affected by the sickness. Incidentally," he added." He was also there and seen speaking with Father Belvieu just moments before your incident occurred." He stated it all so matter-of-factly that I almost forgot who was in charge of the impromptu conference in the first place.

I shook my head a little to clear it and looked back up at the guys. "So, you think that the mayor gave psycho preacher the knife-"

"Athame." Rafe corrected.

I nodded in his direction, acknowledging him. "You think that Jonas Holden gave psycho preacher the athame that he used to poison me?" I hadn't even finished my question when every single person at the table nodded vehemently. "And you firmly believe the sickness is Sin related, I'm assuming?" Once again, everyone nodded.

"It's only logical to assume that he is at the heart of it all." Gatlin agreed.

I noted that Kellan was being more quiet and brooding than usual, so I glanced down the table at him where he sat to Eliam's left. He was staring down at the table with straight up anger in his eyes, his hands clenched into tight fists.

I looked at the rest of the guys and then pointedly at the human - or, non-human, I supposed - skyscraper. Everyone seemed to get the message loud and clear, thankfully.

"Alright, that's it for now. I have a lot to think over. And I think I need a stiff drink after today." I added the last part with a grin and everyone groaned. "Oh, come on! I'm a fun drunk." I winked at the guys and got up from my chair - the chair that only one fucking person noticed - and started for the living room, where I fully intended to jump back into my new favourite video game of all time.

Just when I had reached the couch, I heard Eliam from the kitchen. "Hey, have we always had seven chairs?" His question started the other guys in, debating whether or not the chair had been there the entire time or not. I wouldn't tell him, but I was secretly grateful as all hell for the small gesture. My heart was soaring over something as simple as an extra chair, and I felt like I was walking on air.

IT WAS dark by the time Drea showed up, Chinese take out in hand and confusion all over her face.

"Uh, did you guys know that you don't have a front door?" She questioned, making me laugh over my squealing as Gatlin and Beck attempted to tickle me for the controller. We all knew that they could have easily just snagged it from me, so the torture was intentional.

I swatted at Gatlin's hand for the millionth time as he reached for my sides again. "Oh yeah, someone might want to fix that." I gasped. "Angel, how about you be a dear and fix it? I'm afraid I'm just too small and frail for such a task." I feigned a southern belle faint and he snickered at me.

"Yeah, sure, so small and frail." He rolled his eyes but got up anyway. "Come on, Kel, let's fix the door for the delicate flower over there." He jabbed his thumb back at me and I fluttered my eyelashes innocently, causing the whole room to erupt in laughter.

Drea came over and plopped on the couch next to me, blocking Beck's access to me. I stuck my tongue out at him in victory. "Looks like all of you are getting on like white on rice." My bushy-haired best friend chuckled while handing me little white and red boxes of fried, saucy goodness.

I just grinned at her as I snagged a set of chopsticks from the bag and tucked into a box of chicken fried rice.

Before I knew what had happened, Eliam was reaching around me from the back of the sofa and grabbing the controller from my lap. "Hey!" I objected around a mouthful.

He smirked at me as he waved the controller over my head.

"I don't get a turn, then?" He asked, pretend hurt in his voice and eyes.

I narrowed my eyes at him in return. "Sure, you can have a turn if you're actually wanting to play and not just stage an intervention." I told him, wagging my chopsticks in his direction.

He shook his head as he walked around the couch to sit on my other side. "We've created a monster." He mumbled, making me laugh.

As it turned out, there was someone worse at video games than me, and of course it had to be the most prideful person in the entire room. An entire hour was spent trying to help Eliam master the addictive game over dinner, but he just wouldn't take our advice, go figure.

"The circle is closing in on a wooded area, so set up the launchpad!" I all but shouted at him as he ran closer and closer to the next circle.

He glanced at me briefly before ducking behind an absurdly large tree to avoid being spotted by a few players running past. "What do I need the launchpad for?" He demanded.

I groaned and rubbed a hand over my face. "You need to get up into the trees, Eliam! It'll be harder for them to find and hit you, and you get the surface advantage." I explained, trying to remain calm. "Like those guys on the mountain that shot you down in point two second last game."

Drea yawned next to me, her few wine coolers apparently more than enough for her.

"Hey babe, do I need to drive you home?" I asked her quietly as she was falling asleep.

She shook her head sleepily and smiled up at me. "Don't wanna go home. Sleep here." She snuggled in closer and rested her head right on my boobs, making me laugh.

"Well, those are mine, so you can't sleep there, but I'll have Kel take you upstairs, okay?"

Drea nodded against my chest. "'Kay." She mumbled happily.

I gestured to Kellan to come get her and he quickly obliged, scooping the sleeping girl in his arms like she weighed no more than a kitten, which I doubted she did; she was so small in stature. Kel gave me a quick nod before heading up the stairs to deposit Drea in the guest room.

I stretched a little and yawned myself. It was so rare that I was tired at night, but the insane events of the day and the night before were likely to blame. While I considered myself to be handling everything well, the guys had still been doing everything in their power to distract me from my own thoughts.

"Ria." I snapped my attention to Gray and noticed that everyone was looking at me expectantly.

I cleared my throat and sat up a little straighter. "Uh, yes?" *Smooth, very smooth.* My inner self taunted. Oh, there she was. I had wondered what she had been up to for the majority of the day. It was nice to have my head be quieter than usual for a change. Maybe she had been having trouble wrapping her head around everything, same as me. Which would make sense, since she was me.

Gray was staring at me, assessing me. "You're gonna be okay, right?" He looked so concerned. I knew that they likely weren't expecting me to take it very well, so they probably thought I was in denial or something. Hell, maybe I was.

I smiled reassuringly at everyone. "I'm fine guys, really. It's not like I'm some heroine meant to save the day or something. I'm just a not-so-innocent bystander. I'm cool, promise." I told them all.

They all collectively sighed in relief and I rolled my eyes. "I am, however, gonna head on up to bed. I'm completely done being in the world of the living." I joked.

Rafe chuckled and tapped my knee with a fake punch. "Because you're an undead creature of the night?" He guessed.

"Abso-fucking-lutely." I confirmed with a grin. "Night, guys." I stood up and stretched, then made my way upstairs.

But once I was alone and tucked soundly into bed, nightmares of glassy-eyed people and poison coated blades plagued my sleep, and I knew that I wasn't completely okay.

# 25 RIA

THERE WERE A LOT OF THINGS THAT I ENJOYED IN LIFE, I was truthfully very easy to please. However, waking up with the sun was certainly not one of those things that I enjoyed even one tiny bit. After cracking open my eyes and being bombarded with daytime cheeriness, I all but hissed like a vampire before yanking the covers over my head and begging the sunlight to please just go the fuck away.

Why people eagerly sought out homes with east facing windows was beyond me. Who liked waking up to their retinas burning? Not this girl, that was for sure.

I could smell coffee, but even the dark, bitter, goodness couldn't rouse me. There wasn't a chance in hell I was stepping foot out into the sunlight this early, lest I instantly crumbled to dust. I could also hear the guys making a ruckus downstairs and contemplated how worth it it would be to spend the rest of my life in a state pen.

The thought really made me stop and think. If that horrible poison was the only way to harm a Sin, it didn't seem like there was a way for them to die. And if that was the case, why were the guys - especially Eliam - so hesitant to even mention their seventh? If they couldn't die, they were either lying to me, or something worse had happened.

My paranoia was starting to get to me as I huddled in my little blanket cave. My inner self poked her annoying head around a corner in my head to glare in my direction. Which was all directions, I suppose, since it's my head. *Stop overthinking shit. You can't change what's already been done.* She snapped at me.

*Okay, yeah, but that doesn't change what* could *happen. Whatever happened to the seventh could still happen to one of my guys.* I thought angrily back at her, feeling like pulling my hair out.

When all she did was smirk at me, I realized my slip up. *Not my guys. Just guys. That I live with. And am kinda friends with. Just guys.*

*Mhmm...* My inner self rolled her eyes at me before

strutting away and flipping her hair sarcastically at me. How did one even flip their hair sarcastically?

I groaned and rolled over to my side, facing away from the hell-window. I couldn't even remember if there were curtains to draw, but I sure as shit wasn't getting my ass up to close them if there were any to even close in the first place. Just as I was about fade back out again, my phone rang, causing my to jump out of my skin.

Had I really gone so long without checking my phone? I remembered before my impromptu move, my phone was practically attached to my face. I never went more than an hour without it, and that was excruciating. But here I was, a week later, and I hadn't so much as used it to set an alarm. The realization had my mind spinning. My basic bitch status was on the line.

Well, actually, it was a name that I had never wanted to see again, not in a trillion years.

I picked up the phone and slammed it to my ear under the covers, accidentally smacking myself in the jaw with it. Apparently extended lifespan didn't mean pain resistant. "What the fuck do you want, Mercedes?" I snapped, my teeth grinding together so hard I could have sworn I heard a crunch.

"Ria, OMG, I'm so glad to hear your voice. You haven't been on Insta like, at all. I was starting to think something terrible happened to you!" If I hadn't already seen the kind of snake she really was, I would have thought that I had heard genuine concern in my ex-bff's voice.

"I said, what the fuck do you want?" I repeated, wishing for the first time in my life that I could strangle someone through the phone. I heard heavy footsteps coming up the stairs and hoped to everything that existed that it was one of the bigger guys, so I could get a few angry punches in and not hurt anyone. Seriously. It was either a Sin thing, or they worked their asses off for those bodies.

A strangled sound came through from the other end of the call. "Can't I call to make sure my BFF is okay? I've missed you, boo boo!" She whined.

Someone opened my door and I took a small peek out from under my blanket cave. Gatlin was standing there, watching me with a mixture of amusement and confusion. "What?" He mouthed.

I made a sour face at him and indicated the phone, which only served to confuse him more. Not for the first time, I wished that I could just up and teleport so I could strangle the homewrecking bitch on the other end of the call and be back in time for breakfast.

As fury rose up inside me, I watched as Gatlin's face morphed into an expression of alarm. "Ria!" He shouted, and as he reached for me, I felt a heavy feeling in the pit of my stomach, like heavy stones were being dropped on me, one by one.

Suddenly, the sensation was gone, and I felt like I could breathe. Except, I was laying on my side on hardwood floors, with Gatlin sprawled beside me. "Uh," I whispered. "Toto, I don't think we're in Kansas anymore." I looked around at the familiar room, remembering all the times I had spent the night in it just watching movies and gossiping as if the world were about to end.

I heard a shrieking sound and scrambled to stand up. I saw

Mercedes sitting on her bed, knees pulled up to her chest, phone sitting limply in her hand, and makeup running down her face with her tears.

"For fuck's sake, shut the hell up, you cow!" I roared at her, not really feeling in a chit-chatty mood. Realizing I'd gotten my wish, I lunged at my former friend, claws out and ready to go in for the kill.

A strong, heavily muscled arm wrapped around my waist and held me back, and I practically howled at Gatlin's attempt to contain me. "Ria, calm the fuck down."

I whipped my head around so fast that it nearly gave me whiplash and I stared straight into his gorgeous silver eyes. "No!" I shouted. "That bitch ruined my life! She betrayed me! *She stole him from me!*" I tried not to burst into tears, but I hadn't really realized how much pain and hurt I had been carrying ever since everything went down. I didn't even remember giving myself time to grieve the loss of my relationship or giving myself permission to just have a good cry.

I never gave myself the smallest chance to heal.

"I didn't steal him!" Mercede's cried from across the room, where she was now cowering in a corner. "He said he loved me! It was me he wanted all along and you read all of the signals wrong! You trapped him!" It was so hard to hear those words coming out of her mouth, knowing that even she didn't believe what she was saying. She was red in the face and looking worse than I had ever seen her.

"Oh really?" I drawled, my tone dripping with as much sarcasm as I could possibly pour into it. My inner self was standing in my mind, hands on her hips and fueling my pettiness. "And I read the signs wrong when he got on one knee and asked me, Ria Will Grimm, to be his 'until the end of time'?"

I saw her face fall, a little of the fight leaving her. She was in complete denial and it made me sick to my stomach. As pissed and hurt as I was by her betrayal, I still felt as though she deserved a little less of the blame. When I looked back on everything, all the signs pointed toward my former fiance being a master manipulator. What guy would decide to move in with his girlfriend when he had a perfectly posh penthouse all to himself?

"I didn't know that we were name twins, Merc!" I fake-gushed, smiling too sweetly to even pretend that I was trying to be nice.

She shook her head at me and the rage boiled some more. "He loved me." She insisted, hell bent on believing his end of the story. What the fuck ever, though.

She made her bed, and she was going to have to lie in it - just like she was lying to herself.

"You're disgusting, you know that?" I told her without even a tiny sliver of kindness or emotion of any kind in my voice. "I pity you. I'm so sorry that you never found the love you deserved."

She turned about six different shades of red in the span of about five seconds and I almost wanted to laugh. "Pity *me?*" She screeched, looking as deranged and broken as she sounded, her hair falling in front of her angelic face looked like it hadn't even been brushed in weeks. "You're all alone too! Don't act like you're any better than I am!" Her eyes were wide and wild, and I was actually worried for a second that she was going to snap and hurt herself.

I leveled a hard, determined gaze on her and watched her puff up. "I'm not alone. I'll never be alone, not like you." I told her, keeping my voice steady.

As she moved to open her mouth, obviously to argue with me once more, I turned and softly pressed my lips against Gatlin's, feeling him stiffen as he was caught completely unaware. After a moment, he seemed to thaw, and wrapped another arm around me, massaging little circles into the small of my back.

"Take me home, please?" I whispered against his lips. He nodded once and tightened his hold on me. As I felt the stone-dropping feeling begin once again, I turned to look at Mercedes one last time. I watched as the tears fell rapidly down her cheeks and her eyes seemed to plead with me. I felt nothing but sorrow for her, for the horrible weight on her conscience that she would have carry with her for the rest of her life.

My eyes were closed during the whole heavy, stones-in-my-belly feeling, and once I felt it dissipating I slowly inched my eyes open, shocked to find myself standing back in my room. I turned to Gatlin and was even more surprised my the look of barely restrained fury that shadowed his beautiful features.

I bowed my head sheepishly. "So, uh... I'm guessing that's a Sin thing?" I asked, trying to keep my tone conversational despite how utterly terrifying my Angel looked at that very moment. He nodded once, brusquely in response. "And, uh, I'm guessing I shouldn't have been able to do that?" He gave just one shake of his head and I tried to decipher whether that meant, no, you shouldn't have or no, should have. Words were so much simpler when they were actually, you know, spoken.

"Are you mad at me?" I asked in a hushed tone, more than a little frightened at what his answer might be.

He stayed silent and brooding like that for a long time, making me freak out a little on the inside. He was totally pissed, but the question was more of why he was upset. I mean, I hadn't exactly done anything on purpose. I just sort of wanted to strangle the bitch who destroyed the life that I had built for myself. The entire bubble that I had been living in for so long, that kept me safe and protected from my terrifying past and my uncertain future, she had destroyed in five minutes flat.

It was unnerving. I supposed that if it was so easily destroyed in the first place, it probably was as reliable and sustainable as I had hoped. Though amazing, my existence was flawed and rather lonely. If I didn't convince myself that everything was exactly what I had wanted, then how would I be able to justify all the hardships and trials that I'd had to go through in order to get there?

But then, not all great things are perfect. Looking over at my dark angel, still seething just below the surface, I realized that the best and most perfect things in life are all flawed in some beautiful sort of way.

I took just a couple of steps forward, completely invading his personal space by about negative four inches, and wrapped my arms around his hard, broad torso. Even standing at a normal height as I was, he was quite a bit taller than me, so my head didn't even quite reach his chin. Was being that tall even possible?

"I'm so sorry." I whispered against the fabric of his plain white t-shirt. His entire body tensed, and seconds later he grabbed my shoulders and pushed me away so that he could properly face me. He looked shell-shocked, scared almost.

"Why the fuck are you sorry?" He puzzled. "I just can't believe what I just saw - what I heard." He looked at me sadly, his brow furrowing as if the words eluded him.

"What you went through..." He trailed off, looking more troubled than I had ever seen any person. "I would have killed him if I knew. No one, especially someone as incredible as you, should be treated that way."

And he was back to being pissed, but at least I understood now. If only he understood that my disastrous relationship and its heartbreaking end wasn't even close to the worst thing that had happened to me in my life. Sure, it hurt, but I was strong enough that I wouldn't continue to let it affect me forever. Nothing could affect me that badly anymore.

Not even being nearly kidnapped by a zombie-preacher, which sounded like a really bad movie, if I was being honest. I wasn't really stuck on that little detail, per se, but I was definitely still taking my time wrapping my pretty little head around the surrealness of it.

I shook my head as I looked up at Gatlin, his face, his warm hands on my shoulders, his mere presence, all keeping me grounded and centered. "He's a tiny part of my long past now. He can't hurt me anymore." I took a deep breath as I smiled shyly at him. "I have all of you in my life now. And as much as Eliam's shifts in mood confuse me, I'm positive he wouldn't let that monster of a man within ten feet of me again, if only to protect his... Uh, pride?" I ended on a really bad, unintentional joke and felt like burying my face in my hands. So smooth.

Gatlin's face softened ever-so-slightly, and it warmed my heart. "I know we are a lot to handle, but I swear that we would never try to hurt you. I swear it on my immeasurably long life." He said reverently, squeezing my shoulders a little.

I nodded at him at the same time my stomach growled and I grimaced. "Uh, can we pretend that didn't happen?" I joked.

He stepped into my now non-existent bubble and slid his hands slowly to my hips. "You mean, like this didn't happen?" He growled, his face just centimeters away from my. His hot breath and intoxicating scent washed over me, making me tremble a little.

I started to ask him what exactly "didn't happen", but his lips were already crushed against mine, stealing away my breath and my thoughts. Oh, that. I wrapped my arms over his shoulders and all but fastened myself to him, trying to get as close as possible to his unreasonably warm body.

Just when I thought he was about to pull away, I latched onto the little hair that I was able to reach and yanked until his mouth was back to mine, and it seemed that he got the message loud and clear. He moved his hands just under my ass and lifted me up, startling me, but not even attempting to pry me off of him.

He laid me gently on the edge of my bed, deepening our kiss with the new angle, gravity working perfectly in our favour. Our tongues tangled together, dancing in a way that only our bodies knew how to, and every little touch sent little shocks of electricity through me, making me dizzy in the best kind of way.

I tugged at his shirt and shivered pleasurably, even when he broke the kiss just long enough to pull it over his head. I dug my nails into his shoulders and nipped his bottom lip, which caused him to jerk a little and grind down, once, against me. I moaned against his lips and he swallowed the sound as he adjusted himself between my legs. He pulled away slightly, his eyes dark with desire and need.

"You're not wearing any underwear." He groaned. The sound made me squirm, feeling heat pooling lower and lower inside me and unable to hold out much longer. I needed him. I needed his touch, his warmth, his stability and strength; I needed it all like I needed the air in my lungs.

I made an animalistic, strangled sounded in the back of my throat. "What's you're point? Get over here, like now." I hissed, dragging him back to me.

He nearly drove me insane when he pulled back from me, leaving me writhing in arousal. I was feeling so over-stimulated, just from our kissing and gentle touching, that I almost jumped out of my skin with joy when he made quick work of his jeans and tossed them aside. When his boxers came next, I swear I almost cried out with joy.

Expecting him to resume our activities, sans clothes, I was completely taken by surprise when he began pressing delicate little kisses on the inside of my leg, starting at my ankles and working his way higher and higher. When he got to my inner thigh, my core clenched so hard that I trembled from the incredible ache.

"Gat." I gasped as I writhed from the sudden jolt of pleasure that I received at the feeling of his mouth so close, but so far.

He froze just shy of the target and peeked up at me, his eyes wide and filled with wonder. "You called me Gat." He said in awe. I only shrugged in response. What was the big deal? His brothers called him Gat, and we were, uh, pretty well acquainted by this point. Well, he was pretty damn acquainted with my mouth.

"That's your name." I teased.

His eyes were burning hole into me, intense and smoldering. "I don't know why that's so hot coming out of your mouth." He murmured as he pushed up my nightshirt pressed another tender kiss on my hip bone. "But fuck, it is." He pushed my shirt up higher and I almost growled at him like a rabid dog. It wasn't fair to tease me the way he was and he damn well fucking knew it.

I opened my mouth to tell him to get a move on with that hard-on, but before I could speak, the soft fabric of my shirt was being tugged up and over my head. Gatlin stared at me like he had never seen me before, almost lovingly.

He dipped his head and my breath hitched, my thoughts spiraling in ecstasy when his hot mouth closed over one of my nipples. He caught the other between his fingers and I bucked my hips up toward him, the stimulation alone causing my eager body to react before I even knew what to tell it.

Moaning softly, I arched my back, pressing myself into his touch with a fervor that seemed to entice him, only driving him further. I felt the ball of want and need inside of me coiling, waiting to explode, and I didn't want it this way. I wanted him inside me, sharing in our blissful connection. "Please." I panted, overwhelmed by the scorchingly hot sensations that were consuming me, body and soul, and needing the harmony of the two of us becoming one.

His luminous silver eyes met mine as I silently pleaded with him. Finally, adjusting his position between my legs, he leaned over me and guided himself to my opening. He rubbed his length against my wetness and I made a soft noise of both pleasure and impatience.

Finally, he eased inside of me, filling me with his length and making me gasp at the sensation. He looked to me as if to ask if I was alright and I nodded encouragingly. Once he started moving, it was like I could see fireworks behind my eyelids as they fluttered shut. He withdrew almost completely and then thrust inside me once more, this time harder, making me see stars even as my eyes flew open.

Pretty quickly, we found a steady rhythm between the two of us, a silent cadence that our bodies moved in tandem to. It was obvious all too soon that I wasn't going to be able to hold on much longer and I scraped my nails down his back, feeling a sick sort of pleasure at the fact that I had marked him as my own, if only temporarily. Our eyes met and I knew that he could feel the same need for release.

As if on cue, I felt myself clench and I called his name as I felt my pleasure spill out of me, finding my release. The action elicited an almost predatory growl from low in his chest that reverbrated around and inside me. Quivering in the aftershocks of our climax, we collapsed in a tangle of limbs, slick with our own sweat and the evidence of our...Courtship? Coitus? Lovemaking? Son of a fuck.

I glanced over at Gatlin to maybe catch a glimpse of what was going on in that handsome head of his and he looked nothing but completely blissful. And a little cocky, but he had just bagged himself a stripper in bed - though, I was almost positive that in his very long lifetime, it wasn't the first time.

He caught me staring and I felt the heat creeping up my cheeks. *Oops.*

"So, uh," I mumbled, really wishing that I was as good with words as I was with walking in heels for ten plus hours at a time. "Breakfast?" As if it had been waiting for that one magic word, my stomach grumbled loudly, making Gatlin laugh as he sat up. He looked every bit the role of the carefree, light, beautiful angel with that smile lighting up his face. If he looked that way every time he had sex, I was totally willing to take one for the team - no compensation necessary.

Gatlin stood and began pulling his discarded clothes back on, dressing slowly enough for me to just sit back and enjoy the show. I swore silently and then thanked the heavens that he had been blessed with an ass straight out of a romance novel. I mean, *damn.* When he had finished dressing, he turned to me and raised his eyebrows as if expecting something. *Oh shit, clothes.*

I jumped up and started searching for my night shirt. Gatlin cleared his throat and twirled a bit of fabric in one hand. I narrowed my eyes at him and leapt at him to grab my shirt before he could even consider playing keep-away. "I was just going to say that should, ahem, remember some pants?" He suggested as he waggled his brows teasingly.

His joking attitude had me feeling all kinds of giddy and happy as I slipped into some shorts, which I'm sure did absolutely nothing like my dark angel had intended. I grabbed a bra and tank top too, instead of lounging around in just my pajamas all day. I practically skipped down the stairs and into the kitchen, where an array of fresh fruit and breakfast foods were laid out on the breakfast bar.

"Oh yum!" I exclaimed, a little too loudly. Everyone turned to look at me, but I didn't feel even an ounce of remorse. They made all that ruckus when I had only just woken up, the least they deserved was to hear me fawn over food. I quickly dished up a plate of scrambled eggs, bacon, avocado, and an assortment of chopped fruits before sitting at my chair - yes, *the* chair - and tucking in. Beck made his way over to me and deposited a steaming cup of coffe before me, making my mouth water.

"You may just be my favourite person in the whole world right now." I told him seriously.

Gatlin made a strangled noise from the opposite end of the table and I glanced at him before ammending my statement. "You may be my *second* favourite person in the whole world right now."

Beck's brow furrowed. "Why only second?" He questioned.

I chuckled to myself and tried like hell to keep my

expression neutral. "Gatlin beat me at rock paper scissors." I deadpanned.

The Sin of Gluttony's mouth dropped open with an audible *pop*, and I lost the will to contain myself as everyone else broke out in a chorus of laughter around me.

"I'm your second favourite because he beat you at a *game?*" He asked, confounded.

Not able to confirm nor deny through my rib-cracking laughter, I turned to the guys for help. To my surprise, Kellan was the one who stood and came to link my arm through his – a feat that was extremely awkward as his arm was so much higher than my own. "Want to go with me to see Drea?" He asked me as though his brother wasn't still gaping wildly at me, unable to decipher the truth from my tone.

I nodded to Kellan. "Why, yes, Tallosaurus Rex, I would love to." I laughed as he rolled his eyes and downed the entirety of my coffee before making my way toward the newly re-attached front door. I stopped briefly to pull on a pair of my boots, the only shoes of mine that were downstairs. As we made our way to my car Beck followed us to the front porch and and called after me.

"Hey, wanna play a game of rock, paper, scissors? Ria? C'mon, man!" He shouted. I could hear the eruption of laughter all the way outside, and I made a mental note to bring something special home for the first Sin I had ever met.

We arrived at the coffee shop just before noon. Apparently, it was much later in the morning when I had woke up than I had originally thought. Still not quite as soothing a thought as others might have believed, since the sun was still high in the sky. Even Kellan had taken a pair of my sunglasses hostage as he scowled at the sky like it had wronged him in some deep and personal way.

I peeked over at him as we got out of the car. He had ditched the sunglasses, presumably to preserve his macho status, and he was shading his eyes with his hand, still looking grumpy.

*I get it, dude.* I thought.

We made our way inside and headed for a table at the back of the building after sending Drea an enthusiastic wave in greeting. She made a beeline for us and grinned, but something about it seemed almost forced.

I eyed her up and down for a second. She looked tired, like she hadn't been sleeping well, but otherwise seemed okay. Still, something felt a little off.

She wrapped her arms around Kellan and gave him a little peck on the cheek, then came and did the same to me. "Hey guys. Coffee?" She guessed, giving me a little side eye that said she knew I had a problem. A big problem.

I shrugged, guilty as charged. "Company would be nice too. But coffee first, please. I added with a sweet-as-sugar smile. She only rolled her eyes at me and took back off toward the counter, where the hiss and whir of all my favourite machines were getting to work.

There weren't many people in the shop at all, maybe two tables aside from ours were occupied, and they all seemed to be deep in their own conversations. "Does Drea seem a little weird to you today?" I asked Kellan in a low voice, careful not to be overheard.

Kellan gave me a sad smile and looked back over at Drea where she was busy making coffee for a woman who seemed to order the entire thing with nothing but air. "She has it pretty tough at home since her mom went missing. Her stepfather isn't known to be the best kind of company and he really doesn't give a flying fuck about whether his twin stepdaughters are happy or healthy, so long as they're alive."

"Missing? She told me her mom works at the inn - it was actually one of the very first things she told me." Had something happened just since I had been around? I knew I was still pretty much a stranger, but I thought that we had connected almost instantly.

Kel nodded. "Officially yes, since it's her inn, but she's been missing for about four years now." He explained, keeping his voice just above a whisper. "It was said by the police that she ran off with one of the inn's guests, but no one really believes it. It's just a story to help keep everyone living their ignorant little lives."

I looked over at my friend who was finishing up our coffees and I felt my heart break. I may not have had a very positive relationship with my parents, but that didn't mean that others had the same reservations.

"Who's her stepfather?" I queried, realizing that was something else that I didn't know.

As he opened his mouth to answer me, door jingled as it opened. I turned in my seat to look, because I seriously never stopped being nosy. A tall man with dark, slicked back hair and a navy suit stepped into the shop, removing his sunglasses and stowing them away in one of the inside pockets of his suit jacket. He looked familiar somehow, though I was positive that I had never met this man.

I turned to look at Drea just in time to watch all of the

colour drain from her face, making her already fair pallor look sickly. The man said something to her and she gave a single nod, getting to work on whatever the creepy guy had ordered.

*And fuck.* He was heading straight toward where Kel and I sat.

"Kellan Severin, it's good to see you again." The man smiled the tightest, most insincere smile that I had ever seen pasted on someone's face. It transformed his face, and not in a positive way. When he turned me, I felt a terrifying chill creep up my spine. "Hello, I don't believe I've had the pleasure." He held his hand out toward me and I grudgingly placed my hand in his, feeling like my delicious breakfast was about to end up all over his immaculately polished shoes when he pressed his lips to the back of my hand.

When he released me it was like I could finally breathe again, if only a little bit. "It's nice to meet you mister...?" I let the question hang in the air as I raised an eyebrow. Disgusting human being or not, it was polite to introduce yourself.

He chuckled as he clasped his hands behind his back. "My apologies," he said, sounding anything but sorry. "Jonas Holden, mayor."

Every single hair was standing on end and my nerves were on high alert. After everything that I had heard so far from the guys, I wasn't really really this guy's biggest fan, but at least I knew why he seemed so familiar to me - he was at the club the night that Father Belvieu tried to kidnap me.

Pieces started falling into place, and I suddenly realized that there was a lot of reason to believe this man was suspected to be the one behind the weird illness/coma thing that was going down, other than just being near the victims before it all happened.

I didn't say anything for a long time and neither did Kel. I could feel the Envy Sins's seething hatred from where I sat across from him, and I felt like there was so much more to the story that I just didn't understand.

I looked to see Drea, still white as a sheet, walking toward us on unsteady legs. She put our mugs in front of us and handed one to Holden, refusing to meet his eyes.

"Ah, here's my darling daughter now." The mayor chuckled. He reached over as if to muss Drea's hair until Kellan released a threatening growl - not that I blamed him in the least. I was in shock at the new information laid out before me, but that didn't mean I wasn't equally as pissed. Holden withdrew his hand and the fake smile was back in place after a brief moment of shock. "I'll take my leave now. I have a dear friend to go see in the hospital."

He immediately turned on his heel without a backwards glance at any of us, but he stopped as he placed his hand on the door. "Oh, and Andrea, dear." He said, as if he was just expressing some off-hand comment. "Ana's fallen ill as well, but I'd appreciate it if you stayed quiet. Understand?" The complete and totally lack of empathy in his voice, coupled with the fact that he sounded almost *pleased* made me queasy all over again.

As he pushed out the door, I heard the shattering of glass and turned just in time to watch my best friend fall to her knees, silent tears streaming down her cheeks. "No." She whispered. "No, no, no." She cradled her head in her hands and Kel was there in a split second, lifting her up and into his arms.

"We need to get her home." He told me. His jaw was set and he appeared to be only moments away from completely breaking.

I knew no one else was working, since Drea worked most days alone. I stood up on my chair and cupped my hands in front of my mouth. "Everybody out! We're closed!" I shouted. The few people inside the shop looked confused, but slowly got up and made their way out the door, most of them stopping only to leave their tips on the counter as they passed.

Once everyone was out, I ran and jumped over the counter, grabbing Drea's keys from her tie-dyed canvas bag as I slung it over my shoulder, and quickly locked the front door as we rushed from the building. My car started as we neared, making me thankful for my expensive taste in cars, and I opened the back door for Kel to slide in with Drea cradled to his chest.

DREA WAS sound asleep by the time we pulled up the gravel driveway and in front of the house that I had quickly come to call home. I gestured to Kel to wait while I opened the door, so as not to wake our friend. The hysterical howling and screaming started almost the second we hit the road, and it had lasted almost the entire twenty-five minutes that it took to get to our stretch of twisting, forest-lined road. I was relieved that she was asleep, but it made my heart ache to realize how much crying she had done to expend herself that much.

Once the car door was open, I ran for the front door, pushing it open and immediately locating the other guys. They all turned as one from their spots around the living room and I silently shushed them just as the giant came through the doorway and headed straight up the stairs, presumably to deposit her in the guest room. Honestly, it was probably wiser just to call it Drea's room, since she was the only person I knew that ever used it.

"What the hell happened?" Gray asked, his eyes full of concern.

I took a seat on the floor where I was standing, folding my legs underneath me. "Ana's gotten hit with the sickness thing." I told them shortly. From what I understood about it, it basically made the affected person a glorified zombie and affected them for several days before their brains started shutting down. Which made little sense to me, since I would assume that Drea had seen her sister only very recently, seeing as they lived together.

The guys all started talking at once, making my head pound a little. My inner self was covering her ears, also affected by the onslaught of noise that my poor ears were experiencing.

The whole room went silent as Kellan made his way back into the foyer, facing the living room with his arms crossed over his chest. His imposing posture only made his already intimidating presence even more unnervingly threatening. I could feel the pure, unadulterated fury rolling off of him in waves.

"It's Holden." Was all he said, and it was evidently all that *needed* to be said. All at once, everyone sprang into action, running to various parts of the house and making so much noise that I was worried they would wake Drea.

I turned to Kellan, the only one who hadn't moved an inch. "What are you doing?" I asked him quietly, maybe a little afraid that he could snap at any second and also snap my neck.

He looked sideways at me and smirked, but the expression was devoid of any actual mirth. "*We* are going to make sure that he never does anything like this to anyone ever again." His tone was chilling. I wasn't actually scared of him, but I felt that maybe he wasn't as in control of himself as he perhaps thought he was.

I looked at the ginormous man like he had grown an extra set of arms. "What's this 'we' business? I love Drea, but I'm not going down for murder. That's not happening." I refused adamantly. I realized how crappy it all sounded, even to my own ears, so I made to correct myself. Because I would totally go to jail for her. "I mean, I can watch her or something. My lips are sealed, I won't say a damn peep." I mimed locking my lips and throwing a key over my shoulder.

Before Kellan could respond, the guys were all back downstairs. They didn't look any different at first glance, which made me wonder what they were even doing in the first place, but on closer inspection, I could see the barely noticeable shapes of small weapons strapped to their bodies beneath their clothes.

Eliam stepped forward and locked eyes with Kellan. *Let's go.*

I heard his voice in my head and jumped, remembering the last time I had thought that very thing had happened. At least I wasn't imagining it.

We all filed out the front door and into the glaring light of the annoying sun. Not for the first time, I wondered what the hell I had gotten myself into.

## 28  RIA

If I said that the hospital was crowded, then I would have been the world's biggest liar. I was extremely shocked by the number of people that were crowded around the hospital entrance, spilling out over the sidewalks and into the parking lot. The building itself was small in comparison to a lot the ones I had been to, but it was relatively large for a town as small as this one.

After parking a few blocks down, we made our way inside, pushing through groups of weeping families and friends just to get to the map of the building on the other side of the lobby. The inside was bleak, as was expected from most hospitals, but this one seemed to literally drain the life right out of me. Pictures depicting gruesome biblical events were framed on the walls while little standing signs boasted multiple verses that I wasn't even sure correlated correctly with health or medicine.

It all made me shiver a little bit and I tried to fight back the urge I felt to run from the building screaming. I ran away from the bible thumping and all that, and I still couldn't seem to get away, no matter how far my feet took me. It didn't help that I hated hospitals to begin with - the sterile, plain environment gave me goosebumps.

The guys all clustered around the map for about point two seconds and then were off, weaving their way through the maze of hallways like they had been doing this their entire life. I wasn't even sure if or how they knew where they were going, but I was dragged along for the ride and I trusted them for absolutely no rational reason.

As we rounded one corner, the guys froze. I glanced around for whatever had made them stop in their tracks, but I didn't even get a chance to look past one doctor before I was being yanked into a nearby room.

"Hey!" I objected. "Enough with the manhandling, Goliath!" I pinned Kellan with a glare that I wish could have set him aflame.

He didn't even attempt to look sheepish, as he shrugged in response. *Infuriating fucking men.*

I opened my mouth to give him another earful when I caught a glimpse of the person in the bed behind us. The sight made my heart contract so painfully that I almost collapsed to my knees, and I might have if a strong arm hadn't caught me around my waist. My hand flew to my mouth to hold back a sob as I stared at my best friend lying, unconscious, in the industrial hospital bed, a tube to her mouth and wires surrounding her entire body.

Consciously, I knew that wasn't Drea, it was Ana, but still... No one said being friends with a twin would always be easy. I slowly approached the bed and ran a hand over her forehead, brushing away the hair that was in her face. It was so hard to convince myself that it wasn't really her when I felt so close to crying, and it wasn't really any easier to remind myself that it was her sister. It was so strange to think that I had never even spoken to her, but I felt like I knew her just because I knew someone who looked just like her.

I heard the guys talking in hushed voices behind me and I turned to stare at them over my shoulder. Rafe caught me looking first. "He's here, but it doesn't look like he's visiting Ana." He explained quietly to me, as though he was afraid to wake the sleeping girl before me.

I was going to tell him just to shut the door when an obnoxious squealing sound started ringing around us from overhead.

"Code blue, code blue, code blue..." A mechanical sounding female voice repeated.

As if of one solid mind, we all turned to look at one another, they guys' faces set into lines of grim determination. I hoped mine matched, because there wasn't a chance in hell that I was going to be the chicken of the group.

We all ran from the room just in time to watch Holden's back disappear around a corner at the opposite end of the corridor. Eliam, Gray, Beck, and I all ran for the room that nurses and doctors were rushing in and out of while Gatlin, Kellan, and Rafe took off in the direction that the mayor had went in.

Once we were inside, it was pretty clear that there was no saving the woman that lay motionless beneath the sterile, white hospital blankets. There was another shrieking sound coming from the doorway, but it wasn't an alarm. As I looked back, I noticed the red-headed slimeball trying to push himself through an armed security guard and a number of nurses. My heart hurt for him as I realized that this was likely his mother, Sanya lying in the bed. As bad of a person as Drea had told me this woman was, I still couldn't help but think that she didn't exactly deserve an ending this way.

Unable to behold the sight before me, I begged and prayed that I wasn't in that hospital, that I was back in the safety of the car while I waited for the guys to do their vengeance bit. It had little to nothing to do with me, anyway. As soon as I had thought about my tiny silver car, I felt the coolness of metal pressing against my back.

I opened my eyes to find myself on the other side of the mob of people and breathed a deep sigh of relief. I unlocked my car and slid in, waiting for the heat to kick on. I hadn't relaxed for even two seconds, leaning my head back on the headrest, when there was a knock on my window, and I just *knew* that it was one of the guys.

I glanced at Eliam standing outside with a scowl and rolled my eyes as I unlocked the doors. He walked around the front of the car to the passenger side, and when he reached the door, I locked the doors again with a smirk.

If it was even possible, his scowl deepened and he started to look really pissed. He pressed both hands to the window as he glared at me. I was positive that he could break my window if he wanted to, but I had a little faith that he would respect at least my car, if not me.

Unlocking the doors again, I waited for him to reach for the handle before locking them again. He stared at me, bemused and pissed right the hell off. I started snickering before I could control myself and hit the unlock button quickly as I saw him pull his arm back, as if to hit my beautiful baby.

He hurried inside the car and closed the door a little too roughly. "Hey, be gentle with my baby." I warned as I wagged a finger at him like he was a misbehaving child. He gave me a straight up *what the fuck* look and I giggled like an idiot.

"When did you learn to do that?" He asked me suspiciously.

It was my turn to give him a look. "Uh, well, at some point in history, automobile manufacturers started installing buttons that can lock and unlock doors at the owner's discretion. Weren't you hanging around at that point in time? I feel like you should know these things."

He scrubbed a hand over his face and looked up at the sky. Well, ceiling of my car, but the intent was clear. "Why me?" He grumbled. He took a steadying breath and looked back at me. "I mean traveling. Moving from one place to appear at another in seconds. *That.*" He clipped.

"Oh, that." I rolled my eyes, thinking that he could have probably just been a little bit more specific. "I did it this morning on accident. I feel a little bit like I've got the ruby slippers on." I admitted.

"Well Dorothy, you're still in Kansas, it's just a little more fucked up than you knew it was." He quipped tiredly.

I was a little confused about why Eliam of all the guys would be the one to follow me, but I wasn't going to question it too much. We seemed to at least have an amiable relationship now and I didn't want to mess it up by interrogating him every time he said or did something that resembled concern.

We sat in companionable silence for I don't even know how long, before I finally felt the need to ask. "Holden?"

"The others are looking for him. We don't know how he slipped away without us noticing, but Gray will have found something by now." He informed me. I appreciated him actually communicating with me on the issue.

I thought about Gray chasing down anyone and it made me want to laugh. "Why would Gray be the one to find him? Isn't he Sloth?" I asked.

Apparently, my question was hilarious, because Eliam broke out in a very short spasmodic sort of laugh, as though he hadn't expected something so funny. "The good thing about Gray is that he will always find the easiest way to do something."

When I thought about it, it actually made a lot of sense. If I was lazy, I would find the solution with the least amount of hurdles to overcome. It never really occurred to me that Sloth may correlate with laziness, but neither equaled unmotivated. It was some pretty interesting insight that made me realize how ignorant and blissfully unaware I had been before meeting the guys. I didn't even know that there was a single town still in existence that openly rejected homosexuality.

Proving Eliam right, Gray, Rafe, Gatlin, Beck, and Kellan emerged from the hoard of people and headed straight for the Jeep parked right beside my car. Beck paused at my window and rolled it down.

"Security footage showed him leaving in his car about an hour ago. Our best guess is that he went home, so the plan is to confront him there." He said, looking mostly at Eliam. He glanced at me and I nodded.

"I'll meet you guys there." I told him. He winked at me and made his way back around the Jeep.

I cocked my head to the side as I eyed the blonde, casanova beside me. "I'll ride with you." He said casually, as though he volunteered to spend alone time with me every day.

I shrugged at him and put my car in gear, following behind the guys as we all made our way to the house of a man who completely deserved to burn in hell.

"WOW, I thought *our* place was rural." I said offhandedly to Eliam as we pulled around the paved, circular drive in front of the mayor's mansion.

It was a beautiful house, if it could even be called that; the entire place was built like a museum. If the White House had a younger brother, this house would be it. Upon getting out of the car, I noticed two things at once.

Rafe spoke before I could get a word out, pointing at a sleek, black SUV parked in the drive. "He's here. What's the game plan?" He asked his brothers.

I put my hand up, only to be ignored. "Guys, I-"

"I think Beck and I should go around back and make sure we're there in case he makes a break for it." Gatlin suggested, cutting me off.

As I opened my mouth to speak again, I was cut off once more by Kellan. "I think we should all just go in at once. He's not going to get very far." He rumbled, driving his point home with a cheesy punch in his own hand.

The guys all nodded in agreement, their faces serious.

"Guys!" I yelled, annoyed at the fact that I was being ignored.

They all started walking inside and Gray looked over his shoulder at me. "Ria, you should wait in the car. This won't take long." He turned back to face the house as he continued walking away.

I felt an angry heat creeping up my neck and cheeks as I shook with anger. I tried to recreate the feeling that I had in the kitchen, but couldn't seem to pinpoint it. Instead, I focused on doing that traveling thing that I had done before, thinking and wishing that I was in front of them.

When I traveled to the front door, arms spread wide, the guys all stopped in their tracks. "Eliam, isn't that your fucking car?" I asked angrily, pointing at the sleek, red Camaro, mostly hidden by a car cover.

As one, each man turned and looked at the little corner of the car that could be seen from under the drab cover. Everyone seemed at a loss for words as realization dawned on us.

I threw the door open and bolted inside, mildly surprised that there wasn't a security system activated as it was already dusk. I ran to each room that had a light on, my heart beating in my chest at a thousand miles per hour. I started running up the stairs, following a feeling I had in my gut.

When I reached the top, I ran into the first room I saw with a light on and practically skidded to a halt, my eyes going wide and my breath caught in my throat. I put my hand to my chest and tried to breathe through the itchy feeling in the back of my throat that meant I was about to cry.

"Guys, in here." I called out, looking down at the sight before me and trying my very best to stay standing.

My best friend was kneeling there on the floor, a knife in her hand that was as drenched in blood as the rest of her was. Mayor Holden's body lay motionless on the floor before her, his open eyes glazed over and staring upward into nothingness.

I stepped slowly and cautiously over to my friend, being

careful to avoid the pooling blood on the marble flooring and the body of the man who had caused so much harm. Drea didn't move as I approached, she only stared down at the body of her stepfather with emotionless eyes, her body quivering ever so slightly.

"Drea, sweetie, it's okay." I told her, gently coaxing her with my voice to meet my eyes. Out of the corner of my vision, I could see the guys standing in the doorway, faces grim and turned down in mild disgust. I doubted the disgust was for our fragile friend, but for Jonas, who never had an ounce of compassion in his impeccably dressed body. The mayor had been in the possession of too many sins, and it was ultimately his downfall.

It felt like hours had passed before Drea finally turned to look at me and her eyes were full of unshed tears. "Did I really do this?" She asked me on a whisper. "Is he really dead?" She looked so scared at what my answer would be, so opted for folding her into a tight hug instead. I held her while she cried and brushed her matted, bushy hair back from her face.

I felt a large hand on my shoulder after some time had passed and my friend's hysterical sobbing had calmed into silent tears. "Drea." Kellan's rough voice makes me turn and look up at him and his face is so full of agonizing heartache that I can't stand it. I may call her my best friend, but to Kel, she was so much more. She was his anchor. "Come here, little one."

Drea looked up from her place on my shoulder and burst into tears once more at the sight of her huge Trump wall of a protector. She scrambled out of my hold and practically flew into his waiting arms. "It's okay." He soothed. "We just need to know what happened." He put a finger under her chin and lifted her gaze to his, forcing her to look at him.

Her lower lip quivered and she opened her mouth to speak before shutting it again. She looked to me and I nodded encouragingly, giving her a small smile. "I heard you guys talking and you said that he was the most likely culprit." She explained in a soft voice. "I ran home to look for evidence and he found me in his office. He told me I was a disappointment and that if I had just been normal, my sister and I would have had a happier life." Tears welled up in her eyes again and my heart broke for her all over again. How could one person have so much hate in their heart? I just couldn't understand it.

I stood up and stepped over to where Drea stood in Kel's embrace and rubbed small circles into her back for comfort. "What happened after, babe?" I asked as gently as I could, knowing that this must have been the painful part.

She took a deep, shaky breath and continued. "He told me how Ana would be devastated to learn of my death when she woke up and he rushed at me. I ran for the kitchen, but he beat me there and pinned me against the sink. I got away and ran for my mom's old study, which is where we are now, and grabbed the knife from her desk right there." She pointed an unsteady finger at the huge desk in the corner of the room, looking like someone would be back to do work there any moment. Only, I knew that wasn't the case for this room. Her mother wasn't missing, she was dead. I didn't want to have to tell Drea what we had found out. "I only wanted to defend myself, I swear."

Eliam stepped up to my side and placed his own hand on Drea's arm, gently rubbing the spot with his thumb. "We know, love. You're no killer." He stated in an attempt to console her. Which, of course, only made her cry again. He looked at me, alarmed, and I only shrugged. It wasn't his attitude... This time, anyway.

"Except, I am." She wailed, the pitch hurting my ears. "He told me he killed my mom. He said that he'd bury me next to her to rot together. I just... I lost it. Everything went red and I couldn't seem to stop myself." She fell to her knees, out of Kellan's arms, and buried her face in her hands as she fell into a fit of hysterics.

I dropped to my knees beside her and wrapped my arms around her small, shaking body. "He was a horrible person, Drea. He was consumed by his sins and would never be able to redeem himself. This was a mercy on his soul." I told her gently.

I looked to the guys and each of them nodded in turn. I did good, which seemed to be a first. The whole sin thing seemed to make it a lot easier to explain things. Maybe that's why people clung to that belief.

"We have to go now, babe. The guys will take care of this while we go outside, okay?" Drea didn't look at me, but nodded anyway, her gaze glued to the floor beneath us.

I got to my feet and hauled my friend with me, still holding her as close as I could manage without falling over. She needed me and I was going to be there for her, no matter what. I managed to get us down the absurd number of stairs without falling flat on my face, and once we were on the ground I felt like I could relax a little. No offence to my BFF, but she was a whole lot of dead weight at the moment.

"Can you walk now?" I asked her, trying really hard not to sound as hopeful as I felt.

She nodded back to me and my whole body flooded with relief. *Thank literally everything.*

We made our way to the glass patio door at the back of the massive house and stepped outside into the crisp, cool night air. It seemed to have a strengthening effect on Drea, who was standing there with her arms outstretched at her sides like she was standing in snow. Her mind was probably a little broken with trauma after tonight - hell, her whole life was traumatizing - but I wanted to be there and help her. I knew all to well the struggle with demons that liked to lurk in the shadows of our minds.

I don't even remember how long we sat out there in silence, looking up at the cloudless night sky and soaking in the peaceful, majestic sight of the twinkling stars above us. It was startling to realize that it was also a moonless night. The darkness seemed to make the stars stand out even more than usual, and I felt like it must have been a sign.

Even as I enjoyed the lurking sense of victory over the evil man whose soul was now washed clean from the face of the earth, I felt like something was wrong. Very wrong. How did Jonas Holden do what he did to all of those people? How did he make them all into mindless shells of the people they once were. It just didn't make any sense at all to me. If it was scientific, then the guys would not have sensed magic at play. If it was magical, how did he get his hands on it and harness it? There were too many missing pieces to the puzzle and I didn't like the feeling that this realization gave me in the very pit of my stomach.

Even my inner self seemed uneasy, pacing back and forth, sweat beading on her brow, looking green with sickness. Something wasn't right. But if that was so, what was wrong?

The guys came filing one by one out the back door as I resurfaced from my deep and troubling thoughts. I would have to mention it to them as soon as possible, because I was sure they would realize how right I was and that there seemed to be a bigger threat looming over us all.

Gatlin stepped in close to me and I smiled tightly up at him. I was exhausted and completely drained. I wanted to go home and stop getting interrupted, because a little boot knocking sounded real good after so much fucking crazy. "Everything's taken care of. Let's head home, okay?" He said to me, sounding worn out and nearly dead on his feet.

I nodded my agreement and looked beside me at Drea, who was fast asleep in Kellan's arms as he carried her like a newborn child. I wondered if he had been a dad of any kind in his many years. I remembered Gray's heartbreaking story about his family in Moscow many centuries before and realized that it was a very strong possibility. These guys had millennia to form relationships and build many lives before I came along. I wasn't a very jealous person, but the knowledge definitely stung more than I would have liked to admit.

"Let's go." I told Gatlin as I reached to hold his arm as we walked. We went around the side of the house with Kellan and Drea while the others went through the house and turned off the lights and locked the doors. When we reached the cars, I slid into the back of the Jeep and let the custom leather seats support the weight of all worries that were sitting on my shoulders. I couldn't shake the feeling that something was wrong.

Kellan piled into the back with me, Drea tucked into his arms and sitting on his lap, while Gatlin moved to the driver's seat. Gray climbed into the passenger seat and leaned his head back heavily against the headrest. Eliam, Beck, and Rafe were likely driving my car, but I didn't care. I didn't feel like driving and being near Eliam lately was making my hormones skyrocket like nobody's business. I just didn't have the energy to deal with all that crazy at the moment.

Before I knew it we were on the road and I was seriously contemplating just taking a quick nap, but I needed to talk to the guys, no matter how much my eyes wanted to close.

"Guys." I said while leaning forward and rubbing my eyes to get rid of some of the sleepiness. "Something doesn't feel right." I watched Gatlin's eyes dart to mine in the rear view mirror before turning back to focus on the road. Kellan turned his attention full on me, his bright eyes making my squirm a little in my seat with the intensity of them.

Gatlin was the first to speak, saving me from my own libido. "What do you mean?" He asked, sounding a little concerned.

I rubbed my eyes some more and leaned on the seat in front of me, accidentally catching some of Gray's hair in my hands. "I don't know," I struggled to explain the feeling I had. "I don't think he was our guy. Things just don't add up."

"He's the only one with enough motive and the only one we

could find any real evidence against, Ria. If it's not him, we're back to square one." Kellan interjects.

"He's right. There's enough information in our favour to prove that he was the one behind it all." Gatlin told me, a little too condescendingly. "I think you're just exhausted and it's making you a little paranoid."

I bristled at his words and seriously wondered how guys could be so fucking dense sometimes. "I'm not paranoid, Gat. I can feel it, in my gut. Something is very, very wrong."

"I agree with Gatlin. We've been full-fledged Sins for a lot longer than you have even been alive. We don't sense any danger anymore." Gray said, his heavily accented voice only irritating me at that particular moment.

Gatlin turned his eyes back to mine in the mirror again and I saw the pity there. Why were they suddenly not trusting me? The same guys who had stuck up for me time and time again.

"All that's left is to make sure his victims wake up alright and don't have any lasting damage." Gatlin nods in agreement.

I balled my hands into fists, trying to control my rage just a bit. Not too much, because I was fucking pissed as all hell, but enough that I didn't blow the roof off the shiny black Jeep. "Why aren't you guys listening?" I shouted. "I know something is wrong and you're acting like a bunch of fucking dicks!" I glanced over at Drea to make sure my yelling hadn't woken her and was grateful that she seemed out cold. It seemed like my best friend was always unconscious these days.

"Ria, it's done! Let it go!" Gatlin roared at me, swerving onto the shoulder of the road. Which, out in BFE, was just gravel.

I narrowed my eyes at him, feeling my rage and magic – was it called magic? - boiling just below the surface. I knew I wasn't as strong as the guys because I wasn't actually a Sin, but I was pretty sure it would hurt pretty damn bad if I blasted him with my power. You know, if I could figure it out in the first place. "I won't! You're not fucking listening!" I screeched back at him, mildly ashamed at the obnoxious pitch of my own voice.

Gatlin turned in his seat to glare at me head on, his silver eyes reminding me of the moon that wasn't even present. Except, meaner. Obviously. "Jonas Holden is *dead*. The problem is *solved*. That means it's *over*." He growled at me, his Sin showing in the display of rage that he was putting on.

"You know what?" I grabbed the door handle and pulled, dragging myself out of the car. Eliam, Beck, and Rafe were stopped behind us, clearly confused about the stop. "I'm out. I'll figure out what's going on, and then you'll be sorry." I slammed the door with way more force than I intended. *Oops.*

It was possible that I was being irrational, but I knew that something was going on. It didn't end with the mayor's death, I knew that much. The energy was still out there, the taste of something slimy and evil was still stuck in my mouth like a spoiled drink. I wasn't going to give up, not until I knew for sure that the evil out there was gone for good.

I was still seething after about twenty minutes of walking, and I had zero idea where I was going - not that I cared. I was still trying to formulate a plan in my mind, or really an idea of where to start. I knew something wasn't right. Despite my questionable taste in men, I had pretty damn good instincts, and since the whole Sin thing happened, all of my senses were on high alert. Every single part of me was screaming, begging me to pay attention, but I couldn't figure out what the hell I was supposed to pay attention to.

Was it also acceptable to admit that I was really pissed that none of the guys had come after me? I could nearly get kidnapped again. You know, or actually kidnapped. Why did guys never seem to understand that when women said they wanted to be left alone or stormed off in a rage, they wanted to be followed - not in like the stalking way, but just in the *we love you so much, don't be mad* kinda way.

As I walked, I started kicking loose stones with the toe of my boot and shivered slightly. It was cold as Santa's tits outside and my dumb ass thought it would be a brilliant idea to storm off in a huff while wearing shorts. "Maybe I should just go back and apologize, assuming they're still parked there." I suggested out loud to myself, feeling a little overwhelmed by the night time silence.

*Or,* my inner self chimed in. *You could let them stew and realize that you were right and they should have listened.* Wow, my inner self had no mercy.

"I could have been a little more low-key about everything and not been an asshole." I bit back at her, once again speaking out loud. Whatever. It's not like there was anyone around to listen to me. As I noticed the telltale shapes of gravestones, I shivered. Well, no one that could hear me, anyway.

Despite my innate fear and aversion to graveyards, I felt compelled to go in, which was almost creepier than the land of the dead itself. Who the fuck ever wanted to go into a graveyard? But my body was doing what it wanted, an unseen force propelling me forward, regardless of my very valid reservations.

I thought that the feeling of being lured to the creepiest place I've ever seen would go away as soon as I passed through the gates, like in TV shows and books, instead I was gripped by the sudden feeling of overwhelming fear. I froze in place, paralyzed. A very creepy, very foreboding fog began settling over the mass of graves and I was one hundred percent positive that the corpses beneath the ground at my feet were about to start crawling from their resting places.

What I wasn't expecting, and kicked myself internally for not expecting it, was to see my would-be killer striding through the mist, looking like a frail, decaying Undertaker as he approached me. Even with the lack of light from the non-existent moon, I was still able to see him clearly. Maybe it was a Sin thing.

All I wanted in that moment was to run for my life, screaming bloody murder. I tried to travel back to the house, thinking, wishing, begging for my newfound ability to take me home and get me out of the nightmare I was stuck in. Unsurprisingly, I didn't budge. It felt like a giant bubble had closed in around me, and even I could see the irony.

Father Belvieu was only a mere feet away from me and all I could think of was that fighting would be a whole hell of a lot easier if I could move. I was never going to feel like a victim again.

As he got nearer, his scent of rotting flesh rolled over me and I threw up in my mouth a little. I tried to hold my breath as he got right up in my face and brushed a withered finger down the side of my face.

"If only you had remained a child of God, dear girl." He croaked. "You have sealed your fate and the fate of all those who betrayed the Lord's name in favour of the Devil's temptation."

My skin prickled with goosebumps and I just knew I was going to be sick.

I spat in his face, grateful that I could at least do that. "You're the one killing those people, aren't you?" I demanded, already knowing the answer before he said anything.

It all made perfect sense. He would have had access to anyone in the hospital under the pretense of praying over them. He also could have been around anyone that was touched by the sickness without anyone suspecting a single thing. I also knew that the simplest answer was usually the correct one, and his downright creepiness was enough for me to not doubt the reality of it all. My only question was how anyone could have trusted him. He smelled like death itself and physically appeared to be rotting. How did anyone think that was normal?

He pulled his lips back in a terrifying grin, revealing a mouth full of black, rotted teeth. "Only those born of sin can see Death as the reaper of souls that he is. Heaven demands justice for the atrocities that His children have committed, and I am his avenger." He declared, cackling triumphantly.

Before I could speak again, the psycho had grabbed my arm and begun dragging me behind him. I was simultaneously relieved and frustrated, because even as my feet moved beneath me in an effort to keep from falling on my face, I had forgotten how strong the deceptively frail man was. As he marched on, I tugged my arm back and even landed a few solid punches with my weaker arm, but it was like he didn't even realize I was doing anything. I cocked my arm back and prepared to throw the biggest hit that I could, and when it landed, I felt my hand slip through skin, muscle, and bone. He still didn't slow, even as I withdrew my hand and repeatedly gagged. The hole in his back wasn't even healing, it was just a large, gaping, bloodless wound that stared back at me like a terrifying third eye.

He hauled me up the steps of the church that I remembered seeing when I first drove into town and I started to feel panic rising inside me, the memories that I tried so hard to repress threatening to overtake me. I tried to reassure myself that it was just a building, but the blooming sense of terror in my chest told me that it wasn't.

In a single, fluid motion, I was being thrown across the room, sliding across the wood flooring. I threw my arms up over my face as I slid toward a pew. The wooden frame struck me in my middle and the air was knocked from my lungs.

Finally able to move, I rolled over and gasped for breath as I cradled my stomach, stars bursting around my sight and blinding me for a moment. I struggled to breathe as I scrambled to my feet, ready to protect myself by any means at my disposal. When the explosion of light cleared from my eyes, I glanced down at my feet and found myself in a crudely drawn circle that was decorated with symbols that I couldn't identify. The looked like runes, but not any kind of rune that I had ever seen.

"You're going to pay for hurting those people. I won't be another one of your targets." I hissed at the preacher who stood near the door, eyeing me casually.

He yawned dramatically. "Don't you see? You're not a target, girl, you're a sacrifice." He said as he strode purposefully toward where I stood. "Your essence, your carnal sin, are going to give me the power that I need to rid the world of the wretched blasphemy that stains our once beautiful earth."

I drew up to my full height, which wasn't very intimidating, but it made me feel more confident. "The world is just fine the way it is." I growled. "The only stain on this world is people like you, people who think they have the right to control how others live, how they feel, and who they are. It's not your place, nor anyone's, to say how the world should be or whether someone is good or bad." I positioned myself so that I was ready to pounce at a moment's notice, the second he got close enough.

"God wouldn't want this. He wouldn't want people to die, and he wouldn't put a sorry excuse for a man like you in charge of carrying out his wishes. You're sick, and you're going down." I swore vehemently, searching for a surge of emotion, a spark of the power that I had experienced before. I found nothing and tried to control my breathing, trying not to spiral into despair.

The decaying man stopped before me, appearing completely unfazed by the hatred that I was projecting. "God needs strong men to do his bidding, and thanks to His grace, I am more than powerful enough to purge the world of deplorable creatures like yourself." He sneered, obviously no longer amused by the game he was playing.

Seeing my chance, I charged at him, jumping in the air and tackling him down to the ground with my momentum. We fell to the ground and I heard bones cracking beneath me. I made to wrap my forearm against his throat and he shoved at me, sending me sailing through the air and crashing into another pew. The wood splintered underneath me and I whimpered at the pain in my shoulder. It didn't feel broken, but it sure as hell hurt like a bitch.

I rose to my feet and ran at him again, only to be stopped by a wall of flames. I got too close and wailed as the fire burned my good arm. I looked around to find myself in the circle once again, this time trapped. Through the wall, I could see Father Belvieu looking victorious.

"Just stay put. This will all be over soon." He said. He rose his hands above his head and started praying out loud. My head started throbbing violently, making my vision blur and my legs trembled. I covered my ears to block out the sound as his chanting prayer got louder and louder, until it was all I could hear.

I wanted to retreat into my mind, my safe place. I couldn't see or speak, and all I could feel was searing pain as I crumpled to my knees. There was a loud ringing in my ears and when I adjusted my hands over my ears, I found them slick. I couldn't even care about the fact that I knew it was blood. All I wanted was for the pain to stop.

*Someone help me.* I screamed in my mind, hoping that it would reach the ears of the men that I had somehow come to rely, the men who were my only hope at making it out of this mess alive.

I scrambled to get out of the Jeep as Ria stormed away. I opened my mouth to call after her, but nothing came out. I didn't know what I could say to change her mind, to make her turn around and hear us out. I understood her unease, better than she could have imagined; it was all too easy, too obvious. But we had caught Holden red handed leaving Sanya's room as she died.

Then again, the question remained of how he managed to accomplish the things he did, and *what* he did was still a larger mystery still. I could give her that much as I had my doubts as well, but like the others, I couldn't sense anything.

I stood between the back of the Jeep and Ria's silver car, staring after her as she walked away.

Within seconds, everyone was climbing out of their vehicles and congregating where I stood. Eliam surprised me by being the first to speak.

"What the fuck just happened?" He demanded, staring at Gatlin with a combination of anger and concern. It seemed like I was the only one who could see how much he had quickly come to care for the girl with strawberry blonde hair and stunning green eyes. We all had.

Gatlin was in Eliam's face within two strides, his eyes blazing. "I didn't do anything. She was convinced that we were wrong about Holden and just didn't want to let it fucking go." He snarled back.

As their bickering got loud and more heated, I tuned them out, focusing instead searching for Ria's light in my mind's eye. I couldn't always pinpoint a person's location, but with Ria it was effortless when I looked. Just as she did in my mind's eye, she glowed like a flame and illuminated even the darkest of rooms.

She obviously didn't know it, but our lives were a very dark place just over a week before - well, they had been a dark place for a long time before that. When she walked into our lives, it was like the world turned on its head and showed us a light that we had somehow been missing for so long.

Just over a century before, our seven turned to six, and we were left with all the stress and concern over when - or if - our family would ever be reunited.

Ria took all that anxiety, worry, and pain away just by entering a room. These days, we ate as a family, we laughed as a family, and we worked as one solid, functioning unit. I could count on one hand the number of jobs that had gone off without a single fight since our number dwindled. We weren't whole. Then she came around and just magically fixed us, as if she saw nothing broken in the first place.

It was for that reason that I couldn't help but side with her at least a little bit. Even if she was wrong, we owed it to her to at least look into the possibility of there being a separate culprit. That was the least that we owed her, and everyone else knew it as well. If only we weren't so stubborn.

"I think we should go after her." I said, my voice ringing out clearly over the shouting and name-calling. Everyone stopped to stare at me and I kept my face a neutral mask, despite how strongly I felt about what I was saying.

Gatlin crossed his arms over his chest and glared at me. "She's wearing shorts and heading the wrong way. She'll be back." He insisted.

"He's not wrong." Eliam pointed out. "Plus, she can always travel home at any time she wishes. She's already shown she has a strong talent for it."

"Traveling aside, her feelings are hurt and she's had to deal with a lot in just the measly *week* that she's been around, don't you think?" I scolded as I looked each of my brothers in the eye, daring them to disagree. None of them did. "I think she didn't serve to have her concerns completely invalidated, even if we didn't agree." This I directed at Gatlin who at least had the sense to look contrite. I knew he would never hurt her on purpose, but his anger got the best of him sometimes, and none of us wanted to believe that there was a missing piece in the puzzle.

E crossed his arms over his chest impatiently and stared me down, neither of us willing to back down. He and I had always had kind of a rocky relationship, which was surprising because our Sins were so different. But we were both leaders and we had both lost so much, we just had our own ways of dealing with things.

"Well," Eliam started. "What do you suggest we do, then?"

I sighed, relieved. "Like I already said, we should go after her. Women don't *actually* want to be left alone when they make you think they do."

Kellan blinked slowly. "That doesn't make a damn bit of sense, Gray." He grumbled.

Shrugging, I held back a chuckle. "That's women for you." I stated simply.

We got in the cars and started slowly making our way in the direction that Ria had walked in. Following the road about half a mile we still saw no sight of her and I started to worry a little that maybe she had actually traveled back to the house, then my entire speech in her defense was for nothing.

I opened my mind's eye and searched for her light. I found it immediately nearby and it was flickering wildly. My eyebrows knit together in confusion, having never seen someone's light act quite the way hers did. When it started shrinking, I felt dread course through me like the tail of a fiery whip cutting me to the bone.

My eyes flying wide, I was about to use my link to tell my brothers what I had seen when we all heard it, Ria's voice screaming in our minds.

*Someone help me!*

Both cars skidded to a halt with Eliam almost ramming Ria's car into the back of the Jeep. *Is everyone okay?* He asked over the connection.

I nodded in my frazzled state before realizing that he couldn't hear me nod. *We're all fine. Ria is up ahead about a quarter of a mile. We need to hurry.*

Without any further acknowledgment, Gatlin pressed hard on the gas and we went flying down the road. When we reached the church, the only one the town had, I shouted, "here! Turn here!" I could see her light, flickering and shrinking in size. I was coming to realize that it meant she was in danger; it was her life force slipping away.

I didn't even remember getting out of the car, all I could see was the front double doors of the church and our girl's fading light. Approaching the front doors, I threw out my hand and knocked them clean off their hinges, sending them flying to either side of the hall and crushing pews with the force of the impact.

"Get the fuck away from her!" Gatlin roared, charging at Father Belvieu like a bull in an arena.

The preacher was standing before a circle of flames that rose almost to the ceiling, and according to my light map, Ria was right in the middle of it. I panicked when I realized her light was no more than a little spark, almost no glow to be seen. I rushed the wall of flames without thinking and dove through, spotting her in the center almost immediately.

Stumbling over to her, clumsy in my haste, I dropped to my knees. I lifted her in my arms and cradled her in my arms. "Zvezda moya, please open your eyes." I whispered to her as I brushed her hair back from her face.

I felt like I would collapse when her eyes fluttered open ever-so-slightly. "Hey Gray." She wheezed with a small smile. "You keep saving me."

I choked on a laugh, feeling so much relief that I could have flown in that moment. "You keep getting yourself into these situations, Zvezda moya. You're going to be the death of me." I held her head to my chest, trying to breathe normally. When I closed my eyes, her light was almost completely out and I snapped my eyes open in panic. Her eyes were closed and her breathing was becoming so shallow that I couldn't even see a slight rise of her chest.

Standing, with Ria still in my arms, I looked down at the floor and noticed the crude symbols that were scattered about the circle. He was draining her. I ran for one of the runes and rubbed at the chalk with my foot, trying to mar the shape enough for the spell to stop. When the flames dropped, I saw my chance and leaped over the circle, bolting for the open doorway.

When I glanced over my shoulder, I saw my brothers taking on Father Belvieu. For the first time, I noticed how decrepit he was. His body was totally destroyed by whatever darkness he had been utilizing and was falling apart with each blow that landed on him.

He threw Eliam across the room like it cost him not an ounce of energy. As my brother landed next to me, I nudged him with my foot. "Take Ria and get out of here." I commanded coldly. When I closed my eyes, Father Belvieu had no light, no sign of life. That answered every question I had.

My brother nodded and took Ria from my arms, holding her against him as if she were the most fragile and priceless artifact, which, to him, I supposed she was. I wasn't going to question why he had obeyed me, since it's something we had often butted heads over, but now that I was free from my task of protecting Ria, it was on.

STANDING IN NOTHING BUT BRIGHT WHITENESS, I SAW *myself walking toward me, a perfect mirror image - except for her golden eyes. As she stopped before me, I studied her, unable to figure out what I would be doing staring at myself. There was always the possibility that I was dead, which was extremely feasible from the little I remembered. But if I was*

dead, wouldn't I be seeing Saint Peter or angels? Or shit, even the Devil himself would have been welcome.

"Hello, Ria." Myself said, sounding just like me. She smiled a little bit and it made me feel uneasy. There wasn't something right about the smile she gave me. Maybe it was the fact that it was devoid of warmth or kindness, or maybe it was just the fact that I wasn't exactly used to seeing myself in 3D.

Something clicked to me then. "You're my inner self, aren't you?" I asked accusingly. Of course my brain would find a way to bring this bitch along for the ride. With the whole istory of leaving your troubles and ailments behind, I was a little bit pissed to see that my schizophrenia came with me. Further evidence that there was no way I could be fixed.

I had first imagined my inner self when I was eight, when days would go by without the sight of another person as I was locked in the cellar below. She kept me company and told me all the great things about myself, even reassured me that I wasn't bad. We would spend days and days just talking to each other. She kept me sane.

So wasn't it just ironic that she was driving me insane now?

"What are you doing here?" I demanded, placing my hands on my hips as though that could make me appear any more intimidating than, well, me.

She smirked then and placed a manicured hand on my shoulder, her golden eyes sending little shock waves of panic through me. "I want to be free, and you're going to help me." She said gleefully. Her eyes flashed briefly, reminding me of the way Eliam's illuminated in the kitchen the day everything started really going to shit.

*My inner self seemed to realize that I was scared shitless and that apparently made her very happy. She leaned in close and put her lips to my ear as she whispered, "now wake the fuck up and go save our men."*

*She put both of her hands on my shoulders and I felt a strange energy seeping into me, crowding my internal personal space. It made me feel taller, stronger, and more aware than I ever had. When I opened my mouth to ask her what she just did, she put her hands on my chest and shoved hard, and I started falling, tumbling down into darkness.*

---

BOLTING UPRIGHT WITH A GASP, I wasn't aware of my surroundings and yelped as my forehead connected with something extremely hard and solid. "Ow!" I screeched, cupping my forehead as I rocked back and forth. My whole body hurt, so a little extra pain shouldn't have been the thing to do me in, but I sat up really fucking fast, okay?

"Are you alright, love?" I knew that voice. I tilted my head up and found myself gazing into vibrant violet eyes that made my core melt into a puddle of raging hormones and errant emotions. We were sitting in the backseat of my car and he was cradling me in his lap, something that I would have never expected.

I tried to think, running over my weird ass dream and everything that happened beforehand. I remembered my inner self talking to me, the strange energy she poured into me. I remembered a wall of fire, Gray's worried voice in my ear, a man falling to pieces...

"Oh my fuck." I whispered in shock, the reality dawning on me. I looked back up at Eliam. "Where is everyone?" I was dreading his answer before he even said anything, and I knew what it was going to be.

"They're still inside. You've only been out a few moments and-"

Before he could finish his sentence, I was gone. I traveled effortlessly to the threshold of the church and watched as five of my guys attempted to beat down the thing that they were fighting. Whatever my inner self had done to me, it gave me a new sense of awareness that I had never possessed before then. I could feel that the energy inside of the preacher's body wasn't him, it wasn't even human. It was something dark and otherworldly, something I didn't have a name for.

Augustus Belvieu was no longer on this earth, and what had been left in his place was as devoid of life as bodies beneath our feet. I watched the thing lift Gray by the front of his shirt and Gray swung at him with what appeared to be a flaming sword. Hell, it probably was a flaming sword, I wasn't even surprised anymore.

As I watched the creature's arm stretch and warp into a whip-like shape, I felt the power begging to be let out, the power I cried out for so desperately the first time I faced this thing - and nearly lost. But when he slung his new appendage across the room, smashing benches and pinning the guys against a wall, I felt it really rise in me.

It was like a raging inferno in my blood, setting every nerve ending aflame and turning everything in my sight red. Only, it took me a moment to realize that my sight wasn't actually going red, but there was a red mist-like substance that was stretching from my body and toward the unsightly thing before me.

I grinned, feeling like a total badass as I stepped slowly, purposefully toward the shadow that had taken up residence in the preacher's body. He made to lash out at me with his whip-like arm and I threw a hand up, as if to block it, not even taking my eyes off of him as my power split through the offending limb like it was nothing more than an errant piece of paper.

He screamed, the sound echoing around the walls of the church and shaking the walls. I saw what remained of the arm-whip swinging toward me out of the corner of my eye when I was only a few feet away and I ducked, watching as it swung into the opposite wall.

I glanced sideways at the guys to make sure they were still alright and breathed out heavily when I saw that they were all on the ground, but alive and conscious.

Directing my focus back on the monster before me, I ran for it, jumping into a handspring as I got within a couple of feet and pressed both feet to his chest. I was both pleased and disgusted to see that, not only had I knocked him flat on his ass, but I had also knocked a pretty good sized hole in his chest. The place where his heart should have been was blackened and hollow, as though he was burned from the inside out.

I quickly ran to kneel next to him and pressed my hands against the sides of his chest that weren't crushed in. I tried not to think about the smell as I tried to push my power into him. Well, not him. I felt around with my new sense and found the slimy tendrils of whatever was animating the body. In my mind, I latched onto it and started forcing my power inside of it. I heard it scream in my mind, the sound deafening and making it hard to concentrate.

"Ria, look out!" I heard that out loud and turned to my left just in time to watch Eliam jump in front of the whip-arm as it made another comeback. My mouth was frozen open in shock as I watched it slice through the blonde-haired Sin's stomach.

He turned around to look at me and collapsed to his knees. He pressed a hand to his abdomen and pulled it away, staring at his bloodied hand in surprise. He glanced up at me one last time before he fell forward, as if in slow motion.

A bloodcurdling scream filled the cavernous space and it took me a solid minute to realize that the one screaming was me. Turning back to the task at hand, I pushed with all of my might, sending as much light and power into the creature who dared to hide in another man's shadow. "My name is Ria Will Grimm." I breathed, unable to fully speak through the agony that was consuming me. "I banish you to whence you came, foul creature." I felt strong and powerful saying the words that seemed to spring into my mind like I was reading them off a script. "*Go to hell, you son of a bitch!*" I added the last part because it felt a lot more like me, and being myself always seemed to get the job done.

A burst of white light from the hollow cavity that was once Augustus Belvieu's chest nearly blinded me in it sudden intensity. I shielded my eyes with my arm and felt a strange heat overtaking me, like I was stepping into the sun.

I got to my feet and stumbled backwards, eyes still protected against the light. I fell backwards over some rubble and strong arms caught me before I could land on my ass. Opening my eyes, I blinked a few times and looked around.

"Eliam?" I called frantically, not spotting him on the ground where the rest of the guys were huddled. "Eliam?" I shouted his name louder, feeling panicked.

"I'm right here, love, no need to shout."

I looked up into the eyes of the man who had caught me and nearly cried with the amount of relief I felt. I scrambled to get to my feet and turned to look at him. His neatly pressed button down shirt was ripped, torn, and bloodstained beyond repair, but he appeared fine. Fine enough to catch me was fine enough to be happy about is how I saw it.

I threw my arms around his neck, tackling him in a hug that sent us sprawling backward and into some of the broken pieces of wood. I tucked my face into his neck and tried like hell not to cry. "I'm so fucking glad you're okay." I whispered, not able to trust my voice.

He patted my back a little awkwardly and I barked out a laugh. "I'm fine. I told you that Sins couldn't be killed." He murmured against my hair. "We'll talk later about what you just did over there, yeah?"

A strangled sound escaped my lips because I was torn between wanting to laugh like a maniac and wanting to cry because, shit, I'd just fought and killed an evil creature. "Yeah, sure, we'll talk about it later." I acquiesced

"Then, can we go home now?" I heard someone ask behind me. I sat up, not even caring that I was straddling Eliam right in front of everyone. I did a quick head count and smiled hugely when everyone was accounted for.

I looked at Rafe, knowing he was the one who had spoken. "After this mess is cleaned up, sure. We can go home."

Everyone groaned but me and I just grinned. It was highly possible that I had actually lost my mind at some point, because no sane, rational person would be grinning after an epic life or death battled.

"Do you want someone to stumble upon that?" I raised an eyebrow as I indicated the smoking pile of flesh and bones that was once the preacher's body.

Gatlin started stomping over to the remains of the corpse and grumbled, "let's just get this over with so we can go the fuck home." Rafe and Kellan followed behind him as Gray and Beck headed outside, mumbling beneath their breath.

I was so ready to go home, take a shower, plop down in my bed, and forget this whole night ever existed. Even bickering with the guys over video games and whether or not pineapple goes on pizza sounded amazing, and that probably said a lot about how far gone I was. I didn't care what I did, I just wanted to forget.

Don't forget about me. My inner self chimed in a sing-song voice that was so unlike her. The sound send shivers down my spine and made me want to run for the hills. You're going to set me free.

I could only pray that it was all in my head, and not something much more nefarious.

*The end... For now.*

## ABOUT THE AUTHOR

Jenica Saren is an American indie author, wife, and mother, based in a state that's none of your business. She's magnificent, amazing, an experienced pole dancer, three-time karaoke champion, passionate chef, and entrepreneur extraordinaire. She manages all of this, and somehow is so gracious and humble. (No, she didn't tell me to write that.)

She enjoys books, entire bottles of wine, The Lion King on repeat, video games, her two cats Nala and Sparta, and sometimes even her husband. She doesn't like to admit it, but inside of her is a screaming teen white girl, that craves Starbucks, gossip girl, and says way too many OMGs. Jenica tries to feed her at least twice a week. (She needs her strength up for sale season!)

You can follow Jenica's writing adventure by following her on Facebook (https://www.facebook.com/jenicasaren) or by joining her Facebook reader group. (https://www.facebook.com/groups/JenicasTroublemakers)

## ACKNOWLEDGMENTS

Firstly, I'd like to give a ginormous shout out to Marlee Standard. Without you, girl, I never would have started writing down any of the ideas that I had couped up in my head. They were starving to death, Marlee. Starving. So thank you for pushing a stranger in the right direction, and thank you for being an amazing friend ever since.

Next, I need to thank Cece Rose. International bestselling author and you somehow still managed to find the time to not only help me where I needed it *and* get me a cover when I felt like I was on a dead-end street, but also be there for me *every single day*. I don't know how I existed without my daily dose of Cece and our late night gaming sessions. You're amazing and I love you so much.

And here come the water works. Daqri Bernardo, do you even realize how talented you are? Every time I see this beautiful cover, all I can do is cry. You and your magic hands have a very special place in my heart.

And then there's my beloved Biatch Brigade. Kayla, Tay, Christina, Gem, Meagan, Autumn, and Jamie, I love y'all so much. Thank you for being there for me and never letting me quit, even when I so desperately wanted to.

Now that this has turned into a novel all its own, I just want to thank you all, my readers. If you made it this far, I hope you enjoyed Sinless. Every single one of you that expressed your excitement for this book kicked my ass into gear. I swear I've barely slept since I officially announced its release (I'm currently writing this at two in the morning. Yay!) and you guys have made it all worth it. I love all of you, too.

Made in the USA
Las Vegas, NV
19 May 2021